A.J. SCUDIERE

NIGHTSHADE

FORENSIC FBI FILES ✦ BOOK 5

THE SHADOW FILES

SALVAGE

NightShade Forensic FBI Files: Salvage

Copyright © 2018 by AJ Scudiere

FIRST EDITION

"There are really just 2 types of readers—those who are fans of AJ Scudiere, and those who will be."
    -Bill Salina, Reviewer, Amazon

For *The Shadow Constant*:
"The Shadow Constant by A.J. Scudiere was one of those novels I got wrapped up in quickly and had a hard time putting down."
    -Thomas Duff, Reviewer, Amazon

For *Phoenix*:
"It's not a book you read and forget; this is a book you read and think about, again and again . . . everything that has happened in this book could be true. That's why it sticks in your mind and keeps coming back for rethought."
    -Jo Ann Hakola, The Book Faerie

For *God's Eye*:
"I highly recommend it to anyone who enjoys reading - it's well-written and brilliantly characterized. I've read all of A.J.'s books and they just keep getting better."
    -Katy Sozaeva, Reviewer, Amazon

For *Vengeance*:
"Vengeance is an attention-grabbing story that lovers of action-driven novels will fall hard for. I hightly recommend it."
    -Melissa Levine, Professional Reviewer

For *Resonance*:
"Resonance is an action-packed thriller, highly recommended. 5 stars."
    -Midwest Book Review

This is for all the Smart Chickens. You know who you are.
Thank you for being here from the beginning.

ACKNOWLEDGMENTS

This has been a long road. When I started writing, it was a solitary endeavor. No more. I have my people now, and I love every one of them. They help wrangle the story and close the loopholes. They build a cover and tell me, "No, try this." And they're right. I am the reason you have the story. They are the reason it's in readable English and why the cover gives you the chills. They are the push behind a blurb that makes you say, "Oh, wait. What's happening to Walter and GJ!?!?" They are the reason this book isn't just a document filed on my computer in a format that will one day be obsolete. I would have written it anyway. They are the reason you have it.

And as always, for Guy, Jarett, and January. They live with me. They see every evening when I'm writing. They deal with my surly attitude when I'm editing. They listen when I excitedly tell them I have a new idea for a book, a series, a way to tell a story. And they deal with it when I run off to do it. I love you guys.

1

Walter Reed glanced around the empty conference room. Being the first to arrive made her nervous. FBI Special Agent in Charge Derek Westerfield had invited her to this meeting almost a week ago, yet she still had no idea what he wanted. To calm her nerves, she recited her stats. These were things she knew, things she'd been forced to yell to superior officers, reminders that she could do any of this. Whatever it was.

Born: Lucy Fisher.

United States Marine Corps.

MARSOC.

Wounded in action.

Loss of left arm, loss of left leg, bionic replacements—and now she was known mostly as Walter Reed.

She had saved other troops from IEDs, she'd helped stop a terrorist ring in Los Angeles, so surely she could survive an empty conference room for just a few minutes. She forced herself to sit still.

When the door opened, she turned rapidly to stand at attention. It was a feat on the fake leg, one of the first feats she'd mastered after her surgery. Success had come only after she'd accepted that she was never going to be her old self. She was a new person—maybe less of a person—when she woke up in Walter Reed Hospital. But she'd done her time in therapy and learned to work with her new body and prosthetics. Now, as she put in the energy to snap to attention, she realized her effort wasn't worth it.

The person coming in the doorway was not FBI Special Agent Derek Westerfield, but GJ Janson. GJ's eyes jumped left, then right, as though she, too, had no idea what this meeting was about. However, GJ's mere presence gave Walter a little more insight into what might be going on. She found she didn't like it one bit.

Despite the nervous look on her face, when GJ turned and greeted her, the tone was a little too chipper.

"Hey, Walter. I figured we'd both be here." Her words were relatively confident, but the way her sharp hazel eyes were darting around gave Walter pause. What did GJ Janson know that she didn't? That bothered Walter on a level she couldn't quite define. There wasn't a chance to think about it for very long, because the door swung open again before it had completed its slow, closing arc behind GJ's entrance. At last, FBI Special Agent in Charge Derek Westerfield walked into the room.

He looked from one to the other of them without moving his head, then sat down at the head of the table. GJ scrambled. She hadn't even taken a seat yet. Walter, of course, sat back down fluidly, confidently, and without giving away anything of what she felt inside.

"Special Agent Westerfield," GJ greeted him, her voice still a little over-excited. "It's good to see you again."

Westerfield only nodded. He pulled out two file folders and set them, stacked, in front of him. With thick fingers, he flipped the top one open, and Walter could see a dossier with GJ Janson's picture paper-clipped to the front page old-school style. The second folder, still closed under the first one, was reasonably thicker. Walter could only conclude it was her own.

Westerfield didn't give her time to muse it through, though. Instead, he once again glanced from one woman to the other and then said, "You two have royally fucked up my operations."

Before she'd readily ditched all her non-plans and come here to the FBI Field Office, GJ had been at home. Well, at one of her grandfather's homes. Supposedly, she was doing research. The fact of the matter was, she was actually doing research—it just wasn't associated with any formal institution or any university or anyone else at all. She'd yet to tell her grandfather or even her parents about the serious trouble she'd gotten herself in with the FBI. So when she mentioned she had an interview, they naturally assumed it was with the university. Not bothering to correct this, GJ had successfully dodged questions about where she was going and who exactly she planned to meet.

Though she'd come and gone from her grandfather's estate several times over the past handful of months, she still hadn't quite figured out what was going on with him. To her, he was simply her grandfather; however, the world knew him as the renowned Professor Murray Marks. He had his own bone collection, featuring a good number of full skeletons. While this should have been impressive, GJ was discovering it was more weird than awe inspiring.

All his acquisitions possessed a strange, but relatively consistent, set of anomalies. She'd been trying to figure out what it was. At this point, the best her several science degrees and background in chemistry, biology, and even some psych and sociology could tell was that it looked like—possibly—the people who had the anomaly were double jointed. Their bones looked relatively normal but it seemed they had more than the standard 206 adult bones possessed by other normal human beings. This was due to the failure of some plates and bones to fuse properly despite the fact that, by all other indicators, the skeletons were those of fully-grown adults.

Her grandfather still traveled all over the world collecting human skeletons from digs as recent as several years ago, some from archeological sites that went back hundreds and even thousands of years. However, the only bones he brought home had this one specific anomaly. It piqued her interest, probably the same way it piqued his. GJ, being who she was, was unable to walk away from that—especially once she realized that a particular FBI agent she knew, Agent Donovan Heath, possessed the exact same set of anomalies.

While her grandfather might have skeletons, she had a live human being to study. Needless to say, Agent Heath had not appreciated her inquiries. She'd tried to prove herself useful by insinuating herself with the FBI team of Heath and Eames. Though she'd definitely accomplished *something*, she'd not quite achieved her goal. No, scratch that. She was certain she hadn't achieved her goal. Agent Heath hadn't even admitted that he had an anomaly. He wouldn't even say if he was or wasn't double-jointed. She'd inserted herself into the investigation and even helped crack the case, despite the fact that she still hadn't been debriefed on exactly what the case was. And along the way, she'd clearly done something wrong.

After all, she'd wound up in handcuffs. Despite the fact that the agents left her high and dry once they'd wrapped up their investigation, she continued to dig. And the easiest place to dig was in the basement of her grandfather's estate where he kept a wide variety of human bones.

All her life, she'd simply assumed that her famous professor grandfather had permission to keep the bones in his personal storage facility. That paperwork would have been granted from the university he worked for, or from various institutions around the world, like the British Museum. Her young self had assumed permission. Her older, more educated self knew what to look for, and the more she looked now, the more she didn't see tags. She didn't see logs that tied the bones to any institution. The marking system used to ID each individual specimen in black ink didn't match any system she'd ever been trained on or seen. GJ was growing more and more disturbed by her grandfather's activities.

Though she'd almost gotten caught the first time she snuck down where she wasn't allowed, she'd since learned to turn the power off to that part of the house, mask the cameras, trip the locks, and sneak down the stairs with the light on her camera to show her the way. She would then take photographs and study the bones to her heart's content.

Probably the only one who knew she was doing it was the maid. The maid didn't really seem to care. A reasonable part of his staff had no love lost for the old man, so whatever GJ did—including sneaking into locked basements—was okay.

In the meantime, several other residents of the house had started calling the power company and wondering why they kept having outages. GJ never offered a clue, because what she was finding was far too stunning. While she'd originally thought her grandfather had a collection of several skeletons that had the anomaly, she now knew that his collection was much larger—and the anomaly far more extensive—than she'd originally estimated.

It appeared that every single skeleton in Murray Marks' personal collection was undocumented, without correct provenance to show it belonged to a museum or university collection. It seemed they were all skeletons her grandfather had personally pulled out of the ground and she was beginning to wonder if maybe he'd stolen them.

He had a full setup in his basement lab, including a generator, a table for autopsies—both wet and dry—and a full overhead, sprayer-nozzle system on a pulley so he could wash away bodily fluids as he worked. It was the same kind of rig that one might find in a nice morgue, and he'd built it right into his own basement. GJ had grown up with odd things in the house. She hadn't thought it was unusual as a kid. She didn't realize other kids didn't have grandfathers with full autopsy setups inside their homes. But now, even as a forensic scientist herself, she was starting to get the heebie-jeebies.

Her biggest concern was that, right before she left to come to this interview with the FBI, she'd snuck down into the basement again. Though she'd been planning to take more notes and get more pictures, she'd instead found that the kettle was on.

Her grandfather had left only a handful of hours before and he had a full-sized standard laboratory kettle for boiling bones. A lot of water, a little bit of meat tenderizer, put a skeleton in, clamp the lid down to create pressure, turn it on and leave it for a day. Voila! When you came back, you had a clean skeleton, free of flesh. Any that was still clinging was loose and could be easily brushed or wiped away unlike the fresh, unboiled variety of dead body.

The kettle in his lab was one of the bigger ones she'd seen, about three and a half feet across by four feet tall. It sat up on a slight pedestal so that the top opened up right about at her eye height. She could just peek down inside and see what he had boiling or if it was cleaned out. Normally, it stayed closed but empty—none of the lights would be on.

Today, the lights were on. The lid wasn't merely resting closed, it was clamped, and the gauge on the side indicated the high temperature and the high pressure inside. The numbers revealed that it must have been on the boil for at least an hour and a half. The power being off would slowly let the numbers down. She'd have to get out soon and flip the switch back. Luckily, the kettle boiled for long enough that her small break in cooking time wouldn't get noticed. That didn't bother her.

No. What bothered her most was the size of the kettle that he kept. It was the exact right size for boiling down the bones of a complete human skeleton.

2

G J sat at the conference table listening to Special Agent in Charge Derek Westerfield lay out information for Walter and her. Keeping her hands clasped in front of her, she tried to hide both her excitement and nerves. She did not want to come across as giddy, which she was rapidly getting. On the other side of the table, she saw Walter's hands clasped in the same manner. It must have been quite a feat given that one of Walter's hands wasn't even human; it was robotic. That woman was the fucking Terminator and everyone knew it.

Agent Westerfield went on, even though GJ hadn't quite been paying attention. "I can't have the two of you inserting yourselves into my investigations."

"Sir," Walter interrupted, "if I may."

Just like a soldier, thought GJ.

Westerfield nodded at Walter, and the other woman continued. "I was actually asked to come into the operation."

Acknowledging that with a second subtle nod of his head in Walter's direction, he replied, "That's absolutely true. However, you were inserted into the operation because you went to the home of one of my agents and poked around until you discovered things about this agent that you weren't supposed to. Then you followed him. Does that sound about right?"

Walter only looked back at him. GJ could tell the other woman was debating whether to agree or tell him that he was absolutely wrong. The way GJ had heard it, Walter had gone to Donovan's house and he'd seemed to be missing, so she looked around. As far as she'd been told, that was the whole story—though she didn't believe it. Whatever it was that got Walter into the investigation was pretty big, and GJ was dying to know. No one was going to tell her today, that was for sure.

So she sat patiently with her hands neatly folded and waited for Westerfield to speak again. He'd told her on the phone last week that he was looking to offer her a position with his team. She was hopeful that the position was not as a secretary. If she was lucky, it was possibly as a laboratory scientist, and she couldn't think of anything that would make her any happier than becoming an FBI research scientist.

She'd been on her way to a PhD, and she was currently calculating the number of course hours she'd need, the time it would take her to do her thesis, and how she could possibly balance both—a job with the FBI and the schoolwork to finish that degree—when Westerfield said, "I only work with agents."

Well, there went that dream. But she kept her ears perked, hopeful maybe he'd throw her a bone in some other way. Sure enough, he did.

"My first option, given what the two of you have seen, is to kill you." He delivered it in such a way that GJ felt her own bones suddenly go steel hard and frozen.

Was he serious? He could not have brought them here to an FBI facility with the intent of murdering them in cold blood simply because his agents hadn't done their job well enough.

He interrupted her thoughts. "The other option is to hire you." There it was! She'd known this was coming.

"So I have a proposition for the two of you. I'm starting a new division still under the umbrella of NightShade. While my Night-Shade agents operate with . . ." he paused, searching for words, and GJ wondered what he wasn't telling her. Then she figured if she was going to work for the FBI, she probably ought to get used to it.

"My other agents have certain skills, skills the two of you don't have. But, in the meantime, if the two of you, together, can pass training at Quantico, I'll put you on my team."

GJ felt her jaw drop open, but then she clamped it shut because that was horrifyingly crass and she was desperately trying to look professional here. Walter looked at him. GJ looked at him. They looked at each other for a moment, but it was GJ who found the words first.

"Excuse me, sir, I'd just like to clarify." *There*, she thought, *that sounded good.* "You're actually offering us positions as agents? And we'll go through agent training? Or are you talking about analysts?"

"No, ma'am, not analysts. Agents. I need more agents on my team. The two of you have proved yourself useful at ferreting out details, in fact even details that you never should have been able to ferret out." GJ hid a smile as he continued. "Thus, if you'd like to be a field agent, it's a position I'm offering to you."

She didn't even need half a second. "Absolutely, sir. I'm in. Where do I sign up?"

Well, it wasn't going to be quite that easy, was it?

Westerfield glanced at Walter and then back at GJ. "It's not like that. My team doesn't work that way. This only works if the two of you go through training together. If either of you fails, both of you are out. Because of the situation with my division, the two of you are going to be partners in the field as well. So I'm putting you through training together. It's a bit unorthodox. Usually we pair up agents after training—but usually, we don't have agents who've been involved in major investigations *prior* to going to Quantico." GJ could hear the ire in his voice, but she didn't care. "So as you can see, doing things the usual way isn't quite going to be possible."

Walter spoke again. "Sir,"—this time she didn't wait for him to acknowledge her—"you're offering me a position as an FBI field agent provided I can pass training at Quantico? However, you're suggesting that while I'm passing training, I'm also responsible for *her* passing training?" She pointed at GJ.

For the first time, Special Agent Westerfield cracked a smile. "That's exactly what I'm telling you." Then he turned back to GJ and said, "And for the record, you're also responsible for her."

It took Walter a full week to make a decision. On the one hand, she already had a relatively cushy job. She'd known what it was to be homeless. She'd known what it was to be a jarhead. Now, as a private investigator working out of Los Angeles, she had relatively steady income, an apartment of her own, and the chance to set her own schedule. Why would she trade all that for an FBI job that required months of training and an at-the-hip attachment to GJ Janson?

SAC Westerfield seemed to think that this was an assignment she and GJ *should* be taking. He seemed to hint that Walter was in trouble for snooping—which was both too strong and too belittling a word for what she had done—into Donovan's life. Walter knew a lot about Donovan, but that was only because he'd been missing and there had been a wolf in his yard. What was she supposed to do? It wasn't her fault she was smart enough to put two and two together and get *Donovan.*

While she enjoyed her work as a P.I., she had to admit, some of it was beyond dull. That was probably true for all jobs. She hadn't held many different ones herself, just Marine, homeless person, and private investigator. All three had involved interminable stretches of down time. She could surmise there would be times as an FBI agent that she would sit around and do things she absolutely abhorred, like paperwork. She'd not had to do so much of that as a Marine. If she took the FBI job, she'd *almost* become like a recruit again. She'd once again be beholden to a large organization that didn't feel it was necessary to tell her what she was really doing or why, only that she needed to do X, Y, and Z.

Probably the thing that tipped the whole decision for her was the fact that she would once again be part of a unit. That's what Walter Reed was made for. In the very end, though she was a great P.I.—and while she had an excellent head sitting on her shoulders—she worked best when she was part of a team. As of right now, she had no team. She had friends, and that was good, but she had no unit to work with. She had no orders to follow.

What she had were clients, and she had to admit there were a lot of days that she just wanted to tell them where to stick it. The only reason she didn't was because she knew if she did, she wouldn't get paid. And once she'd started getting paid, it had become addictive.

An FBI agent job would mean a steady paycheck and even vacation days. It meant a full, one-eighty shift from where she'd been just a little over a year ago. An FBI job meant flying off to new and exciting places in the middle of the night, and an FBI job meant a holster and gun on her hip again.

Still, she peppered Donovan with questions. What was it like being an agent? How was working for SAC Westerfield? Had Westerfield ever threatened to kill Donovan? That had gotten Donovan a little bit riled up.

"He threatened to *kill* you?" he asked. "This is the FBI. This is a federal agency. They can't do that. This isn't MI-6 or James Bond or anything."

Walter had laughed. "He didn't really threaten to kill me. Well, *us*," she corrected, since Westerfield had been talking to GJ, too. "He just hinted at it. He said we were a problem for the agency."

"How are you a problem for the Bureau?" he asked. "The main office hardly even knows the NightShade division exists. If you two came out and told everything you know, my guess is the FBI would say 'Agent Westerfield who?' and then 'Agents Heath and Eames, and all the others who work under him, don't even exist!' So I'm not sure how much of a problem you could possibly be. Can you even imagine telling people what you've seen? I hate to say it, but only the conspiracy nuts would believe you."

"You're right." She took a deep breath and tried to let the SAC's veiled threats roll off her.

"Don't let Westerfield bully you into anything you don't want to do."

She'd taken that under sincere advisement—but in the end, Westerfield wasn't bullying her. And despite the fact she was going to have to drag GJ Janson kicking and screaming through Quantico training, she was really looking forward to it.

3

G J packed her suitcase. She'd packed some things from her grandfather's estate, some things from her own small apartment, and some things from her parents' house. It had taken four days to get to all the different locations and gather all the items she might need as a recruit at Quantico in the newest FBI Training Academy class.

While she'd said yes to Agent Westerfield's offer right there in the conference room, Walter had not been so quick to jump. GJ had waited, alternately twisting her fingers and taking time to sneak into her grandfather's basement lab. She tried to read as much as she could to keep her mind off the fact that her entire future hinged on the decision of a woman who was a former solider, and very clearly was not a fan of GJ Janson.

It had taken a full week for Agent Westerfield to call and tell her they were going to be in the next class. GJ had no idea if that was how long it had taken Walter to decide or if that was how long it had taken her new SAC to bother to call and let her know. She didn't ask.

Of course, once that interminable week had passed, she had only a week left to get ready and show up on campus. A new class was already entering and Westerfield wanted the two of them in training as soon as possible. He told her he'd pulled strings to get them in and that their butts had better show up on time. So GJ had kissed her parents goodbye two days ago and headed to grandfather's to pack the last of her things. Then she'd hugged him like she meant it. The fact was, she did mean it. He was her grandfather. He'd inspired her to become a scientist and go into forensics. Unfortunately, while she loved him more than anything, she worried about what he was into. GJ had to admit it didn't look good.

This training would last almost six months. But it wouldn't feel too long if she was lucky enough to win Walter Reed over and turn the two of them into a real team. The problem was, she had no idea how to go about doing it. She had a distinct feeling Walter Reed didn't suffer fools or nerds lightly, and GJ Janson was definitely a nerd. Her father had taught her the common right triangles at the dinner table. At three, when she'd asked him why the sky was blue, he'd answer with a detailed description of refraction. Her grandfather had taught her all the proper anatomical names for every organ in her body and she was able to list all two hundred and six bones of the adult human skeleton before she was seven years old. Long before high school, she'd known about tendons and ligaments and why fighting dogs had that ridge at the top of their skulls. By senior year, she still could not catch a ball to save her life, but could readily explain resistors in series and parallel and why a dielectric helped improve a capacitor.

On the drive to Quantico, she loaded up on Cheetos and Coke, certain she wasn't going to get anything like this for the next few weeks. Even if it was offered, she was going to turn it down. She had to look like she was serious. More than just looking like it, she needed to actually *be* serious. But she had a handful more hours and Cheetos to go before that happened.

Physically, she was in pretty good shape. A forensic scientist often had to drag a dead and bloated human carcass however many yards to a flat surface for study. Or she would have to pull it up out of the earth where it had been buried five or more feet deep. That was physically taxing. People didn't realize how strong she was. Still, she would bet dollars to doughnuts that ... well ... that Walter Reed hadn't been eating any doughnuts.

She stayed in a hotel overnight and timed her arrival so she'd get to Quantico during the morning hours. Once past the gates, she went through a series of background checks to get in. Since they were expecting her, GJ figured it was just a tactic for intimidation. So she smiled and stood her ground until they directed her to the FBI agent portion of campus.

Several groups were being trained simultaneously, as was apparently always the case. The DEA and other agencies also held extensive trainings at Quantico. So while she was getting a new inauguration into class, other agents were graduating, or close to it. Police were learning advanced techniques. SWAT officers were upping their game. There was noise from the firing range. There were people running in groups out on the trails—something she was actively not looking forward to.

It took several hours to get through all the red tape. Even so, GJ was the first to arrive at the dorm room assigned to her and Walter. Apparently, when Westerfield said they were going to be partners, he'd been dead serious. He made sure they were roomed together—absolutely no questions asked. Well, actually the agents had asked her one question: they'd asked her where Walter was and when she was expected to arrive. GJ had been confused for a moment, since they'd inquired after "Lucy Fisher." It had taken her a moment to remember that was Walter's real name, and she began wondering if things were going to go a little bit wonky when everybody called the woman "Lucy." From what she'd gathered before, Walter wasn't a fan of her given name.

Being the first one in the dorm, and seeing that it was perfectly symmetrical, GJ wondered if she should wait for Walter to make a decision about who got which side of the dorm room. Then she shook off the feeling. The room was perfectly symmetrical; there was zero difference between the two sides. And Walter would likely appreciate a decisive partner. So, after looking back and forth rapidly, GJ made a snap call and set everything on the bed on the right-hand side. For a moment, that was all she did: put the suitcase on the bed and looked at it. There. She had staked her claim. Putting aside that thought—which was as dumb as it could be—GJ opened the suitcase and began unpacking her things into the drawers and onto the shelves. She was three-quarters of the way done when Walter showed up. Without so much as a knock, the door opened and there stood her new partner.

There were no squeals, no welcome hugs, no "Oh, it's been two weeks since I've seen you!" Honestly, GJ hadn't expected anything different. There was nothing girly or soft about Walter Reed.

Walter's amber-colored eyes tracked from one side of the room to the other. Without any expression at all, she asked, "You've already decided? You picked that bed?"

GJ nodded, standing firm in her decision. Walter slowly examined the room though she didn't move from her spot just inside the doorway. Then she looked to GJ and took a breath. "Is it possible we could trade?"

GJ thought for a moment, *Stand your ground* and *You're as strong as Walter.* She smiled and shrugged. "I'm mostly unpacked." Then she waited for a good reason.

Walter nodded accepting her decision. *Good.*

Then her new roomie spoke again. "It's okay, but I prefer to sleep on that side of the room. My left leg and my lower left arm are removable. I have to take them off at night. Having my right side away from the wall is actually safer for me."

Oh, Jesus, GJ thought. Here she'd come in and made a firm decision and she hadn't even begun to think about the fact that Walter Reed, while bionic, was also technically handicapped. Trying to be as straight-forward as she could be about it, she said, "Well, that makes sense."

Then she slowly undid all the work she just spent the last twenty minutes doing—pulling her things, one by one, out of the drawers, walking them across the room, and putting them away on the other side. *Wow, what a way to make a great first impression.*

4

Two weeks into training, Walter reached her limit. "You have got to be fucking kidding me." She turned and looked at GJ.

GJ was loading bullets into her magazine. All the NATs—New Agent Trainees—had to hand-load each magazine. The first bullets—because of the spring mechanism pushing upward inside it—went in relatively easily. The last ones were harder. Much harder. That made perfect sense. However, GJ was practically whining.

"I can't get them in. My fingers are not this strong. I'm not sure I can push them down in."

Two weeks. For two weeks, Walter had been watching this. They hadn't been allowed to fire a gun yet. Instead, they'd taken them apart, cleaned them, reassembled them. They'd been given a set of pieces and told to make a gun out of it. Sometimes, the pieces didn't actually all belong to the same kind of gun. It was their job to figure it out, to know that—for example—the firing pin was missing. They had to know the difference between rimfire and center fire ammunition. They needed to know full metal jackets versus hollowpoints.

Walter had no problem with this. She had been trained in weaponry before. For the first time, she was the star pupil in a class. When she'd been in the Marines, she'd been very good. But, like everyone else, she'd been learning the material for the first time. This time around, it was just review for her, and it was fun to get to play with all the guns again. She could assemble an AR-15 in her sleep. In fact, she was pretty sure she'd had that dream just last night.

So, she'd spent a reasonable amount of the first few weeks feeling bored. The good news was, they had some other classes that challenged her. While GJ took copious notes, Walter tried to sit back and listen and understand.

There was coursework on psychology, on victimology, and an amazing amount of information to be absorbed and fully understood on legal issues. As a serviceman, Walter had been told, "Shoot whoever they tell you to shoot." Apparently, that was no longer the case. Now she was going to be put out into the field.

She would not only have to read people their rights and cuff them instead of shooting them, she would now have to make decisions about who she could and couldn't shoot. If she did shoot somebody, she was going to have to be able to defend that decision in a court of law. This was more than she had bargained for. And so was GJ.

She'd expected to be dragging her new partner along behind her for a good part of training. Though she'd understood that from the start, it wasn't any easier than she'd expected. Now, having filled her own magazine to capacity, she turned and looked at GJ. Taking the piece out of her partner's hand and grabbing a bullet, she pushed it down into the clip.

It was an art form, she had to admit. One GJ had yet to master, or even get close to passing level on. Walter pushed another bullet into place with her left—fake—hand. She'd spent a long time in rehab, and then she'd spent a longer time learning to use her prosthetic. The prosthetic itself was a modern miracle. It could grasp with amazingly inhuman strength.

Using the muscles in her arm and flexing or not, she could twitch the first finger. This allowed her to actually hold and fire a gun with her prosthetic left hand.

By a series of movements ... twisting, pushing with her whole arm and using the flexion that was granted from the prosthetic ... she was able to push the bullets with relative ease—if not human-like movements—into the magazine that she held in her right hand. She pushed in a third bullet and then handed it back to GJ with a hard stare.

"Okay," GJ said. "That was nice. But you have to admit that your metal finger doesn't hurt. In fact, it doesn't even squish. I'm pushing and pushing and my finger's going to break before the spring at the bottom of that stupid magazine gives."

In answer to this, Walter picked up the magazine in her prosthetic hand and used her human hand on the right side to push more bullets in. GJ was not amused.

"Look," Walter said, "you have to do it yourself. It's not my job to do these things for you. You have to pass. I guess I could do it for you now, but I can't load your magazines for you all the time. You just have to get stronger fingers."

"Yeah, I just have to lose the *nerve endings* in my fingers," GJ muttered under her breath. Then, louder, she said, "Since you're bitching about this, maybe you don't borrow my notes after class today or tomorrow or ever again."

They'd been sniping at each other like this for days. It didn't help that they were together almost twenty-four/seven. In the end, Walter only watched as GJ managed to get the last two bullets down into the magazine. Her junior partner took a break between each one and she swore a bit under her breath.

By the time the instructor made it around to check on them, Walter had been sitting with three full magazines for quite some time. GJ had just barely finished getting the last bullet into hers. Apparently, her precious fingertips were bruised.

Then their firearms instructor said the one thing that could make Walter happy. They were going to pack up all the guns they'd assembled and all the magazines they'd filled. While they wouldn't get to use a wide variety of firearms today—only the nine millimeters they'd been assigned by the FBI—they finally got to go to the range.

They were started off on paper targets, something Walter knew well. Once you were in the field, once your targets were moving, that was a whole different game. And if your targets were human, that was another level she wasn't looking forward to repeating.

She was petrified as she watched as GJ picked up a loaded gun and aimed for the target. She wasn't sure that GJ was physically strong enough to handle the recoil on the nine-millimeter. But her little partner put both hands on the gun and held it steady. Walter had to admit that she was impressed when GJ emptied the entire magazine right into one small hole through the paper man's heart.

"Good work," Walter said.

GJ turned and looked at her. "You weren't expecting that, were you?"

"No, I wasn't."

GJ shrugged. "It's not my first rodeo. I've shot before."

"Clearly," Walter replied. She didn't say anything else.

GJ was a little slow on the trigger, especially when compared to Walter, who'd trained herself to shoot first and shoot fast. Walter emptied her magazine in a quick, steady rhythm. GJ had paused to take a breath between each pull of the trigger. When each NAT finished, they set the gun down, turned, and stepped back, waiting for one of the instructors to come and inspect their work. Even GJ earned praise. Walter thanked the gods. Each thing she didn't have to drag her junior partner through was a blessing.

It was part of the training to watch the other NATs fire, to listen and learn as the instructors helped others. Honestly, Walter was surprised when she got several corrections herself. Apparently, the way you killed people as a marine was not quite the same way that you needed to kill people when you were an FBI agent.

But she took the corrections and easily changed her stance, shifted where she was shooting, and did as she was told. She and GJ made several comments to each other about how to improve their own shooting. Then, when their next round came, they were placed side-by-side again.

"All right," the instructor said in his firm, clear voice. "This time, I want a head shot. If possible put it right between the eyes. Go."

Though she had ear protection on, Walter heard as gunfire echoed from the positions next to her and down the line. She fired two bullets, leaving two neat holes in her paper man's face: one in the middle of the forehead, and one just at the top of his nose.

Having heard the shot on her left, she moved her eyes over to check out GJ's target.

"Shit," she heard from the next aisle over. "I parted his hair."

Sure enough, it was hard to see at this distance, but the tiny bullet hole ran right across her paper perp's skull according to the picture.

"One more," GJ muttered. Then she pulled the trigger and left a nice neat hole between her picture's eyes.

5

G J raised her hand in class. As a perpetual student, the gesture was natural. As soon as she received the nod, she began speaking. Her instructor—she always thought of them as "professors" though technically they weren't—did not have correct information.

Looking around, she informed the class at large, "There's new technology that's able to break down the protein complex in a human hair. Hopefully soon we'll be able to do it with a single human hair, but right now we need several from the same subject to do the testing. Soon, that protein breakdown will be able to identify an individual person just like a DNA electropherogram would."

The instructor eyeballed her. "That technology hasn't come to full testing scenario yet. It doesn't yet meet the Daubert Standard."

"Actually, it does," GJ corrected him and went on to describe which phase of testing current trials were in, what the likelihood of a multiple protein match was being found to be, and so on. "They've identified over a thousand unique proteins that can be isolated in the hair shaft—no rootball or DNA necessary. Statistics alone says that should be able to reveal a single human individual. Though, yes, it would be important to be scientifically certain there isn't too much overlap in profiles before it was admissible in court. But I suspect that day is soon coming."

Apparently, the instructor was not keen on her new information.

Well, too bad. She had a brand-spanking-new degree in this. She'd been trained by the best in the business, and she'd been partly raised by her grandfather, the esteemed Dr. Murray Marks. She'd been fed forensics since she was an infant, and she wasn't going to let any FBI instructor tell her what science did and didn't exist.

When she finished explaining the new stages of hair analysis, the instructor over-politely asked her to cite her sources. Apparently, he thought he was going to catch her. She cited them. She'd done scut work in the lab that was performing the initial trials. But she just listed the university where the studies were being performed, information about results of current trials, and the names of the three lead professors on the case, as well as another university where repetition studies were already well under way.

The students sat in neat rows at long tables, taking copious notes during class, though they'd all stopped writing when this "current state of the science" debate broke out.

She was opening her mouth to speak again when Walter elbowed her in the ribs. Though GJ didn't care that she'd started something, she did shut up for the rest of class even though she really wanted to tell the instructor that he needed to be more forceful about emphasizing the care with which an evidentiary skeleton should be removed from the ground. When they walked out at the end of the hour, Walter turned and said, "That wasn't your smoothest move."

"Oh, really?" GJ quipped. "But explaining yesterday to the instructor how to build a firing pin out of a paper clip, when he'd just said it couldn't be done? That was *your* smartest move?"

Walter at least had the decency to shrug.

They were supposed to have the upcoming weekend off. GJ had never looked forward to a weekend more. Generally, weekends were for studying and sleeping in and eating pancakes and capping the day with a drink. She had plans to do all of it—except the damn studying—in spades for two whole days.

She found herself wondering again if anyone at her grandfather's house noticed that the power never went off when she wasn't there. More than that, she found herself wondering what had been in the kettle when she left several weeks ago. And she wondered if anything else—any new skeletons—had shown up in her grandfather's home lab.

She and Walter talked for a while. Though they didn't really like each other, they'd been thick as thieves out of necessity. While GJ was explaining the procedure for pulling protein from hair using chemicals and a breakdown process, she heard footsteps behind her. She didn't need to turn to know that Brian and Hank were following them down the hall.

The two guys had been gunning for top position amongst recruits. Though there were no official awards, it was an honor to graduate at the top of their class. To GJ, it wasn't an honor she was expecting to get anywhere close to achieving. Her physical abilities were at the barely-passing level. Academically? Well, that's why Brian and Hank had come after her. Walter was out-ranking them physically. They'd been bitching about her having an unfair advantage. GJ didn't think there was anything less attractive than bitching about being outperformed "by a girl"—their word, not hers. And Hank and Bryan did it while wearing preppy uniform khakis and blue polo shirts.

To be fair, all the NATs wore them. It was required. But GJ and Walter were both convinced it was a test to see just how badass you could be when dressed like you worked the door at a big box store. Brian and Hank were rocking the look with their preppy haircuts and whiny asses. Their goal was to take everyone out on the way to their final showdown, which they naturally assumed would be against each other. Walter clearly did not appreciate their confidence.

"So, ladies," Brian said as he came up on one side of them, Hank on the other. Each man was taller than even Walter's 5'8" frame, which made them exponentially larger than GJ's tiny form. The flanking maneuver was straight out of class. GJ almost called them on it, but Walter offered a subtle nod of her head.

"Ladies," Brian said again, and then he turned to GJ. "Do you care to explain how one might extract these proteins and why, since in the past no one has been able to do anything more than identify a hair as being consistent with those found at a crime scene. So why do you think you can now identify a person, from all of the world's population, by a single human hair?"

GJ gave him a dirty look. This was juvenile. She was an adult, despite the fact that she might look eighteen a lot of the time, especially with her hair pulled up. So naturally, that was the way the NATs were made to wear their hair during all days of training. She was going to wear it down this weekend, just because—but in the meantime, she was glad that Brian wasn't able to yank on her pigtail.

"Actually," she said, smiling sweetly at him, "we know this from a cool thing called science. It's always improving our world!" She adopted an overly-excited tour guide voice. Then she continued with more trepidation in her tone. "I already cited my sources. You're more than welcome to go and read the papers yourself. Or are you not able to remember the sources? Or maybe it's that you can't read. You can get your AI to read them to you!" She offered it like a sincere suggestion.

Beside her, she heard Walter smother a sharp giggle under her breath. *Holy shit, Walter Reed had just giggled.* Giggled. It was almost worth the harassment from Brian and Hank.

"Now, Arabella Jade, that was unkind." Of course, he insisted on calling her by her given name. While she'd once thought Walter wasn't going to handle being called "Lucy" very well, it turned out it was she who had the problem. She didn't go by her birth name either. Her grandfather had called her GJ, for Grandpa's Joy, and though these two had teased her mercilessly over the weird, random-seeming combination of initials, she'd never told them what it stood for.

Finally, Walter managed to get her expression back in order and she turned and looked each of the men in the eyes for just a moment. "Are you trying to intimidate us? Are you suggesting that we back down and not do our best? That's against the code. Or do you just want us to not try to graduate at the top of our class? Because that would insinuate that you weren't actually able to beat us by any other method than intimidation." She put her hand to her chin as though she were thinking. The men had them boxed in, but Walter wasn't afraid of them.

GJ decided she wouldn't be, either. She stayed silent while Walter continued.

"I would like to point out that we just sat through the exact same series of courses on maneuvering, intimidation, and psychological tactics that you did. And I'd like to remind you that my partner here outscored everyone else in the class."

This time, Hank's fair coloring showed off the lovely shade of red creeping up his neck. Walter apparently had had enough, and GJ decided she had, too.

Walter was the one who turned to her and said, "Do you think they underestimate us because we're female, or do you think it's because we're cute?"

Hank guffawed. "Actually, you're neither."

He had barely gotten the words out when he suddenly slipped and fell, or at least that's how it appeared to GJ, until she realized that Walter had snatched his hand and was squeezing one knuckle between just two of her fingers.

That move alone had taken Hank down. It happened so fast, there'd been nothing Brian could do to defend his asshole of a buddy. Hank was on the floor, and while he should have been getting up, the hold that Walter still had on the knuckles of his right hand kept him there, squirming. He looked to be in some serious pain. GJ worked not to smile.

"Hey," Brian said, "Don't ... *Hey!*"

He apparently hadn't yet been taught the technique Walter was using. Neither had GJ, but she was grateful that her new friend knew it. After half a moment—too short a time for anyone to really see what was happening, or for anyone to gather incriminating evidence against Walter—she let go.

Hank scrambled to his feet, and Brian turned and looked at her. "What in God's name?"

GJ stopped. She looked at him, tipped her face a little bit to the side, and said, "Brian, I finally figured it out."

"What are you talking about?" he sputtered, unable to keep up with the conversation change. She was seriously beginning to wonder how these two had gotten into FBI training in the first place. Maybe on an asshole scholarship.

She peered at him as though investigating his face. "It's the eyes and the mouth. Look, Walter. See the wide set of the eye sockets, the slight downturn at the outside edges? Do you see how his mouth is a little bit wider set, too? That's in the bone, not just on the skin and the musculature over it. That's a defect from birth. And if you look, too, you can see how the lines of his face don't follow the golden ratios. This is indicative that his mother imbibed a large quantity of alcohol while she was pregnant with him. Did you know about that, Brian?"

Brian didn't respond, and for a moment, GJ stood stunned, realizing that she had hit the nail on the head. Whether or not it was true, Brian was afraid he had a touch of Fetal Alcohol Syndrome.

It was Hank who muttered under his breath, "My fucking hand!" and turned, taking his friend down the hall. There were threats issued under their breath as they walked away, but for the first time, GJ and Walter had stood up together and acted as a team.

6

They hadn't been able to leave the Academy yet. They were stuck at Quantico one more night before the weekend, but Walter was counting down the hours.

Right now, she wasn't too far from where Donovan lived, and he was between cases at the moment. Though that might change before she made it to his place tomorrow night, she kept her fingers crossed.

He told her Eleri had found something that might lead to information about her missing sister and was researching that. Though Walter didn't know the whole story behind it, she was hoping to hear some nice, leisurely updates from her boyfriend this weekend. It had been far too long since she'd seen him.

She'd been lying in bed, staring at the ceiling, thinking sleep would never come when an alarm sounded and woke her from the deepest dream possible.

Shit. They'd been told this would happen. One of the NATs had heard this was a common drill and asked about it in class. The minute their instructor shook his head as though he had no idea, the rumors had begun flying. There would be midnight drills. Of course there would. FBI agents were often called on a moment's notice to go immediately to a new location to start or join a case. They always had a go-bag prepared. Walter understood this, but that was not what a midnight drill was like.

A midnight drill was a torture device.

She looked at her clock. It wasn't midnight—it was two a.m. She'd actually managed to get to sleep the night before their weekend break, and now these fuckers had to wake her up. She was quite certain they were going to have to attend a full day's worth of classes tomorrow on very little rest. *Lovely.*

Still, she was a Marine at heart, and she was good at doing what she was told. She rolled upright, watching as GJ Janson put both feet on the floor, stood up, and slid fluidly into her khaki pants and academy-issued polo shirt.

Though Walter was bionic during the day, at night, it was as entirely different story. Her prostheses were off. They had to be. She couldn't function if she slept in them. So she now sat on the side of the bed, one foot on the floor, the other partial leg dangling, and slung herself into the polo shirt. At least she'd had it handy. She'd been ready.

As she pulled one pants leg up, she saw GJ tuck her shirt in and buckle everything up her pre-threaded belt. Her roommate wasn't the strongest or the fastest or the most intimidating, but she was sharp. GJ was at the door with her hand on the knob before she seemed to fully wake up and realize what was going on.

Though Walter was mostly dressed now, she was still missing two limbs. Reaching out, she grabbed her leg prosthesis, and began the task of settling it just so, then buckling it into place. It wasn't the long, arduous process that many veterans dealt with. Few people had her level of tech. She'd agreed to be a guinea pig at Walter Reed Hospital. While it had meant a longer stay and longer recovery, it also earned her the best non-flesh limbs money could buy. But even with all her advantages, putting on her prosthetics still wasn't a process that could be termed "fast."

Worried and wondering why she hadn't heard the door open— why GJ wasn't already out it, since she was dressed and ready— Walter looked up. She'd moved just in time to see GJ holding out the left arm prosthetic.

"You should go," Walter said, "I can do this."

"I know," said GJ, "But I'm here. We go out the door together."

"That's not necessary." Walter shook her head. "You have to pass these things, or neither of us will graduate."

"I know. I'll pass. I know you may not believe me and I know that I huff and I puff when we go on the five-mile runs. And I hate every step of it while you seem to think it's just a walk in the park. I'm the one who takes excellent notes in class and understands all the scientific concepts. I'm the one who makes everybody concerned that I'm a sociopath because I'm actually really good at interrogating people. You're good at intimidating.

"But the deal is: we have to start being a team. It isn't just about training. When we get out in the field, Westerfield's going to leave us on our own. If we don't have each other's backs, it won't be about flunking out, it will be that we're actually not going to survive. It hadn't really hit me until earlier today, but we can't afford to keep going the way we've been going. So here's your arm. How can I help put it on so that we can be faster? Because we're going out that door together."

For a moment, Walter sat in stunned silence. In all her life—even before she'd even been missing a limb or two, before she'd ever needed an extra five minutes to get a prosthetic device on—everyone went out the door for themselves. That was how she'd been trained to operate. It was what she'd always done. Despite being part of a team, she was expected to go on her own.

No one had ever waited for her.

Walter woke up in bed naked next to Donovan. However, she was thoroughly disappointed. She was naked for no good reason, and that sucked. She had been so tired when she arrived, that she'd walked through his door and basically shed every piece of clothing before saying hello. Then fell face-first into his bed. At some point during the night, he must have climbed in with her, but she would not have been able to answer what time in a court of law.

Luckily, when she woke up, the morning played out a good bit better than the night before had.

Later, over breakfast, Donovan commented, "I'd expected you to arrive earlier. And I expected you to be awake. I'm just glad you made it safely."

"Yeah." Walter fought a sigh. "It was a bitch. I think I drank fifteen sodas trying to stay awake on the drive down. I'm surprised I didn't have to get up five times in the middle of the night to pee."

He laughed at her and she appreciated the ability to speak with frank candor about peeing in the middle of the night. She appreciated having a boyfriend. It had been a long time since that had happened. The last time Walter had a significant other, she'd also had four intact limbs. But if anyone understood her, it was Donovan.

She explained to him about the middle-of-the-night drill, how they'd been roused from their beds and lined up in the hallway like cadets in a military academy.

"I remember those!" He almost looked nostalgic. "I remember having these contradictory thoughts at the time. One was, *I survived med school just fine, and I can survive this.* And the other was, *I fucking went to med school. I do not need this shit.*"

That time, she laughed. At least midnight drills and cold practices were something she knew and understood well. She told him about GJ waiting for her and then she told him how the two of them had arrived, last in line, last to stand at attention.

While everyone waited silently ready for the drill/torture to start, the instructor yelled at GJ. Why hadn't she come out first? Why had she waited for her partner? GJ had stayed motionless—all five feet and two inches of her—and stared the man down. She said, "That's my partner. I don't leave without her."

Walter could tell that Donovan understood how touched she was by the gesture. He also understood she was never going to say so. Though the instructors threatened GJ with failure of the exercise—which meant a repeat of it—GJ didn't budge. They next threatened to flunk her out of the physical portion of training, giving her bad marks and putting her at the bottom of the class. GJ still stood firm. She only repeated what she'd said to Walter earlier. "She and I, we're going to be partners in the field. If we don't have each other's backs, we'll be dead. So you can yell at me all you want, but it's not going to change the fact that every time we leave the door, we'll leave it together."

Walter's final assessment was that GJ was slow, she was relatively weak, she was quite smart, and sometimes she was a holy terror with a gun. Walter was still afraid her partner was going to accidentally hurt someone in the roll-and-shoot drills. Walter wanted to be nowhere near her when that day happened. She was simply grateful they hadn't gotten there yet.

"That," she told Donovan, "is probably going to be the day that GJ flunks us out of Quantico."

Walter was unprepared for when he laughed at her. "I don't know, Walter. The girl's got spunk; you've got to hand it to her. My thought is, you can pull off the academy courses and study. It's not that you're not smart, you're just not a student like that. If you can pull off the academy classes, she can pull off the physical side of it. You just watch. The two of you will graduate just fine. After all, I did, and honestly, some days I don't think I'm in any better shape or any more coordinated than GJ is."

They ate a little longer in silence and then Donovan changed the topic. "I'm assuming since Westerfield put the two of you together, he'd also set you guys up to spill all your secrets to each other, right?"

Though he hadn't completely meant it, Walter knew what he was fishing for. "No," she said. "He sat us down together and offered us the position together and GJ accepted right away. When I took longer to decide, he talked to me a couple of times that week. He made it very clear that I was *not* to tell GJ what I knew about you and the others like you."

"Are you serious?" Donovan asked. "That's like pitting the two of you against each other. Like making you partners and then making you keep secrets. But surely, she's figured it out. Right?"

"No, I don't think so." Walter shook her head. "GJ still seems convinced that you have an extreme case of double-jointedness that you don't even know about yourself."

"What?" He blinked a few times as though reconciling the idea. "GJ did ask me about that before, and I brushed her off. She's still stuck on that?"

"Looks like. Her grandfather has a collection of bones like yours," she said. "But she doesn't think there's anything to it other than some plates that didn't fuse and some ligament attachments that make it look like you should be pretty flexible."

"Holy shit," Donovan said, though Walter wasn't sure if that comment was from finding out about the collection or from GJ's current inability to put the pieces together. "What's going to happen when she finds out?"

"Who says she's going to find out?" Walter asked. "If she and I are partners and we're not put on the same cases with you, how would she? If she doesn't see you or the other agent Wade or, you know, someone else *like* you, what would happen? If we don't run into the Lobomau, then who's to say she'll ever figure it out?"

Donovan didn't seem as convinced about that possibility as Walter did and honestly, Walter wasn't sure. Apparently, GJ had cracked a nearly uncrackable code when they'd been working a previous case. She'd cracked it partly through sheer smarts and partly through dogged determination. Maybe Donovan was right. Walter wondered what would happen if she just told her everything, but what would Westerfield do if she defied his specific orders? She asked Donovan what he thought the repercussions might be.

Shaking his head, he stood up from the table and carried his plate to the sink. "I don't know," he said. "All I know is that Westerfield's being an ass. He's put you in a damn hard position, Walter."

7

GJ's grandfather wasn't even home. He was out on a speaking tour and she'd known it. He'd managed to leave just prior to her arrival and he'd be back Tuesday, after she'd already left. So no one was here for the weekend, except herself and the staff. The staff loved her almost as much as her grandfather did.

She could've gone to her own home or seen her parents. However, since she hadn't even told them that she was at Quantico training to become an FBI agent, she wasn't about to try to explain where her bruises had come from. Or why she was so sleep-deprived. They would likely assume the sleep issue was from being a graduate student, but the bruises were much harder to explain away. And what could she possibly say about why on earth she kept putting her hand to her right hip?

That's where her gun was holstered. They wore heavy plastic, brightly colored, molded fake Glocks that wouldn't do anything in a fight except bounce off someone's head if thrown. But the NATs had to wear them at all times, Quantico regulations for new academy trainees. The problem was, after just a few short days of wearing the heavy pieces at their sides, all the trainees began to act as though they were walking around with actual guns.

The men got more macho, which was honestly a tough thing to do given the amount of testosterone that was flowing through her training class already. But GJ found even she began to reach for her hip. After so many times practicing the release of the holster, drawing the weapon, and firing on sight, it had become perfectly natural to her. Once they'd been allowed to actually pull the trigger on the real guns and loose some bullets on things, then they'd started pulling the fake guns out of the holsters. And that was the point, though she wasn't sure she liked it.

They practiced aiming, even though the plastic guns couldn't shoot. Despite all the fake parts of the drills, she'd still become adept at reaching for her gun. It was an odd sensation—one she'd never expected to feel as a scientist and she *had* expected to be a scientist. It wasn't that she wasn't one now, but she certainly had entered a whole new realm.

She'd made the drive to her grandfather's house because she hadn't wanted to go to her own place. GJ could've gone to her apartment and seen some of her friends and she would have loved it. They would have wanted her to come out to party, to hang out, to talk, to stay up late, and she would've wanted to do it. She would've returned to Quantico more worn out than when she'd left—and those assholes kept them up all night running trainings.

After lining up the NATs along the length of the hallway the night before, they'd taken them to the practice room. There, they'd spent hours practicing jiu-jitsu take downs. They practiced hold maneuvers, and pressure-point applications, and finally, everyone was let in on the little trick Walter had used to take Hank to the floor. That was a shame. Though GJ appreciated learning the hold, she wished it was something Walter still could lord over Hank. Hank had smirked at Walter as he'd walked by at the end of training.

The only thought GJ had was that—while Hank had one trick— Walter surely had a hundred more. You didn't come out of MARSOC, you didn't come out of Afghanistan or Somalia—or any of the other places where Walter had apparently been stationed, but couldn't breathe a word about—without knowing all kinds of wonderful little things like that. Maybe after they graduated GJ could get Walter to teach her a few more. Maybe after they graduated, she and Walter would be closer to being friends. At least they'd improved from always sniping at each other to at least being partners. They sure as hell weren't friends, yet.

She probably slept fourteen hours the first night at her grandfather's. Her original plans included walking in the door, hugging the staff, and telling them a lie about where she'd been. If she could get them to ignore her bruises—though that was difficult, as they were no less nitpicky or concerned than her parents—she'd thought she would go down to her grandfather's laboratory that first night.

No such luck. She slept so soundly that she didn't wake until the sun crested the top of the sky. She hadn't done that since finals. Having slept so long, she certainly couldn't run right down into the basement lab. She had to check in and assure the staff there was nothing wrong with her, she'd simply been extremely busy. And that, though she'd been looking forward to her weekend, she had not been able to get a good night's sleep the night before she left. That part was true. The *why* was not. She was lucky she'd gotten some sleep on the plane or she wouldn't have made it home without falling asleep at the wheel and driving off the side of the road, though she didn't tell them that part, either.

The staff had made her a hearty breakfast at the usual time, but when she didn't show, they'd set it aside and kept it warm. She ate it served up at noon: French toast casserole, sausage, bacon, and an egg, because what growing grad student didn't need all that? She finally managed to sneak away. It was almost two o'clock by the time she'd showered, gotten dressed, and managed to get everyone else out of her hair.

Once again, she'd flipped the breaker to the wing that housed a full lab inside the large home. Leaving the power off kept the camera at the end of the hallway from recording her as she walked down. It also tripped the switch on the coded lock that had shown up on her grandfather's basement laboratory door, replacing the old combination lock she'd figured out opened with her own birthday. The new lock didn't.

Maybe he was getting suspicious. Maybe he'd always been paranoid. She wasn't certain what it was, but she knew it wasn't a good sign. She tried to ignore the feeling in the pit of her stomach. Tried to ignore the fact that the person she was spying on was her own grandfather. The man who'd taken her for walks and Planet Earth movies in IMAX. He'd told her about animals and people and ancient cultures. She just didn't know what else he was doing.

With a little bit of research, her specialty, she'd managed to find an online video and figure out how to flip the lock. While it was a nice, heavy, digital padlock, it had an emergency code so it couldn't lock anyone in or out if the power was off. It was a design flaw, she thought, but her grandfather—while very smart and good at many things—was no technical expert. It made perfect sense that he'd bought a lock that his own granddaughter could pick.

In the middle of the day, enough light came in through the high windows to see around without her camera. The windows had been frosted so that no one could sneak around the outside and peek in to see what he was doing—another design issue that she hadn't fully considered the first time she'd come down here. Back then, she'd thought the place incredibly cool and wondered why he locked it up. Now, each time she visited, she encountered or spotted yet another feature designed to keep the world out.

The more she walked around, the more she looked, the more she realized that this place was a fortress of its own. Despite the glow coming through the high windows, she still needed the flashlight on her phone when looking in the backs of drawers, or under papers and stacks of files, where the light wasn't quite enough to make up for the shadows that always haunted the room when she was down here.

Scanning the space at large, she saw the kettle was once again open. Standing near it and peeking down inside, she could see it was back to its normal, clean, shiny self. Whatever had been boiling in it had been removed. Nothing was lying out on the tables. That was also a normal facet of her grandfather's lab. The more she'd learned about other people's labs, the more time she'd spent with other professors, the more she'd learned that they left their bones out. They simply left the bodies lying on the table. They considered it enough to lock the lab when they left. If that was enough precaution to cover their end of the responsibility, why did her grandfather always put everything away? She didn't want to think he was hiding his work, but there was no other conclusion she could draw. Ironically, he was the one who'd taught her to rule out all other options to arrive at the logic of a situation.

Now she had the task of sorting through what she knew, what she remembered, and what she had in the record on her cellphone. She had to figure out which things were new in the lab. Pulling open drawers, GJ saw some had full human skeletons laid out, bone by bone, recreating the anatomy of the figure when they were alive. Others simply held pieces. Some had a femur, a tibia, a handful of foot bones, each laid out as well as could be done with so many missing pieces. Still other drawers were smaller, holding only partial limbs, and eventually, some pieces were just kept in boxes, labeled on the ends and stacked to the top of the ceiling. *So many lives were cataloged in this room*, she thought. And so many of them—in fact, almost all the ones she could specifically examine—had one singular, massive, full-skeletal anomaly.

For all full drawers in the lab, for all the bones it held, it still had many empty boxes with no labels and drawers with no tags on the end. GJ began searching through these first. Sure enough, thirty minutes later, she discovered one of the untagged drawers held a full, clean, fresh skeleton that likely had been in the kettle when she'd left. She couldn't be certain, as she'd never seen the body before it went in, and had no information other than something large had been in the kettle the last time she was here.

She frowned at it now but dismissed what she was seeing. She had to check everything first. As the body was already laid out in anatomical form, she did what she'd been trained to do. This meant first she looked it over and made certain her grandfather had gotten it right. Were all the carpals in the right positions for the hands? Had any of the feet bones been mixed up or swapped? Had he been going too fast?

She didn't expect mistakes from her grandfather, but she'd seen enough from undergrad students and even the occasional careless error from other scientists that she always checked first. What she saw wouldn't mean anything if it was a mistake. In a moment, she assessed that the skeleton appeared to be laid out correctly. Knowing she couldn't fix any errors if she did see them, she began taking catalog-style pictures with her phone. Though the power was out, she worked in the eerie silence, filling the air with the soft bumps and thuds of opening and closing drawers, the slide of wood on wood, and the sound of cabinet doors. With the camera, she added a technical sound—the fake whirring sound of the shutter that didn't actually exist on her phone camera.

Even as she continued snapping photos, her eyes darted back and forth. This was another skeleton that had the same anomaly. She'd started at the feet and worked her way up, not pausing. She had to complete her round of pictures. If she heard anyone from upstairs coming down this often unused hall, she'd have to stop, be quiet, and make sure no one heard her. But nothing sounded from overhead and she continued clicking away.

Eventually, she was able to look at the weird thing she'd spotted first. Though the maxillary plate had a fissure that normally was fused on humans at a very, very young age, in infancy even, this one remained in separate pieces. Though the limbs and torso and head were all in the right places, her grandfather had altered the skull. Using putty and wires, he'd moved the maxillary plate out. The jawbone had more than an average cleft. In fact, it appeared to have cartilage between where the two sides of the jawbone had come together during formation in early fetal development.

Much like a cleft palate, sometimes jawbones—which grew simultaneously from both sides and met in the middle—didn't fuse in the center or fused incompletely. When they met and grew into one piece but failed to do it fully, it was called a Staphne Defect and was considered the only aesthetically acceptable birth defect. In fact, most people simply called it a "cleft chin." This skeleton had far more going on than that. Though it appeared nothing would have been noticeable on the live person, the mandible was very different. It wasn't just that the jaw hadn't fused, it was that she could see a very thin line of cartilage down the center holding together what were now two separated pieces of bone together.

The way her grandfather had wired the skull and mandible, the whole front of the face jutted out. She noted again how the jaw, while thicker than an average human jaw, was possibly narrower across the base as well as longer front to back. She thought of Agent Donovan Heath's physiology. She could see that his jaw wasn't narrower, but it *was* longer front-to-back than average.

Could it jut out this way? She looked at the temporomandibular-joints, where the jaw rested into the skull, and noticed more, smaller anomalies in the otherwise standard anatomy there.

Yes, it was possible Donovan Heath could do this. She frowned. This was more than just double-jointedness. This meant the entire front of the face could move forward. Then she looked down at the skeleton's arms and noticed something even more startling.

8

"Sir, tell me about your wife." GJ spoke into the microphone sitting on the desk in front of her. Next to her sat three different open notebooks detailing the situation she was trying to talk her way out of.

"No," the voice replied into the headset she wore. He sounded like he was so close, just like he would in a real scenario. Both their voices also transmitted to the room at large, so everyone could hear everything— every word, every tone, every inflection in her voice—as she negotiated the faux hostage situation. The man in question had taken his entire family into their home, boarded the doors and the windows, and informed everyone that he had multiple weapons at hand. He threatened to kill his own children if his demands weren't met. But GJ had noticed he made no threats made specifically against his wife, though she could hear the woman crying and screaming in the background.

"Isn't your wife the reason that you're doing this?" GJ prodded. "Wouldn't she want you to—"

She was cut off by the sharp retort of a gun into her right ear. She startled, dropping her pen and almost knocking her seat over.

"You failed," her instructor announced sternly. "He just shot himself."

She looked up into the stadium seating of the classroom, finally seeing the faces of all her fellow NATs as they watched her try to work the situation. Yes, they were all looking at her like she'd done exactly that—failed. Big F. She was wondering if, however, the loss was a *complete* failure when she saw a hand go up from the back of the room.

Lauren, a fellow NAT who'd been nothing but kind—although not overly friendly—asked the instructor, "Is it truly a failure? Sure, he shot himself, but he was the one holding everyone hostage. He was the terrorist. His family is okay, aren't they? Isn't that the goal?"

This time the instructor turned narrow eyes onto Lauren and responded with a criticism just as harsh as the one's he'd previously leveled at GJ. Though GJ was grateful to be out from under his stare, she didn't think things were going to get any better after Lauren was taken down a notch or two.

"What was the assignment?" the instructor asked Lauren.

Sounding less certain, Lauren replied, "Talk the man into throwing his weapons out the door, then talk him into coming out the door with his hands over his head, with his family intact and unharmed."

"Exactly. Did agent Janson achieve this?"

"Well, no," Lauren said, "But—"

"No. There are no buts. We do it again. Who's next?"

No one volunteered. *Shocking*, GJ thought.

The fact of the matter was that GJ seemed to have a natural knack for this. She'd been great in their interrogation classes, practically able to climb into someone's lap and pretend to become their best friend. It had disturbed her how easy it was to talk to agents posing as child molesters, serial killers, and all the dregs of humanity that she'd once thought she'd never have to deal with. She tended to work with humans in their skeletal forms more often than as live human beings. Particularly live, awful human beings.

The instructor simply pointed, pegging his next victim by that move alone. This brought Hank down to the front of the room. His swagger was unmistakable, even if GJ was still shaking a little bit from the gunshot that had been fired. It still sounded so close. Shaking, she removed the headset, closed the folders, and happily vacated the hot seat.

Hank put on the headset, obviously confident that he could do better than she had. Three minutes later, he'd managed to get the man to shoot his entire family *and* himself. Well, at least she hadn't failed as heinously as Hank.

Sitting calmly next to her, Walter leaned over and whispered, "You know, Hank blew it even harder than you did. And to be fair, he had your example of how to at least get the guy to not kill his family, so that's pretty epic. Can't be sad about that."

On the one hand, GJ agreed. It was a fake situation; no real children were harmed in the making of this failure. However, out in the real world, they would all have to perform better. One by one, the NATs went through different scenarios, and one by one, most of them managed to get everyone killed.

Quantico sucked. Lunch was usually relatively jovial, but today it was a somber affair with most of the trainees thinking over their failing grades from the morning. GJ looked around the lunchroom. This was a class full of overachievers. You didn't really wind up at Quantico being a lazy ass, that was for sure. But all these overachiever/Type A personalities were now stuck in one room sucking down the spate of failures from this morning and no one was doing anything other than chewing and swallowing. Even GJ was grateful later that day for the punishing five-mile run.

She was at the point where she thought maybe if she spoke to anyone at all, they might take other people hostage and kill themselves. The instructor had ended the class by informing all of them they'd have another chance the next day. That didn't make anyone any happier.

Still later that afternoon on the range, GJ found she was disturbingly soothed by the ability to shoot bullets out of a nine-millimeter Glock. This was not the life she'd chosen. And in bed that night, staring at the ceiling while Walter slept softly—in fact, like a *baby*—on the other side of the room, GJ contemplated all of it. Walter probably slept better because the people she'd killed today were merely fictional. She'd shot and killed live humans before. Probably often. However, fictional deaths were the closest that GJ had ever come. Previously, she had zero responsibility for the deaths of any of the bodies she dealt with. She was always there after the fact. Never at the tipping point.

As a forensic scientist, she considered herself a warrior for justice. She was often the only voice a dead person had. She was the one who found evidence and sought justice for the crimes committed against them. She was the one who proved that the person on the floor was not the killer, so that they could be buried in peace with the rest of their family rather than their family dealing with the shame of believing they had a criminal in their midst. She proved the perpetrator was the one who caused it all and deserved to be dead on her table.

Coming to Quantico had seemed, to a certain extent, a natural extension of that soul-deep need she had for justice. However, after today, she was beginning to think maybe she'd taken a wrong turn. She was shooting targets that had drawings on them of actual human beings. She was training to kill *people*. Previously, it had been the bad guys they were training to kill. She knew one of these days, it was going to be the good guys, because today, she'd killed someone in the middle. Today's death lay somewhere in the wide gray line that so much of Quantico training was about. The hostage-taker wasn't truly one of the bad guys. He was troubled. He was frightened, and she hadn't been able to save him.

She was wondering if she would be able to save her own family. Her grandfather was into something strange, that—the more she looked at it—the more concerned she became. The more she learned, the more illegal it appeared.

Her parents didn't even know where she was. Most everyone else wrote home excited. They called and told their parents, and even had parties when they got accepted into FBI training. She'd lied. And here she was in the middle of the night, when she was supposed to be getting sleep for the brutal day that faced her tomorrow, and instead she was staring at the ceiling. She'd washed actual human blood off herself before, but this was the first time she'd understood the real meaning of "blood on her hands."

Walter stood at the edge of Hogan's Alley, Quantico's training grounds for the NATs. It was built to look like a real town, and to be fair, aside from the fact that nothing in the town worked, it looked pretty good.

She felt like she'd stood here a thousand times before. Training simulations were absolutely the name of the game, and when she'd been in theater overseas, they'd done them even in the areas where they might actually wind up walking out the door and fighting insurgents. In closed spaces, they'd trained against each other, so that they would be ready. She stood now, her fake gun at her side, waiting to hear her name called. The instructors appeared to be pairing people at random.

GJ stood next to her. In rapt silence, they listened to the sound of gunfire coming from inside one of the buildings. It had been staged for some particular purpose they still didn't know. The trainees were sometimes let in on what that purpose was. The first several rounds of action they'd worked on here, in the early weeks, had been relatively simple. Clear a room. Find a bad guy. Cuff him. Read him his rights. Kill him if you had to.

Lately, things had gotten much more intense. Sometimes they were given only the briefest rundown of the situation. Sometimes they were sent into buildings with no instructions whatsoever. Then they had to walk in, guns on their hips or in their hands, and try to figure out what was going on. Sometimes, it got ugly.

Silently, the NATs standing at the edge of the simulation watched as Hank and Olivia came out from the building. According to the rounds of *simunition*—simulated ammunition—fired and the marks on them, both of them were badly wounded. By the expressions on their faces, they were actually dead.

In previous rounds, the NATs left outside had been given live camera feeds into the action so they could learn from what their fellow trainees had done or failed to do. Now those were gone, so while Hank and Olivia had been graded and set free, the others were still waiting their turn with no idea what they were facing.

"Fisher, Janson," the instructor called out, pointing then holding up two fingers in case they couldn't count. "Two of you, head in."

Walter got a bit of a funny feeling. Just two nights ago, GJ had asked before they fell asleep, "Do you notice how they put us together more than the others?"

"We're roommates," Walter shrugged it off. "They often pair up the roommates. They're training to make us partners."

"No, I know that," GJ said, "and they do pair up the roommates more often than other pairs, but they also put the NATs in a variety of other pairs. They're trying to get us to work with other agents. They're trying to throw us into new situations. But the fact of the matter is, I've been collecting data, and you and I are put together far more often than the other roommate pairs are."

Walter hadn't noticed, but then again, she hadn't been *collecting data*. Since GJ had said it though, she'd been keeping a silent score for herself, and it looked like her partner was correct. They walked to the front door of the schoolhouse wondering what they were facing. Then the instructor opened the door and simply ushered them inside. Weapons drawn, ready for simunitions fire, they slowly entered the space.

They called out, as they had been trained to do, using short, barking phrases in authoritative voices. Even GJ could now scare the piss out of anyone they ran into with only the sound of her words. Just two weeks ago, they'd gone through pop-up training where they ran, jumped, crawled, and rolled through a staged scenario where good guy and bad guy targets popped out. The trainees had to make split-second decisions whether to shoot or not. Wrong decision, you killed a civilian. Right decision, you scored a point. Wrong decision, you were dead. There were places to duck and obstacles to jump over or roll under. This was the part where Walter had most feared being anywhere near GJ Janson with a gun. Instead, GJ had surprised them with a nearly perfect score. It turned out, she was using her tiny frame to her advantage, fitting into places others would never be able to. It gave her a slight advantage in decision time, as it made it much harder for the "bad guys" to get a clean shot at her.

Later, as she looked at her partner, Walter realized something. While no one had been paying attention, GJ Janson had bulked up a little bit. She'd become slightly less klutzy, definitely more coordinated, and a lot safer with a firearm.

Inside the school building, they called out into the empty space. And Walter had to admit that, while there were other NATs in their class that she might have preferred to be on the range with or that she might have wanted to take notes off of more than GJ these days, when it came to having someone at her back, she considered Janson a pretty damn good ally.

They walked together into the empty space, and though they continued hollering out, no one hollered in return. Together, back to back, they cleared the room. Walter knew her own stride was slightly less than human. She didn't limp the way she had in the beginning, when she'd first learned to work with the prosthetic. She'd learned to twitch her muscles in certain unnatural ways to make her gait appear more natural. She could walk, run, and jump, but while she did all of this—and while she did it now without thinking—she still didn't have quite a normal stride.

What she noticed though, was that GJ had matched her stride. Walter couldn't match to GJ, so GJ had fixed the problem. Together, they opened a door. Standing clear of it on either side, they swept in, checking angles with their guns. No longer did GJ swing her gun to mistakenly aim at a live human being, but now brought it up just shy of the mark, swept her angle, and cleanly entered into the room.

They didn't yell out, "Clear." There was no one to yell it to.

By the time the fourth room turned up empty, Walter had begun to wonder what they'd gotten into. That was when all hell broke loose. Five armed assailants, actually some of their instructors, popped up from behind well barricaded positions in the room, each of them holding a nasty-looking firearm. Because they were FBI agent instructors, they knew what they were doing. Walter and GJ ducked, covered, and rolled. One of them would lay cover fire while the other ran in a short burst, and then took turns retreating out of the room piece by piece.

They made it from the first room safely and were just gathering themselves when two more agents popped up. Despite the fact that they cleared this room before, and they knew it, bad guys must've come in while they'd been in the other room.

"Shit," Walter yelled.

GJ echoed the sentiment and ducked, propping herself up behind a metal desk for cover. With short, sharp hand signals, she showed Walter exactly the path to take and laid cover fire. Though it felt like an hour, it was probably less than twenty seconds before they managed to maneuver themselves outside of that room as well. They paused, stopping on either side of the door, breathing heavily, weapons clutched tight to their chests. GJ looked at her with an expression that surely mirrored her own. *What do we do now?*

When a hand fell on Walter's shoulders, her first reaction was to turn and shoot at it. Luckily, she had slightly better reflexes than that, because it was their initial instructor, the one who'd opened the door and led them into this hellhole, who was clamping on her shoulder and letting the two of them know that the drill was over.

The other agents, armed to the teeth, came out of the back room and smiled at the two women. As her breathing and heart rate slowed, Walter looked around at all of them. She and GJ were the only students here. Everyone else had just tried to lay waste to them.

"Hells bells, that was a shit show," she said.

"Well," one of the senior agents said, looking between the two of them, "you're still alive. That's a passing score on this exercise. In fact, it's the only passing score."

Holy shit, Walter thought, but didn't say. This time biting down on her tongue and glancing at GJ as she saw her friend try not to smirk. The next morning when she showed up for breakfast, Hank and three other trainees had disappeared.

9

It was several more weeks before they were given a solid break again. In the meantime, they'd had more hostage negotiation classes, and GJ had managed to kill fewer people and get more of them to surrender. No one had a perfect record, but hers was getting pretty good. Needless to say, she still hated it. While she worked, she always knew that it was a fake situation with terrorists and hostages played by her instructor agents. Despite the fact that every scenario was based on a real encounter, she couldn't actually kill anyone. But that meant that, if she were ever in a real situation, it was going to be an entirely different ball game, and one she was not looking forward to.

The next week, when she'd almost decided she'd learned everything she could about firearms, they dragged out something new. She could jump and shoot, roll, hide behind things, and cover her partner, even if it wasn't Walter. The one time Brian had been assigned as her partner, she'd kept that fucker alive, even though he didn't deserve it. She could make split-second decisions about who she should shoot and who she shouldn't. It would've given her no small amount of pleasure to let Brian die in the exercise and then shrug later and say, "Well, it couldn't be helped." But no, she'd saved his sorry ass. Then he'd turned around and claimed he'd saved hers.

When that was all said and done, they turned their attention to making bombs, throwing grenades, avoiding IEDs. They had to practice with several different types of gases. They entered a specially built house wearing their full complement of tactical gear, including gas masks, heavy vests, and more. They had to walk into the "Gas House," which was entirely dark and had already been bombed with OC gas or CS gas, both of which burned like a motherfucker if you didn't have your mask on. GJ knew this because that had been their first gas training: stand there and take it.

When they'd started, Quantico had been exciting. It had been new. It had been challenging. Now, it was just exhausting. It was hard to believe she once thought the people they were learning about during the first weeks were the dregs of humanity. Those people practically seemed like regular family members after the stuff they'd gone through this past week. No wonder agents were often cold and hard.

She did not want to profile another serial killer. She did not want to hear about how he tortured animals as a kid. In fact, she decided to buy a pet bunny when she got home, just to make up for all the ones that had been gutted by psychopaths building their way up to a good murder.

As class went on, the tally on how many pet bunnies she was going to have to buy rose. However, by the time their next break— four full days on a long weekend—rolled around, she had managed to squash the idea of saving all the rabbits in the world. She also realized she needed to see her own parents again.

After flying to her grandfather's house for the first break, she was now approaching far too long an absence without her Mom and Dad knowing where she was. It was tempting to let the omission stand a while longer, since her parents thought they knew where she was— but if she didn't correct that soon, it would roll from *omission* directly into *lie* and she didn't want that. Still, the way her parents always tolerated her and let her grandfather indulge her, led her to believe that it was entirely possible she could probably hold a job with the feds for two or three years before she mentioned that she was an FBI agent. However, if she did that, it would be a shit storm of epic proportions when it did hit the fan. Since she was already exhausted, GJ decided she might as well deal with it now.

Even so, she was not planning to spend the entire four days at her parents' house. She wouldn't go to her grandfather's house either; she'd had enough of him, too. Perhaps the way to not get in trouble with what she'd found in the basement lab was simply to not go to the basement. It almost shocked her that it was an idea she'd simply never considered before. Had she told Walter her problems, her roomie would have stated the option as a matter of fact a long time ago. Maybe she should have told Walter...

Though GJ would never have expected it, Walter had shocked them all by becoming an expert in serial killer and serial offender profiles. Whatever it was about Walter, she just understood these guys. GJ wasn't sure if that was comforting or scary as fuck. Maybe it was because Walter didn't have GJ's sensibilities. These people didn't really scare the former Marine. Walter had no doubt about her ability to get away from anyone who might try to attack her or take her down. GJ, on the other hand, still had plenty of concerns in that department. Walter also managed to completely disengage herself from the perpetrator and the series of victims, while GJ never fully could. Maybe it was an advantage of having been an armed fighter in the past: the ability to look at human life in simple terms of commodities and losses, the same as she might if her groceries were stolen. Ironically, Walter was the one who'd worked with live people. GJ was the one who'd worked with the dead.

"If you look at it like a puzzle, and you know these certain kinds of pieces go certain places," Walter had said, "it makes sense. We know they tend to drive white or silver cars. We know they tend to have certain types of histories. We know Child Protective Services was often called on them when they were children. Those are records we can look up and put together. We know what a disorganized killer does versus an organized killer." Walter had gone on and on while GJ sat there stunned, feeling like she was being "mansplained" to, or *Waltersplained* to. Wasn't *she* supposed to be the star student?

"I understand," she replied. In fact, she'd studied some of this stuff before she'd ever set foot in Quantico. The knowledge helped with determining how a body had been positioned, or how deep it was buried, things like that. Forensic anthropologists and human forensic scientists like herself understood a good deal about these things.

"It's just, *Walter*, I can't look at that person and not think *that's a living human being*. Now I'm dealing with them *before* they're dead," she'd explained. "If we screw up, more of them wind up dead. That's a heavy burden."

But Walter had remained very much disengaged and said, "There's nothing we can do about that. We just catch them as fast as we can."

Damn, GJ wished she had that ability. Walter would probably get reassigned to the serial killers division and GJ would go on to—oh God, please not!—hostage negotiations.

So for the break, she'd headed back to her own apartment, figuring she would spend the first two days there, probably the only way she was going to get any relaxation. Once again, she slept a long night. Sadly, this time she dreamed she was assigned—of course—to a hostage negotiation team. In the dream—a nightmare, really—they sent her from one fraught situation to another with zero sleep and an epic number of failures. She woke up feeling no more rested than she normally did after a night drill.

This time, she did all the things she had eschewed her last break. She went out with friends. She partied. They saw a movie. *Oh my God, sweet blessed relief, a movie.* She drank a bit too much at a party that trailed into the wee hours of the night and she slept in late again. That was going to kill her sleep cycle when she got back. But before that, she was going to kill herself by going and telling her parents.

She arrived at her family home late the following night. After a brief round of hugs and zero confessions, she slept straight through the night again. Her silence didn't last five minutes into breakfast. She'd thought of fifteen different ways to casually work the idea into conversation. She was looking for a topic where they were already proud of her. Maybe something they were already asking questions about, like her academic advancements at the new university where she was supposedly working. She had it all laid out. If they did A, she did B. If they did C, she had D, and so on.

Instead, they said, "Tell us what you've been up to, GJ," and she blurted it out.

"Mom, Dad, I've been at Quantico!"

"Oh, are you teaching forensic science there?"

GJ had not expected her mother to ask that, although now that she thought about it, it was a perfectly fair question. She didn't have a PhD, but she did have the background and a pedigree to certainly be capable of teaching at these universities and training grounds.

"No, Mom. I'm a student. I'm actually a NAT—a new agent trainee."

"Oh, what are you training to be an agent of?" her mother asked between serene bites of pancakes and bacon.

GJ rolled her eyes. Good lord, had her parents never heard of the

Federal Bureau of Investigation? "The FBI, Mom." Then she smacked her fork down. Man, she had escalated that shit all on her own. *Way to go, GJ.*

In the end, she mucked things up so badly with her parents that by the time she was headed back to Quantico, she found she was actually looking forward to it. However, that sentiment changed relatively rapidly upon arriving at her dorm. While she started the first day back with a renewed sense of purpose and an I'll-show-them attitude, it didn't last long. After a handful more weeks of training and far more midnight drills than she'd been counting on, and she was more than ready for their third break.

The next time, she planned to hop a plane for Peoria, and beeline straight to her grandfather's. She wanted to believe she could go and just relax, hang out in her apartment in the south wing, not go in to the basement, just be fed wonderful food, and be nice to her grandfather. She was all set to do exactly that, but she got a call the day before she left from her grandfather.

"GJ, honey," he said through the line, "I hate to tell you this."

"What?" she'd asked, her voice probably low and weary over the phone. She'd yet to tell him that she had joined the FBI. Given the way he was speaking and the way he hadn't asked, he had not yet had that conversation with her mother. GJ was wondering how that was going to go down, too. This weekend wasn't looking any better than the last one she'd had off. "What's going on, Grandpa?"

"I got called away, again. They offered me an amazing chance to lecture over at the Sorbonne."

"The Sorbonne? What are they doing with forensics?"

"They've opened up a whole set of classes to visiting professionals," he explained. In the end, if he wanted any part of it—and he did —he needed to be on a plane the day after she arrived. She would get to see him and give him a hug for about fifteen minutes in the morning. He would not be awake in the evening when she got there because he needed to get a good rest. All these things she understood. They were a part of her grandfather's regular life. It was GJ who was out of whack.

She dragged herself through the few remaining days before the break, managing to scrape out some passing grades and not have to retake anything. Then, she'd flown and driven another exhausted, dreary journey to her grandfather's house. She went into her apartment and slept face-down on the pillow, exactly as she'd predicted she would. Over breakfast the next morning, she spoke briefly with her grandfather and learned what more he'd found out about his assignment.

As soon as he left, she scraped her plate, put it in the sink, and headed down to his basement laboratory. There, something new awaited her—a new body was in the walk-in cooler.

10

While Walter had seen Donovan for the second break as well, when their third break rolled around, she had nowhere to go. Donovan had been pulled by Agent Westerfield as a backup resource on another case and wouldn't be home. Walter wanted to go to Los Angeles, but she wanted to go to see her old friends. The problem was, she couldn't call her friends back home.

Almost two years earlier, she'd been homeless, living in a caged-in city block in the downtown area. The block was chained to protect it while it waited for a building to be erected. Instead of keeping them out, the fence had offered safety to those who congregated behind it. Though the high-rise had never been built, and the block remained much the same, and she lived in Los Angeles most of the time, she didn't visit the downtown block much anymore. This break, though, she found she very much wanted to go back. She'd lived in a tent there, with other veterans protecting their space, eating when they needed to and could, and generally taking care of each other through some serious postwar mental and physical illnesses.

The problem was, she couldn't call ahead. She couldn't check to see if her old friends were going to be around or even if the people that she'd known were still living there. She would just have to go by the old block and find out. Unfortunately, Los Angeles was too far from Quantico to make the trip for a weekend. There was no way she could catch a flight to LAX, then catch a ride downtown, check the place out, find a hotel room. No, she did not have the energy for it, so it was just going to have to wait.

While Donovan had offered her the use of his place for the weekend, even though he wasn't going to be there, she'd refused. There was no point in driving that far simply to save the fees on a hotel room. That idea amused her. How far she'd come. The first time she met Donovan, she'd been eating fried chicken, sitting on a crate turned upside down, outside of the tent that she lived in. Now she decided she'd pay for the hotel rather than driving the extra couple of hours. But fortunes changed and she knew that.

Taste changed with it too. She didn't go far from Quantico, just far enough to be away and then, when she found the first cheap motel, she stopped. She checked in and promptly went back to the desk and checked out. She'd slept on dirt cleaner than that bed. She stepped up her game, finding a nice hotel with clean, white sheets, full pressure in the shower, and basically pampered herself. It was a very un-Walter-like thing to do. But these days, what was she doing that wasn't un-Walter-like?

She was sitting on her bed wrapped in the hotel bathrobe reading a romance novel—of all things—when GJ called.

"Walter."

GJ didn't sound frantic but there was something in her tone that made Walter set down the book, adjust the towel on her head, and pay close attention. "What is it?"

"Where are you? Are you at Agent Heath's?"

Walter always referred to him as Donovan. GJ had never quite gotten around to referring to Eleri and Donovan as anything other than "Agent" and their last name. This was possibly because, when they'd first met, GJ had wound up handcuffed to the safe in Eleri's hotel room. Walter still wondered how long it would be before she would live that down.

"Walter," GJ continued, "can you get here?" And she rattled off an address that was three states over.

Jesus, Walter thought. She'd come this way so she could avoid all that driving and, in fact, she'd gone west from Quantico. Now GJ was sending an address that was north and even farther west. *Lovely*. But since she hadn't been doing anything important—not even just hanging out with her boyfriend—Walter had a hard time just saying, no, she couldn't make it.

"What's going on?" She fully expected GJ to be having some kind of minor crisis that truly didn't warrant getting Walter out of her bed and bathrobe. However, she should have given her partner more credit than that. Though she often thought of GJ as a girl—her bubbly exuberance and diminutive size lending to that idea—if she'd learned anything at Quantico, it was just how wrong that perception was. GJ was an avid student, an intelligent woman, and a scientist. She brought all that to her studies, even the physical ones she didn't excel at, even the ones she downright hated. Honestly, she'd pulled Walter along as much as Walter had expected to pull GJ along.

GJ hadn't answered and the dead silence was concerning. Walter asked again, "What's going on?"

It only took a few moments for GJ to explain the situation at her grandfather's house. Walter hadn't realized, or maybe she hadn't paid enough attention before, or maybe she simply didn't have GJ's steel trap of a memory, but GJ's grandfather was apparently a renowned forensic anthropologist and archeologist. He went on digs all over the world. Walter remembered some of this from Donovan talking about the bones that GJ's grandfather had found. So while she'd known the grandfather had been looking into Donovan's "kind" before this, she really hadn't put all the pieces together.

It turned out that GJ's grandfather was currently lecturing at the Sorbonne. That was very different from the professor hobbyist she'd thought him to be.

"What do you mean, he has a full laboratory in his basement? Is he rich?"

"Yes," GJ answered simply. "He has a house with three wings and I live in a separate unit over the garage, with a fully furnished apartment that he built just for me. My parents aren't as wealthy. But between his non-fiction books, his research, textbooks, and consulting work, his career is really broad and it pays him a lot. Even his speaking fees for the Sorbonne right now are covering the cost of all this. He's used some of his money to build a full forensic laboratory in his basement. I've known about it for a handful of years, but recently I've been investigating. So I told you about the skeletons that have the same anomaly as Donovan?"

Walter didn't really have time to answer before GJ kept right on going.

"Well the last time I was here, there was a body in the kettle. Well, no, *scientifically*, I don't *know* that it was a body, but the kettle is really only used for full human bodies. The kettle was on once, and then when I came back the second time, there was a new skeleton laid out in one of the drawers. It was untagged and it was pretty clear it had been freshly washed. So I think there was a body in the kettle the first time I came. And now this time there's actually a body laid out on the table."

"What?" Walter said, startled. "Isn't that illegal?"

"Walter, we both just had Legal 2 class. *Yes! It's completely illegal.* Whereas, previously I thought maybe what my grandfather was doing walked the edges of legal and moral and was maybe a little unortho- dox. I wanted to believe he had permission from universities and institutions."

"GJ, slow down," Walter said.

"No! There's a body on the table here!"

"Wow," Walter said "If there was anyone who *wouldn't* be upset about finding a dead body on the table, I thought it'd be you."

"Ha ha, very funny. I'm not upset about the fact that there's a body. I'm upset about the fact that I've learned just how very illegal this is. And this body's partially burned."

"Can you report it?" Walter asked.

"Really, Walter? Is that what you want me to do?" GJ's voice had dropped almost an octave in the question.

"Well, why not?"

"Because you know exactly what kind of skeletons my grandfather collects. What is going to happen when somebody comes down here and finds this *whole collection*? Agent Heath keeps brushing me off like he doesn't know anything and I'm about to stop believing him. And the last body I found down here had the face shifted. I really do not know what the fuck is going on here, Walter! But if I report it, I'm blowing this whole thing wide open. Not just this body, but this whole damn collection! Does Agent Heath want that?"

Walter sat back, stunned all over again. GJ made a very excellent point, "You're right. I'll be there soon. Give me that address again."

GJ did and, before she hung up, she added one more thing, "Wal- ter, the body still has some of the clothes on it, so some of the body is burned and some isn't. I can't examine the face, but I found a wallet and more in the pocket and…it has an FBI badge."

11

GJ examined the body while she waited for Walter show up. Normally, she would never have called Walter for a situation like this—but the fact of the matter was she had nowhere else to go. While Walter was no scientist, she had a good head on her shoulders and would help make the right decision. There had to be another option besides calling the FBI or calling the police and turning this all in.

Everything is fine, she told herself. Her grandfather surely had papers somewhere for the bodies, and everything would be easily resolved if he would just show them. However, if everything was fine and her grandfather did have papers, GJ would ruin it by calling this in. Because, until her grandfather could return and show his paper-work, the police would have confiscated the dead body that he was doing research on. They would almost certainly destroy evidence in the process. If that happened, she was going to be in a metric shit ton of trouble. Whether this set-up was legal or not, simply by notifying the authorities she would be letting her grandfather know that she'd been snooping into his business. She wasn't ready to do that.

This dead body might change all that.

As of that moment, she had no endgame plan for letting him know what she'd been doing. It was unusual for her grandfather to leave a body lying out on the table like this, especially while he was gone. What she would have previously called his *thoroughness*—and what she now was thinking of as his *secrecy*—would not have allowed this to happen. However, this was not a skeletal body. This body must have come in relatively recently, because it still had the skin and muscle intact. Not her grandfather's forte. He liked to joke that he only dealt with the dry stuff. Other people got the wet stuff—human identification specialists like GJ.

While the lower part of the body's legs, the shoes, the pants even, were fully intact, the upper body had suffered severe burns. From what GJ could see, it appeared someone had poured an accelerant onto the guy and thrown a lighted match at him. At least, that was her scenario assessment according to her FBI training. Scientifically, she could say there was a liquid accelerant and that it had been lit.

Given the position of the body, she couldn't have said for certain if he'd been dead or alive or maybe conscious at the time that he burned. Her initial visual assessment had her leaning toward "unconscious."

Burning tended to make the limbs pull in, into what was known as a "pugilist stance." His limbs hadn't done that. This indicated the fire had not been too hot, as it was the high temperature of the fire that constricted the muscles. However, that curled-in/almost-fetal position was also a common one for people in pain. So, conceivably, the man hadn't struggled against the fire much. That would mean—*blessedly*—he hadn't burned alive or hadn't been awake to feel it.

Still, the whole thing was odd. There were a handful of reasons to burn a body, and this one didn't seem to have any of the usual issues. This was not an old body being burned for concealment of identification. Hell, whoever had done this had left the damn wallet in his pocket. So that was out. There was no rot. Prior to the fire, this man had been very fresh. Because the lower portion of the body showed no sign of smoke or any trace burn evidence, GJ concluded that he was the only thing in the vicinity on fire when he'd burned. That meant he wasn't the victim of a house fire or probably even an accident. Most people would say it wasn't possible, but GJ had seen the dead bodies of people doing some seriously stupid stuff. They thought they were invincible or that the science was wrong, and then they were dead. This, however, did not look like a case of "the stoopid."

Given the lack of burning on his back, and the way the burn pattern faded out around the edges of his shoulders, she could make an assumption that he had been lying down, face up when the accelerant was poured. Also when the fire started. None of this was provable yet, but she was grateful it was another point in favor of the argument that the man had not been conscious when he fried.

It was because of this odd burn pattern that he still had intact legs and pants pockets. She'd done a standard, cursory search of his things, pulling out his wallet, ID, and then a second, folded black billfold. When she flipped it open, she'd been stunned to see the shield that she'd come to know so well over the past weeks. She could now easily distinguish it from police shields, DEA, and other that looked very similar to the untrained eye. She hadn't even needed the accompanying ID card, the kind she hoped to carry one day herself.

More than the body, more than the fact that her grandfather had done something unusual and left it lying out, more than the fact that it was down here, those three blue letters were damning. She could not imagine a scenario where the FBI would hand a corpse over to her grandfather willingly. Sure, they might ask him to investigate a situation. She was confident they had called him in to consult many times before, but he did so on their turf. The bodies went to the morgue. They were followed by an agent. He occasionally went on site for the recovery. But at no point could she ever recall any scenario, either from her grandfather's past or from her new FBI training, where an FBI agent's body would be distributed to a private residence.

When her stomach growled and Walter was still more than an hour away, GJ headed upstairs and met up with a few staff members in the kitchen as she made herself a sandwich. She ate it rotely, not conversing, not tasting, and barely chewing. It was just enough food to get her stomach to shut up so she could go back downstairs.

She watched her phone like a hawk, hoping that Walter would arrive soon. She knew the mere arrival of a friend of hers, and a friend like Walter specifically, would surprise the staff. Still, GJ didn't think they'd think anything too much of it, though it would certainly be out of the ordinary.

She headed back downstairs to continue examining the body when the message came in from Walter. Her new partner was only thirty minutes away. Setting a timer, she tried to stay at her work for as long as possible.

It was difficult to tell if this body had the same anomaly as the others, given that the flesh was either still intact or burned onto the bone. Most of what she understood said the anomaly was not visible at the surface. While she hoped Agent Donovan Heath had not gotten too concerned with the thorough way she checked him out, she had watched him like a hawk. She noted the way he moved, the way his joints flexed, how his feet rolled against the ground when he walked, *all of it*, looking for some outward evidence of the small changes that added up in his skeleton. She wanted to see if she could find something, since her grandfather was likely hoping to put his name on the mutation.

As the timer went off on her phone, she gave up. Unable to make the distinction with this dead body while the flesh was still attached, she shoved the body back into the cooler, headed upstairs, out the front door, and down the drive to wait for Walter. She guided Walter's car in and did only the barest of formalities of briefly introducing her partner to the staff before the two of them disappeared into her apartment. Her apartment was on the exact opposite side of the house from her grandfather's lab. Now she was beginning to wonder if that was no coincidence.

He'd had her apartment built specifically for her. She was the other family member who understood the science like he did. Yet it now seemed that he'd wanted to keep her as far away from his work as possible.

Did he not want to incriminate her? Or was he concerned she'd figure it out? Unable to quell the questions in her head, GJ tried not to let them show in her frustration. She and Walter snuck out the back door of her apartment and around the back lawn, hoping the gardener wouldn't see them, and down into the basement laboratory.

At the bottom of the steps, Walter paused and looked around, her expression a combination of wonder and horror. GJ tugged her along, pulling the body back out of the walk-in cooler and showing Walter what she'd already found. Then she handed over the wallet.

As she examined the badge and the FBI identification, Walter stopped dead in her tracks. "I know him. That's agent Wade de Gottardi. He's one of Westerfield's."

12

W alter stared at GJ. "I know this man. Or .... I *did*."

There was something in the way that GJ looked at her that let Walter know that she was used to people not having the correct verb tense when speaking of the newly departed.

"You actually know him?" GJ asked. "Or you just met him once?"

"Somewhere in between," Walter replied. "We have to contact Westerfield."

"No! We can't contact Westerfield, I already said we can't call the authorities."

"You've got to be kidding me!" Walter looked at GJ like she'd gone insane. "This man is not only a federal agent, he is an agent that I *know*. He's an agent that works—*worked*—for the same division that you and I now work for."

"We don't work for NightShade yet," GJ countered as she began pacing the room. It was the first time Walter had seen GJ Janson nervous.

Shit, Walter thought to herself, *this is going to be tough.* In order to do the right thing, which was turning over the body to the FBI, they were going to have to incriminate GJ's grandfather. It wasn't something Walter was looking forward to. On top of that, it looked like she was going to have to override GJ in order to do it. But that was Wade on the table. She had met him and worked alongside him. He was like Donovan, she knew. Then she paused. *Wade is like Donovan.*

The thought ran through her head, reminding her that Walter knew it but GJ didn't.

"Do you think he's down here because he's like the others?" Walter posed the question as innocently as she could. She wasn't as good a liar as she wished, and she wasn't as good a liar as the FBI agency had tried to train her to be. Certainly not to GJ. It turned out lying to GJ Janson was hard.

One, she was this woman's partner. GJ knew her well, since they'd been living in each other's pockets for the past months. She had a very good meter on what Walter's "normal" should read like. GJ would recognize anything that was off from "normal" in a heartbeat. Two, Walter had to add in the fact that she actually liked GJ. That made it harder to lie, harder to force that needle back into position than it would be to lie like that to another person.

Luckily, GJ—too worried and caught up in the ramifications of what they might be about to do—didn't notice. "I don't know, he might be. I can't tell from what's here. I still haven't been able to find any outward signs of what the anomaly does in a live human being,"

Walter almost startled at that.

She knew. And GJ *should* know. Right about the time that the thought was passing her brain, a second one dogged its heels.

Damn Special Agent in charge, Derek Westerfield! He'd put her in this shitty position. She should be right now explaining to GJ exactly what the anomaly was. Instead, she was concerned that if she told— and certainly if she did it before they graduated Quantico—that she and GJ were going to get kicked out. Then again, if they held the body of a NightShade agent without reporting it, they were also going to get kicked out. This was a lose-lose situation every way she looked at it.

As a Marine she'd been in unwinnable scenarios before, but in that training she'd also been taught to deal with them with one tactic: if you can't win, burn the place down. Sadly, that was not an option here. There were way too many problems with burning the place, even metaphorically. On top of the fact that it was GJ's family home, it was actually a civilian's home and not a war zone. There was also the problem that Wade de Gottardi's body was here and someone would want it back. What was his boyfriend's name? ... *Randall*, his boyfriend's name was Randall.

For some reason, Walter found it comforting to try to remember everything she could about Wade, as though she had somehow now become his keeper. Burning even just the body would mean concealing the death of an FBI agent, let alone that of a man who was friends with her boyfriend. She'd just had a class on the charges for interfering with law enforcement. She could do it under the guise of the FBI, but that umbrella would not reach to this decision.

Another problem with burning the place down was that this place was evidence. This place held a wealth of information about Donovan and his kind. Since it was so far from her own profession and hobbies, Walter had no idea how much of this evidence—how many of the things in the drawers and boxes—Donovan might want or at least want to know about. Burning it down would mean burning down what Donovan needed to know.

"What if we move the body?" GJ offered.

"Okay, that's an option," Walter conceded. "Where do we move it to?"

"Anywhere! Anyplace where we can claim that we found it. Then we turn it in, get it the proper processing. That keeps it away from here and away from being tied to my grandfather."

"On the one hand," Walter offered, "that works pretty well. But there are two other hands."

"Oh good, we already have a problem. We have too many hands," GJ quipped, sounding more irritated than snarky.

"Listen to me," Walter told her, trying to get her to focus. "One big problem is moving the body. How do we remove it without leaving evidence that we moved it?" She watched GJ's face and knew that if they couldn't pull this off to her partner's satisfaction that the evidence wouldn't trace back, then they couldn't do it at all. "That's just part of the issue. The other part is, how do we sneak a *whole human body* out of this house?"

"Well, I don't know." GJ snapped, "but I bet we can figure it out. Because the fact of the matter is, my grandfather routinely sneaks whole bodies in. There's got to be a way."

Something about GJ's face made Walter stop for a moment.

Her partner sighed, her expression crumbled, and for a moment she looked so young. "It's all illegal, isn't it?"

"Maybe not." Walter didn't believe that, but she wasn't going to twist whatever knife GJ seemed to have just found plunged into her own gut.

"Yeah, it is. He keeps sneaking them in." She practically yelled it as she waved her hand, gesturing around the lab. "If it was legal, he would have showed me. He would have called me, excited, every time he got a new body. *Shit!*" She cursed the last part out with the weight of world on it.

This was her family. Though Walter didn't really have one, she understood. Instead of going on down the sad path GJ had just taken, she steered back to her original problem. "Okay, one hand, we can probably move the body. Maybe not so it looks undisturbed, but at least so that it doesn't specifically trace back to here. But the other problem is worse: what happens when your grandfather comes down here and finds his latest specimen missing? I mean, is he going to walk in *now*? Is there any chance he's going to show up while we're sitting here yelling at each other?"

"I'm not yelling," GJ replied at a high decibel level. "I am calmly debating."

That was a load of crap if Walter had ever heard one, but once again, she didn't contradict GJ.

"No, he won't come back now. He's out of the country," GJ replied to the question. "But yes, when my grandfather comes back and his body's gone, this whole thing turns into a massive shit show. I have no idea what that means. Honestly, there's still a mild possibility that this is all legal somehow, and that everything is on the up and up. If we steal the body and my grandfather has paperwork for it and now it's gone, we're in trouble."

Walter thought of another thing, something else she needed but could not find the answer to on her own. Looking at GJ she asked, "How long has he been dead?"

"Well, he's been in cold storage. He's still below forty-degrees. Grandfather must've taken the body down to a level close to freezing for preservation. Maybe because he was leaving and he needed it to keep. You wouldn't want to hit the freezing point or below, because that could cause ice crystals that would burst the cells."

"Not now, GJ. Just tell me time since death." And there was Walter now throwing around forensic terms almost like GJ. Quantico had changed them both.

"Right," GJ continued. "He is very cold. The lab itself is being kept colder than usual and the body has been in and out of cold storage—I can tell. However, my grandfather left the body on the table, which I assume means he wants the decomposition process to start, though it will be incredibly slow. The cold makes it harder to determine time since death, but I'm thinking probably in the range of four to seven days."

GJ started citing evidence and information again, things she saw on the body that made her think of this timeframe. Once again, Walter shut her up. She didn't need a full report. She took GJ's analysis at its word.

Shit, she thought to herself, remembering Donovan had just been called away as backup on a case. Was it related? Was it specifically because Wade had been killed?

"Wait a minute," she told GJ. "I know what to do. Let's call Donovan first and see what he knows."

Thirty minutes later Donovan called back, answering the summons she had sent out via several frantic voicemails and texts. That was unlike her, but she was struggling to keep the quiver out of her voice. *That was Wade on the table. Burned. Dead.*

"Walter, is everything okay?"

"No, Donovan, it's not." She tried to keep her voice calm and regretted getting him all stirred up by way of the texts. "Long story short, I'm in Dr. Murray Marks' basement. He's got a huge mansion with a hidden home laboratory inside it. I'm calling from there with GJ. GJ came home and found a body on an examining table. It's got a billfold for an FBI agent. Donovan...it's Wade."

There was a moment of stunned silence on the other end of the line, so she said it again. "Donovan, I'm looking at the wallet. I'm looking at the ID. It's Wade."

"I heard you." The reply came back solemnly. "I just need a minute."

"Donovan, what can you find out? Can you figure out what's going on? If we call Westerfield, if we turn this in, we are opening a jar of I don't even know what. This is a shit show down here."

They hung up with a mutual promise to report back as each of them learned things. Another thirty minutes passed before Donovan called a second time. "Walter, Wade has been missing for eight days."

13

GJ listened as Walter held the phone up. With the speaker on, Donovan's voice came through loud and clear.

"We have to tell Westerfield," he said. "I don't know what's going to happen, but that body on that table is Wade. I can't find any record of him being dead. In fact, no one quite realized that he was missing until I started checking around."

"So, what you're saying," GJ spoke into the open air above the phone, "is that you've already alerted Westerfield that something is up with Agent de Gottardi? You raised an alarm enough to get everybody to pull all the strings so you could find out this kind of information inside of thirty minutes?"

"Yes," Donovan agreed, his tone disturbingly flat. "I had to. It's Wade."

"You told him we had this Agent de Gottardi's body?" GJ asked. Walter made a look at her, as though to cut her off, to tone her down, but GJ wasn't taking it. She demanded again, "No authorities."

This was her grandfather's lab. This was her family, her home, and it shocked her how aggressive she felt at the idea that it might be invaded, even though she knew what was going on here was wrong.

"No," Donovan replied, and she almost found herself missing his response because of her anger.

"What do you mean *no?*" Walter demanded, jumping back into the conversation.

"I mean, *no*, I didn't tell Westerfield that Wade was dead. Or that you had the body. I just said I had reason to believe that something was up and I needed to contact him. I said it was urgent and that every string needed to be pulled. That was all."

"So Westerfield doesn't know that we have the body," GJ clarified, already feeling a little better.

Before anyone could answer, Walter chimed in. "But Westerfield does know that something is up with his agent. And he knows that something—at least something associated with Donovan—is at the heart of it. That, in some way, Donovan has become alerted to a problem with Wade."

"Do you think he'll trace that idea back to this lab?" GJ asked Walter now, and Walter shook her head before saying *no*, so that Donovan could remain part of the conversation.

"Look, I get it," Donovan said, clearly speaking to GJ this time. "You don't want your grandfather taken down. You don't want his lab dismantled. But the fact remains, that's my friend."

"I get it, too," GJ said. "And let me tell you something Agent Heath. This laboratory is full of skeletons bearing the same anomaly that you have. The skeleton I found lying out just last week had the face *pushed out*. The maxilla was disjointed. The jaw was in an alternate position. And I noticed for the first time that it's longer than normal on all the skeletons. There's something else on the arms, indicating that this isn't just a simple issue of double-jointedness.

"Now, *I* don't know exactly what's going on with you, but I'm getting closer. And your bullshit about *you* not knowing what's going on with you...Well, it's just that. It's bullshit."

A silence hung in the air for a moment before GJ continued.

"If you bring in the authorities and they come through this lab, I don't think you're going be able to pull off your innocent act much longer."

Wow, GJ thought. It turned out she swore like a sailor when she was angry or afraid. She hadn't been afraid when Heath and Eames had taken her into custody and handcuffed her in that hotel room. She hadn't been afraid out in the snow or stealing bones from a branch office of the FBI.

But now? *Now* she was shaking in her shoes.

"I understand that you don't want authorities in this, GJ. And you're right," Donovan responded. "In fact, neither do I. Which is why we have to tell Westerfield. It's his agent. You think he doesn't know what's going on with me? You think he doesn't know about Wade? He knows all of it."

Across from her, Walter looked up at the ceiling and whispered, "Thank you, baby Jesus."

"What?" GJ looked bewildered, wondering what the hell Walter was talking about.

Walter didn't disappoint. Staring at GJ, she answered. "Just so you know—before Westerfield descends upon us—I think you should be brought into the loop on what we're dealing with. Westerfield specifically forbade me from telling you about Donovan."

"What? That you're dating?" GJ looked at her. "I knew that. There's much more going on here than the fact that you and Donovan are in a personal relationship."

Walter shook her head; so that wasn't it. GJ looked back and forth between her partner and the phone, wondering what the hell they were holding back. Then she caught on.

"So, what you're telling me is this anomaly isn't simple extra flexibility. Which I'd pretty much already figured out for myself. And given the way the joints move, and the where points of attachment are on the bones...He can completely shift position, can't he?"

Walter nodded and whispered a soft "yes."

"Thanks, Walter," said Donovan.

"Well then, *you* tell her! She really already figured it out."

"What do you shift *into*?" GJ asked him, her brain racing in a variety of different directions.

For a while, silence reigned and no one answered her.

She demanded again, "What do you shift into?"

She looked at the body on the table, wondering if she could manipulate the bones and get it to subtly slide one way or another to give her a hint. The elongated face came back to her, the bones jutted out. The jaw, the slightly longer canines.

Something niggled at the back of her memory, and she tried to grab onto it, but it didn't want to fit.

"Are you ... a *dog*?" she asked.

"Why would you say that?" The tone of Donovan's question caught her off guard, making her think she was close.

"You don't want to know."

"Tell me." The tone of his demand was flat, dry, almost angry underneath.

Too bad, she thought, somebody should've told *her* these things a long time ago. "Because my grandfather used to hunt big dogs. Wolves, maybe."

"*What the fuck?*" His voice came through the phone, sharp and quick. "He *hunted* them?"

"He said he was a hunter," GJ replied. "But all he ever brought back were dogs...or wolves."

The agents appeared, one by one, at her grandfather's house. Though they tried to dress casually, they didn't really pull it off. None of them looked like she'd suddenly invited over all her friends from school. It likely appeared to the staff as though GJ was impulsively throwing a party at her grandfather's estate. Only she was throwing a party for the stodgiest people she'd ever met.

Agent Eleri Eames arrived first. Apparently, she'd been at her family's home, Patton Hall in Kentucky, and had not been too far away from Dr. Marks' estate. *Oh goody*, GJ thought. *Just as everything falls apart, the first person I get to see is the agent who hates me the most.*

"Janson. Fisher," Eames greeted them using Walter's real last name.

"Agent Eames," GJ replied, trying to be respectful. She did not want to wind up handcuffed to anything this time around. She had to admit she'd deserved it before, but right now she was standing in a laboratory over the dead body of an FBI agent that she hadn't wanted to call in. Sadly, she could easily see herself winding up in the cuffs again.

The two women stared at each other for a moment before Walter physically stepped between them and said, "Can we please end this pissing contest? We have work to do. That's Wade on the table."

Agent Eames visibly swallowed. That was clearly not something she wanted to hear. She and Agent De Gottardi went back for well over a decade, and as GJ watched, small tears formed in the corner of Eames' eyes, though she fought them back. Still, it was Agent Eames who spoke first, showing herself to be the stronger woman, GJ guessed.

"Look, I just want to clear the air. Before he hired either of you,

Westerfield asked what I thought about each of you individually." She looked back and forth between Walter and GJ. "I recommended you both. I have no idea if it carried any weight, but he asked and that's what I said."

"That's a shocking turn of events. You handcuffed me to a safe in a hotel room," GJ replied, only a moment later wishing she hadn't let that one out of her mouth. Now was not the time to bring it up.

"Yes, because you're incredibly intelligent and you were likely going to run off with something else from the evidence locker if we didn't. I had no idea how to bribe you to help and shut up or leave and shut up. It was the only option left. Motivations aside, you did good work."

"Hmm," GJ said, before turning back to the task at hand. Unfortunately, her eyes had darted to the right, checking once again the body on the table, the body Agent Eames couldn't quite bring herself to look at.

About forty-five minutes later, Special Agent in Charge Westerfield showed up. The three of them had only been talking, not touching anything, not sure what they should do until the boss arrived. His arrival meant another round of introductions with the staff, who were starting to get concerned looks on their faces as more and more cars pulled up. GJ wasn't sure how to explain to them that they didn't need to notify her grandfather. But saying that was probably the surest way to get somebody to pull the trigger and call him. Then they would tell him what was going on. So GJ didn't say it.

The staff had a right to be concerned. This was their home, too. They lived on the grounds. They watched out for the house. Her grandfather sometimes left for months at a time, leaving the place entirely in their care, and though they might not care for him too much, they did care about their home. Today's events were incredibly unusual for them.

GJ led Westerfield into the basement laboratory, where Walter and Eleri Eames were already speaking. He looked around in a bit of wonder.

"Holy shit, this is state-of-the-art."

GJ only nodded. This man was, after all, her boss, and the laboratory did belong to her grandfather. She was between a rock and a hard place if there ever was one. After taking a cursory inspection of the setup, Westerfield got on the phone and called Donovan, who was already en route, only another thirty or forty-five minutes away. Donovan recommended that they begin inspecting the body without him. Though he was a former medical examiner, Eleri was a forensic scientist and had plenty of practice. She knew what she was doing.

So did GJ. They had probably two of the nation's top forensic scientists in the room already and a Special Agent in Charge of an entire FBI division. They were more than ready to go.

Donovan recommended they begin by taking x-rays. They would need them for a thorough record if they were going to try to leave the body in place. Given that they didn't find anything that suggested a need to do otherwise, they were going to get in and out with their analysis. Hopefully their work wouldn't trigger anyone to call GJ's grandfather and alert him that something was up. Or leave behind any evidence that would let him know they'd been there. It was a more difficult job than it might seem at first glance. It helped that they were all trained in exactly this kind of operation.

Westerfield wanted their work to go unnoticed, which was why only Eames and Heath were in with him. He was only pulling the agents already closest to the case. Eleri apparently had been on leave, following a lead on her sister's case. GJ didn't know the details. She sure hadn't kept up with Agent Eames since they'd last seen each other.

"I'm guessing there's an x-ray machine down here?" Westerfield asked, looking directly at GJ as he waved his hand at the walls behind him.

"Of course, one second." She darted to the side of the room, trying to be helpful and quick. She did not want to blow this. Opening a cabinet, she pulled the portable machine out and then rolled the table over to where the swing arm would reach over the body. Next, she started to fire up the generator down here. It was for just this kind of thing, and GJ could only hope her grandfather wouldn't notice all his equipment had been used.

The x-ray machine needed the generator since the power was off. It was a slightly larger version of the one that might be found in a dentist's office. With it came much larger, digital plates than the dental versions, though he had those, too. Here however, a big-box store version of cling wrap, approximately 1,000 meters long, was used to cover and protect the plates. Apparently, her grandfather had not invested in the hospital-grade clear covers.

It took a moment for them to get the hang of it and find a rhythm for the group to work, but all of them were familiar with the equipment except Walter. But she fell in line, doing what was needed as they asked. Bit by bit, they moved, lifted, and scanned the body. By the time Agent Heath showed up at the front door and GJ had to go fetch him, they were finishing the last of the x-rays. Given that the tech was all digital, there was no wait time needed to see the films.

She led him downstairs to where Agent Eames, Walter, and Westerfield were all looking at the screen she'd set up for them before she ran out. Eames was examining the chest and skull.

"I don't see any bullet wounds. I don't see anything that indicates that he was shot first. What I do see is something here on this side." Using her finger, she pointed at the screen to an anomaly on the right side of the picture. The patient's left. GJ saw it, too. There was a change in the arc.

"We need a different angle," she said and almost headed toward the body to get the shot.

"Well, let's look directly." Agent Eames followed her back over to the table. For a few moments, they'd managed to ignore the body. Agent Donovan Heath had looked at the x-ray films first, as though he couldn't yet look at the body of his friend. Eleri had been avoiding it, too, but now she bent over, getting a close, clinical perspective on the side of the skull.

"It is hard to see through the burn. However, it appears that there is what's probably a fatal head wound here."

"But not bullet wound," GJ added. It looked more like the kind of damage sustained hand-to-hand. A hit with a blunt object, direct to the head.

They proceeded to take another x-ray from a different direction which more easily illuminated the circular area that had been slightly caved. From this angle, it was clearer.

"I don't know," GJ said it at the same time she heard the words coming out of Agent Eames mouth. They looked at each other.

"I don't think that injury necessarily looks fatal."

Eames agreed. So maybe GJ wasn't going to get handcuffed to anything this time. She was going to work hard to keep that the case.

"What else is there?" Walter spoke up though she'd remained relatively quiet. This was not her forte.

"Over here," Donovan said again having turned his back to the body in favor of looking at the x-ray films. He pointed to a fracture at an angle in the ulna of the right forearm. "Looks like a defensive wound. Maybe a knife mark?"

Right beside the fracture where Agent Heath pointed, was a shadow on the bone. It could be the slight kind of cut that wouldn't necessarily show up well on an x-ray, but only faintly. Only when they de-fleshed the bone and examined it directly, would they know if the shadow was an old birth defect, a mutation of some kind, or perhaps, as events suggested, a defensive knife wound. Burned flesh made it difficult to distinguish and that was probably the point. Since no one else had said it, GJ said exactly that to the room at large.

"Are we in relative agreement that the burn was intended to hide the damage to the body?"

Though no one agreed verbally, everyone nodded their heads.

"Over here." Donovan pointed to the x-ray for the other forearm. "This could be one too. It's just too hard to tell from x-ray alone."

Once again, they nodded in agreement and then turned to the x-rays of the legs and feet. But as the rest of them moved to the screen about three feet down the row, GJ stayed put. She could not stop looking at the image of the forearm. It wasn't right. She looked at the lower legs. She looked at the skull and reexamined the area that had been bashed in, and then she turned back to the group at large.

"Wait, I thought you said Agent de Gottardi was like Donovan. Like every other skeleton in this room. Right? One of those changing wolf things. What's the word?" Why hadn't she thought of it before? She looked Agent Heath directly in the eye and said, "*Werewolf*. You're a werewolf."

Heath gritted his teeth, saying, "There's no such thing as were-wolves." And for a moment, GJ thought she saw Eleri almost smirk through her sadness. But that wasn't what she wanted to talk about.

"Fine, a changing-wolf-man-thing then. Is he like you?" she demanded, pointing at the body, though that wasn't really the right idea. "Is he?"

After looking to Westerfield to check if he could reveal his friend's secret, Agent Heath said, "Yes."

But by then, he'd given it away. GJ didn't need the confirmation. What it did give her was answers. She looked at each of them briefly, wondering that they hadn't caught it. "Then this isn't Wade."

14

W alter watched as Donovan and Eleri both suddenly turned pale at GJ's words. Then, in the next moment, their expressions changed completely.

Speaking at the same time, Donovan almost yelled, "Then who the hell did he hunt?"

And Eleri yelped out, "This isn't Wade?"

Leave it to GJ to manage to confuse and startle an entire roomful of FBI agents in less than thirty seconds. If it wasn't so shocking, so scary, Walter would've laughed.

GJ was still looking at the x-rays and hadn't seen the expressions she'd inspired. She was pointing out various issues, things Walter didn't really follow, even after her forensics class at Quantico.

"So if you look here, at the epiphysial plate," GJ said, pointing at the end of one of the long bones...and after that she lost Walter.

She talked about fusion points. She talked about the maxilla. Then she said, "I mean, I can't be positive without completely defleshing the body, but I really do not think this has the anomalies associated with this group. It doesn't have any of the *signs* of the anomalies. I mean, if we could deflesh it and actually see all the bones and the tendon and ligament attachment points, that would be conclusive. But according to the x-rays, this isn't one of Donovan's kind."

It was disturbing how easily GJ used the term *deflesh*. For all the things Walter had seen, and all the things she had done, even all the surgeries she had undergone, that word gave her the willies.

Though Walter always believed GJ wanted to impress the senior agents around her, now, when the time came, she seemed to be completely ignoring them. Such a nerd, so lost in her own little world, that when something exciting happened, even her own goals were pushed aside in favor of the discovery. It was probably why she'd stolen the bones from the Bureau branch office in the first place.

That was almost a year ago now, Walter thought, although it did make her wonder what would happen in the future, when the next discovery came along. Would GJ forget all about the oath she'd taken at Quantico and think only of the discovery in front of her? Walter couldn't fathom a guess right now.

It was the second time Donovan questioned her that GJ turned around and paid attention.

"Is your grandfather *hunting* us? And if he is, why is this person not one of us?"

"I don't know," GJ replied. "I was a kid when I saw it. He's my grandfather. I do remember him coming home with carcasses of wolves or big dogs. And he *said* he hunted them. I remember I didn't like it. I mean, who hunts puppies?"

Walter cringed as she saw the expression that passed across Donovan's face at that term. GJ, however, completely missed it. She'd turned back to the x-rays and was still examining them, even though she was answering Donovan's question.

"But that's what it was. I mean, I don't see any dog bones around here." She absently swept her hand to the large lab space behind her. "So he certainly didn't keep them and put them in the pot."

Suddenly, she stopped dead. Then Walter caught on as well.

"So maybe he *does* have the dog bones here," Walter mused, inadvertently mimicking GJ's term.

It was Donovan and Eleri who looked at her, strangely. Interestingly enough, she had a moment of feeling smart, right in the middle of all these brainiacs.

"He did keep the bones." Walter said it again, as she looked from face to face.

"He kept them?"

"He put them in the kettle, I guess," she said, now trying to use GJ's terms. It did not roll easily off her tongue. "And when he put them in the drawers and the boxes, because they're like you, they look just like all the other bones in here."

GJ looked up for a moment. "Do they transform back into people after they're dead?"

Donovan rolled his eyes. "No. Just like a fractured arm doesn't unbreak after you're dead." He said it through gritted teeth.

GJ, once again, seemed oblivious. "Oh, that makes sense." And she turned back to the x-rays again. Then she muttered to herself what a dumb question it had been. "They were brought here as dogs. So clearly, they didn't transform back. Sorry."

She pointed out a few more points on the x-rays, again supporting her theory that this was not someone who had Donovan's anomaly, and therefore, could not be Agent de Gottardi.

Then she turned around, her eyes questioning. "What do we do?"

It was Walter who spoke up. After all, she'd just been through Quantico training. She knew exactly what they were supposed to do. "We need to identify the body. We can rule out Agent de Gottardi right away if we've got any kind of records on him."

She looked to Agent Westerfield, who nodded his head. "Yes. We have records on all our agents."

It seemed just a matter of course, but at the same time, it also seemed relatively morbid. Walter didn't say that, though.

She looked to the others in the room. Donovan, the medical examiner. Eleri, with a forensic science degree. GJ with another forensics degree. And herself, a Marine. She was out of place in the middle of all this brainpower.

Yet here she was, the one talking. She was afraid if she didn't talk, Westerfield would get an idea, or Donovan would. And they would close this place down. She had to argue in favor of keeping it open. It was GJ's grandfather's lab, after all.

"What do we need to collect from the body in order to identify it?" She was looking at each of them, keeping their attention on her and her idea. Let them explain it to her, whether she needed the answer or not. If she had them engaged, she could steer them. The only question was, would they catch on that she was using techniques straight out of class?

"Well, normally, I would just take the body to the morgue," Donovan said. "Why are we not doing that?"

Well, shit. That gambit lasted all of five seconds. Probably because her boyfriend didn't manipulate well. He was a little shy on his social skills, never having mixed well with others as a kid.

"We have to leave it here," Walter argued. She hated this. She hated making a point against Donovan. "If we take it, then her grandfather knows we were here. Which means he knows that she was down here. And right now, he doesn't seem to."

"I don't care if he knows," GJ sighed out the harsh words. "We need to bring him in. He's hunting humans."

That was the first time Walter saw GJ fully realize the impact of what she'd said.

GJ spoke up into the small space that opened.

"I don't know that he was *hunting* them per se. He said he hunted, and he brought them back, and they were dead. Some of the bones are far too old to have been hunted. Not by him. Maybe he's stealing them from sites, or from where he finds them."

"I think he's hunting at least some of them," Donovan said, and Walter noticed he said "them," not "us," still not putting himself in the same class, even though his revulsion made it clear that, at least on some level, he did. He didn't have evidence to support his claim either, unless he knew something she didn't.

"We have to leave the body here," Walter said again. "We don't know that her grandfather is hunting your kind. We don't know exactly what he's into. And if we take the body—if we take or leave *anything*—we tip our hand. Then we'll never know. We have to leave it here and we have to find the rest out on our own."

She turned to GJ, thinking about what the woman had said to her while they were working so hard in the early weeks of Quantico. *You've got to play to your strengths.*

Well, Walter was a Marine and an investigator. "We need to put a tracker on his car, so that when he comes back from the Sorbonne, if I remember correctly... Anyway, when he comes back, we'll know where he goes."

She looked to Westerfield for confirmation. The man nodded his head, seemingly looking at his new agents more closely now. She could feel him assessing them.

"Next, we gather all the information we can from this body without damaging it in any way or leaving any evidence that we were here."

"What do we need?"

Though it was GJ who spoke, Walter looked to Eleri, hoping to put Donovan and Eleri a little more at ease, or at least distract them with a task to do.

Eleri immediately answered, "I'd run dental records. We've got the skeletal x-rays. We'll need to get a full dental set. Then we'll print and take them all with us. We need to erase them from the computer system, too."

GJ sucked in a breath. "I hadn't thought of that."

"Anything we leave behind will tell him we were here. If he comes down and finds a full set of x-rays on his newest skeleton up on his computer, he'll know."

Though Donovan was still angry, and though his need to stop the person who was hunting his kind had not been assuaged, the group immediately set to the task of getting dental x-rays.

The x-rays of the teeth and gums were only good if they had a record to match them against. They had to already have an idea who the deceased person might be. Then they had to have that person's x-rays to match or rule them out. They would immediately rule out de Gottardi, but after that, right now? All bets were off.

As far as Walter knew, there was no clue who this guy was, unless Westerfield was holding out on them.

When they finished gathering dental x-rays, as well as taking digital photographs of the hands and the feet, they collected a few last pieces of evidence. This included some skin-scrapings that Eleri said would not be noticed missing from the body, especially given that GJ's grandfather had a tendency to boil the bodies down. Walter again tried to hide her shudder.

Then, with everything in hand, Westerfield handed all the evidence they had collected to Eleri and Donovan.

He said, "You two are in charge of this. You'll be responsible for making the identification from this information as soon as we get a tip as to who this body might be. In the meantime," he turned to face Walter and GJ, "you two get out of here. We have to find Agent de Gottardi. He's been missing for eight days. And this definitely isn't him."

15

GJ found herself back at Quantico on Monday and utterly stunned to be there. She'd watched as agents Eames and Heath gathered evidence from her grandfather's basement lab and left in search of Agent de Gottardi. She'd helped Walter and Agent Westerfield pack her grandfather's lab up. They did their best to put everything back exactly as it was supposed to be in hopes that the man would never notice they had been there. They scrubbed the computers, exactly as Eleri Eames had suggested.

But then, GJ had expected to do *something*. She'd expected to be tasked with helping to identify the body. Or she'd thought she'd help hunt for Agent de Gottardi. Instead, Agent Westerfield sent them back to Quantico, back to school. Told them to do nothing. She'd gotten no texts from her grandfather, though he was just as likely to call as anything else—an artifact of his generation. Still, that only meant that he hadn't decided to let her know if he knew anything. It was entirely possible one of the staff had alerted him of her activity and he was coming home even as she sat there in her class, trying desperately to pay attention.

SAC Westerfield seemed to think that she and Walter would just be able to come back here and focus on their lessons. GJ could've told him that that wasn't going to fly.

She'd paid little to no attention during class on Monday. And Monday afternoon, during their drills, she'd been flat out murdered by one of their bad guys. It was the first time she'd been shot and killed during a simulation with absolutely no idea that it was happening.

Sure, she'd tried and failed to dodge bullets before and had wound up "dead." But this time, the shot had come out of nowhere. She had no clue she was dead until she felt the hit. So, on Tuesday afternoon, she was repeating the exercise. To make matters worse, her partner in failure was none other than Brian. Normal Brian was an asshole. Brian doing repetitive makeup work was an even bigger ass, and a threat to her life, at least in the scenario.

Forty-five minutes later, GJ had survived the scenario, although only barely. Brian had not.

"You bitch," he accused her. "You threw me under the bus so that you could get out. We're supposed to be partners."

GJ stood there, stunned. He'd literally tried to use her as a human shield in several situations. He'd ducked behind her, holding her arms to keep her in front of him, letting her take any oncoming bullets. Inside the exercises, there were cameras everywhere. She thought about saying this, but bit her tongue. Surely, the instructors could see what he'd done. No one needed a defense from her.

Unable to resist opening her mouth, at least a little, she replied in a calm tone, "Yeah, that's not how it happened."

"You're trying to get me flunked out," he snarled this time, spitting the words at her.

GJ, still tense from the exercise, on top of her tension from the weekend she'd just endured, didn't have it in her to hold back anymore. This time, she laughed, "Brian, you don't need my help with that. You're doing a fine job of failing all on your own."

And it sounded like she was right. The instructor hooked a thumb over her shoulder. "Parks, you're out. Pack it up."

She wasn't sure if that meant Brian should pack up his things from the exercise, or pack up his dorm room, but she was pretty sure that Brian had failed three times in a row—this time being number three. Full failure—one that wasn't made up, like today—led to removal from the NAT class. GJ was pretty sure she'd just watched Brian Park kill the last chance he had at becoming an FBI agent. *Couldn't happen to a better asshole.* Still.

No wonder he was so mad. No wonder he wanted her to take the blame for it, but really, there was nothing she could do about it.

Trainees either survived the exercise or they didn't, and Brian was wearing the mark of a dead man. He stalked off, throwing his weapon onto the ground as he left. *That was not FBI protocol*, she thought as she watched him go, her own breathing still heavy from the exertion of the exercise and the confrontation.

She wanted to yell after him, "Why don't you go meet up with Hank, and the two of you can cry in your beer together?" or "Try not to become a mass murderer!" but neither seemed appropriate.

She was still standing in front of three instructors. The lone NAT still at the exercise, the last one to pass. The lead trainer barked at her. "Janson, back to the dorm. I don't know what's got you these past two days, but you need to have a better day tomorrow."

"Yes, ma'am," she replied and turned, setting down all the equipment from the exercise into the proper containers. She stripped her gear next and walked back to the dorm. It was an effort just to keep her back straight, just to hold her head high enough not to be considered moping. She'd had enough of this.

It was a long walk and she made it alone. Brian had stomped off somewhere a while ago, and she wasn't going the same direction as him, thank goodness. Hank had left long before.

Everyone else had passed the exercise yesterday. Walter had whizzed through with flying colors, and GJ envied the other woman's ability to compartmentalize what she'd seen over the weekend to let it go and focus on the task at hand. It was certainly a skill GJ would like to pick up. Then again, Walter wasn't compartmentalizing her own family. She wasn't compartmentalizing her trust fund, her grandfather's respect, her parent's web of social ties coming down if anything she'd done came to light.

GJ made it all the way through to Friday night. Not having heard anything from her grandfather, and finally beginning to let go of some of the worry that plagued her, she managed to bring her scores up and stay in line with class for the rest of the week. Though she wasn't as good as she'd been before, she was at least getting close.

When the knock came on their door at two a.m., she and Walter quickly rolled into their routine. Walter groaned her usual, "Jesus, another midnight drill," to kick them off and they got ready at lightning speed.

Everything was within easy reach. GJ stepped quickly into her own clothes. Tying her shoes and buckling her belt to get her own uniform completed, she stood to find Walter with her prosthetic leg almost entirely situated. GJ picked up the arm—as had become their regular routine for getting out the door as fast as possible—and helped Walter get the metal and plastic limb in place. They were always last and she knew they'd be last again. This usually got them yelled at, and usually got her yelled at specifically, because Walter had a clear excuse for being last. GJ's only excuse was Walter.

The two hopped out into the hall in their khakis and blue NAT polo shirts, to discover they were the only ones there. They'd even managed to line up in their usual spots out of pure rote habit almost before realizing that the only person who stood waiting for them was SAC Derek Westerfield. He looked at them and spoke in his usual gruff tone. "Grab your things, you're coming with me."

Walter had ducked back into the dorm room and grabbed her go bag, returning to the hallway as soon as Westerfield told them to gather their things. But he only looked at her oddly.

"No, pack everything."

For a moment she stood there, stunned, the bag hanging from her good hand while she stared back at him. "*Everything?*"

"They're clearing you out. I need you. Now." He'd looked away while she absorbed the statement and it was only later that Walter really began to question things. He'd put the two of them into the back of his car, all their belongings shoved into the trunk, and driven them away from Quantico at three a.m. with no one the wiser.

"Are you failing us out, sir?"

"No," he replied, but it was all he offered.

"So, we're not going to graduate," GJ. said.

It should have been a question, Walter thought, but GJ had merely stated it, unable to keep the disappointment out of her voice. Walter felt it, too. They were pulled" She couldn't see or think of anything they'd done to cause their Quantico experience to go the way of Hank and Brian.

Westerfield's voice remained gruff, his eyes glued to the road, the darkness pushing in around them. Walter had no idea where they were going, and the words he said startled her. "You just graduated. I graduated you."

He said nothing else for almost thirty minutes and the two sat in the back, more stunned than they'd been when they thought they were failing. They occasionally looked at each other, as though that would answer any of their questions. When it didn't, they spent their time glancing out the windows. Walter turned the evening over and over, wondering what the hell was happening.

At some point, they must have passed a mark that Westerfield had predetermined because he suddenly began speaking. It seemed he wanted to get a few things cleared before they arrived wherever they were going.

He directed his first question to GJ. "Do you know how much money your grandfather has?"

Her partner shrugged, and Walter assumed they were truly partners now.

"I don't know. I mean, he's wealthy. That's obvious from the estate. He's made a lot of money from his lectures and his books. I don't think he was always this well off. My mother didn't really grow up with that much money. She was raised more modestly, as far as I know." Then GJ faded off, running out of information.

It was Westerfield who filled in what Murray Marks' granddaughter didn't know. "That's actually not true."

"What?" GJ's startled tone bit into the darkness around them.

Westerfield didn't even notice the yelp. He barely looked into the rearview mirror but kept talking. "We'd been looking at him before this but now, with that body on the table and it having a wallet that contained all of Agent de Gottardi's credentials, Marks' case moved to high priority. That means we put analysts on it full time and ramped up our efforts in our fieldwork as well. The fresh bodies mean this isn't someone we could simply keep on our radar but someone we needed to actively follow."

Walter watched as GJ slumped back in the seat.

"Where was he last weekend while we were roaming his lab?" Westerfield asked, but it appeared he already knew the answer.

"The Sorbonne." Walter put the word in for GJ, knowing that GJ was struggling to absorb everything Westerfield was saying.

"He wasn't at the Sorbonne." Westerfield dropped the words like a brick at their feet. "We don't know exactly where he was, as he eluded our tails." Westerfield produced a short, sharp sigh that expressed his irritation about his agents being given the slip. Maybe more so because they'd been given the slip by an old anthropologist. Once he'd expressed it, Westerfield went back to his information dump. Surely, he was expecting them to memorize this as they listened. Walter tried.

"He has bank deposits of large amounts coming from a variety of sources. Many are in Europe, many across the U.S., some in Canada, a handful in South America, some in Africa. Know about these?"

GJ. was shaking her head, but her answer sounded like she did know. "He's had speaking engagements all over the world."

"That's not it," Westerfield quashed her response immediately. "There *is* money from the occasional speaking engagement. Do you know how many he went on last year?"

Walter watched as GJ calculated, then said, "About eight."

Again, he shut her down. "No. He only did three and they only netted him about forty-five thousand total."

Even Walter frowned at that. There was no way that kind of annual income would support the house in which they'd found the basement lab. That income wouldn't support the lab alone or even just the kitchen or the grounds. And it certainly wouldn't cover all of it.

As GJ. appeared to struggle to find information and put pieces together, Westerfield changed the topic. "We found de Gottardi. He's safe but shaken up."

Walter dove into the conversation head first now. "De Gottardi's alive?" Her heart was beating fast at the news. She'd held off asking, fearing she wouldn't like the answer. There was a dead body with Wade's FBI badge. She'd first dealt with the idea that Wade was gone. She'd liked him when she met him and more importantly, he'd been a friend to Donovan. He was a friend of Eleri's going way back, but Eleri had been willing to share. To help Donovan understand that he wasn't alone.

"De Gottardi went home to visit his family. He took his new boyfriend, Randall," Walter supplied as her brain searched to find what she'd last heard from Donovan's updates.

"Yes," Westerfield agreed. "Randall Standish. Apparently, Wade told them about what he was, maybe more. Took him home to meet the family and it didn't go well."

Walter understood it in her head. "Is that who the body is? Is it Randall?" she asked. It was the only thing that made sense. Maybe it was a different family member, but someone had gotten ahold of either Wade's pants or his wallet and badge and taken the ID with them and gotten killed in the process.

"It's Standish," Westerfield confirmed with no emotion behind the words. Next to her, GJ flinched.

"It's his boyfriend?" she asked.

Walter nodded. "He and Randall—" she tried again. "I think Randall is the first one he really loved."

"Well, shit," GJ muttered under her breath.

And that's the thing, Walter thought. In their jobs—in their old ones and now in this new one—they disconnected from death. They looked at bodies. They killed people. They removed themselves as far as they could from the idea that these were actual people with families and loved ones. They'd examined the body with the respect they thought it deserved when they thought it was Wade and once GJ had told them it wasn't, they'd disconnected. The body became, for Walter, a thing. For GJ, a piece of the puzzle, a mystery to solve. To Eleri and Donovan, it was evidence. Now it was Randall—a man she'd never met but heard so much about, all of him tied to Wade and the fact that Randall was the first one that made him want to tell his family they were together. Walter's heart broke, and she'd gone a long time not sure that it could.

Looking back, she thought about all the things they hadn't done. For Wade. For Randall.

"Randall's body," GJ began, softly posing into the dark of the car what would become a question. "What will they do with it? Can they get it from my grandfather?"

Walter too was wondering the same thing. *Would they be able to get it back? Offer Wade some kind of closure, a funeral?*

"No idea," Westerfield said in that flat, emotionless tone that was beginning to bother even Walter. She'd been a Marine and sat in her ghillie suit with a sniper rifle, waiting for hours to take out insurgents at 600 yards. Never seeing their faces. Never knowing if they had families or not. Only knowing that she'd successfully ended their lives. But right now, she was bothered by what she'd done.

"We left the body there. We couldn't put any trackers on it. We'll have to go back down again and find it. See if he's boiled it down."

Jesus, Walter thought, *He probably boiled down Randall. Holy fuck.*

But Westerfield kept going. "Surely, he's added it to his collection.

I have no idea if we should use this to go in and raid the place, figure out what he's doing or leave it and watch him."

"Maybe we can switch it out," GJ said. "Perhaps he's not familiar enough with it yet. If he hasn't had a chance to do a full exam, we can find another skeleton and swap it out."

"I like the idea," Westerfield said, "Can we make a resin cast and pass that off?"

"No. He'll notice that right away," GJ said, shaking her head in the dark in the back of the car.

Walter barely caught the movement and added her two cents. "My thought exactly. He's too much of a professional to be fooled by a fake, which means we need to swap it with another skeleton with nearly identical marks."

"I'm not sure where we're going to get that and how we're going to get in and out and swap it. Do you know when he's coming home?" Westerfield glanced briefly into the rearview mirror.

"No, I don't," GJ said. But she pulled out her phone and seemed to be checking the date as though she should have known. She muttered again under her breath.

"What do we do?" Walter asked.

"That is the million-dollar question," Westerfield told them, taking a right-hand turn down a lonely road and into a dark area. Finally, Walter recognized the place. He was taking them to Donovan's.

Off the beaten path and down dark roads, the home of the man who was probably her boyfriend sat at the edge of a national forest in South Carolina. The location was near where he'd previously held the position of medical examiner, though Walter hadn't known him when he held that position.

"Agents Heath, Eames, and de Gottardi are already here waiting on us. We're the team. This is now your case as much as theirs."

As they pulled up, Walter looked at the familiar little house where she had spent many a weekend recently. Only this time, it looked a bit sinister.

16

G J hung back. They'd left all their belongings in the trunk of the car Westerfield used to drive them here. *Too clean to actually be his, it must be a rental,* she'd thought.

Though Walter seemed comfortable walking into the home, GJ wasn't. This was the home of a superior agent, and while she didn't have innate respect for a lot of things, she understood this. She watched as Wade stepped forward, clearly grieving the loss of his partner, and hugged Walter. Walter stepped readily into his embrace. "I'm so sorry, Wade."

He had tears pushing at the corners of his eyes, as did Eleri, and the two hugged for a moment. GJ hung back in the awkward space around them. Westerfield also did not hug his agent, but he did it out of sheer brick-headedenss, not the feeling of misplacement that GJ seemed to have embraced while everyone embraced each other.

Did Agent de Gottardi know that she'd handled his boyfriend's remains, that she was the one who argued that it be left there, and that he not be given it back for a proper burial? *Shit.* She had no idea. All she could do was hold out her hand and say, "Hello, I'm ..." but she was cut off.

Westerfield began more formal introductions. Everyone else knew each other already. Walter had worked with Agents Eames and Heath before, in a more formal capacity than GJ had. Walter apparently had never been handcuffed to anything, and she had even worked with Agent de Gottardi once before as well. GJ was the only odd man out, but Westerfield held his palm out toward her in a more formal introduction.

"De Gottardi, this is Agent Arabella Janson."

Holy shit. The sound of the words stunned her. She should have been unhappy. She should have been sad for Agent de Gottardi. However, at that moment, the new idea ricocheting through her brain was that she had just been called *Agent Janson* for the first time. He really had graduated them. Holding her hand out, she returned her brain to the situation and shook Agent de Gottardi's hand.

"Thank you for helping," he said, seeming to hold no ill will against her or her decisions, and she wondered again if he knew about them, and if his feelings would change if he did.

De Gottardi offered a small smile and said, "Call me Wade. Seems like you're going to be up in my business quite a bit for the next few days."

She nodded and decided it was best to come clean early. "I know one of the people involved is my grandfather, and it may have been him who killed your boyfriend."

Wade nodded, "I understand"

GJ felt the need to apologize for her part in all of it, for how she'd admired and studied the skeletons her grandfather brought in, for how she'd been stupid enough to think it was all legit for so long. "I thought the skeletons were on loan from museums, and only recently did I discover that he didn't have the proper provenance for them."

She rambled for a little bit before Westerfield put a hand on her shoulder, effectively stopping her. "We've given him the information." Then he turned to de Gottardi. "Wade, Agent Janson tends to go by GJ."

And that was it. Her apology was effectively ended. Wade only nodded his understanding, and they got down to the serious business of figuring out what the hell had happened to Randall. They all sat around Donovan's dining room table, a beautiful old piece that he must have picked up or inherited from somewhere entirely unlike the places he had found the other pieces of furniture, but GJ only got a moment to glance around. Westerfield naturally seated himself at the head of the table, which put Wade on his right.

"De Gottardi, you'll have to tell them what you know."

Even Eames and Heath leaned forward as though they had not yet heard this story, and for a moment Westerfield looked around and seemed to assess his agents. Then he explained to GJ and Walter, "They only got here twenty minutes before us. They found Wade in.... well, you tell it, Eames."

Eleri looked around the table.

"We tracked his cell phone. So we found his last known location by triangulating it, and we simply went there. But it took three days to locate Wade."

Wade shrugged. "I'd been running. Once Randall didn't come home, and I knew he'd taken my wallet, I'd gone out looking for him. By then, the others had started coming in, telling us there had been a problem. Hunters. So I tracked him to his last known place, but he wasn't there. I smelled blood, but the trail was cold."

"You told him about you, right?" Westerfield asked. "About your family? About the anomaly?"

Had they adopted her term? GJ wondered. She'd always referred to it as an anomaly, not a mutation, not a trait. It was a full set of changes that always seemed to come together and were clearly linked. She turned her attention back toward the conference table.

Wade had nodded. "I was in love with him. He said I was keeping secrets, and he was right. I figured the relationship couldn't move forward if I didn't tell him. I thought he'd leave. Hell, I would have. So I told him."

The confession came out with a world of pain behind it. GJ could hear it from further down the table and across the space.

It was Wade who looked at Donovan. "Remember when you asked me about telling people what I am? This is why I don't tell." The words came out with a painful rasp. "I got him killed."

"You didn't get him killed, Wade." Eleri put a hand over Wade's, reaching out easily from where she was sitting next to him. She leaned her head on his shoulder, though GJ wasn't sure which of them was leaning on the other for comfort.

"Ell, I did get him killed. I told him everything. I took him to meet my family, and he realized many members of my family can do this too. They changed in front of him. They showed him everything. They took him in as a family member. Probably assumed we'd get married. I know that, by then, I was thinking along those lines. So they didn't think anything of it when he asked if he could go with them. And then they went out for a run."

Wade looked around the table. Apparently divulging information no one had yet heard.

"They started out together. Randall must have gotten curious about whether there were things I hadn't yet told him. Or maybe he just understood that it helped to see it." The tone of Wade's voice told of loss.

He'd never know now, GJ thought. He'd lost many things with Randall's death. Things big and small like this. Why had Randall gone? Wade's words interrupted her morbid thoughts.

"He grabbed an old pair of my pants. I didn't know he had my wallet and my ID for quite a while. I was completely asleep when he left. I had no idea."

That was clearly something that weighed heavily on Wade's shoulders, GJ could see.

But the man didn't let it stop him from giving information. She and he had something in common, she discovered: they were both inextricably intertwined with this case. He'd already suffered his loss. She feared hers was still to come.

Wade continued. "He didn't come back. The family did, and they told me something terrible had happened. My cousin was seriously injured by a gunshot wound he'd gotten at very close range. He said some of our people had gotten into fights, hand to hand, but since they were in form then, *hand to hand* isn't the right term." Wade said it bitterly, without a scrap of humor.

"My cousin barely made it home. He came back in wolf form because it was easier to move. They all said they smelled someone else, someone else's blood. They thought it might be Randall, but they didn't have time to go back and check. They weren't all accounted for because their homes were in different places depending on who you were talking to. So we didn't know who was missing yet or who Randall might have been following when everyone scattered.

"When I went back, he was gone. I changed form and tracked him as best I could until I gave up. Some of the family suggested he'd run off, scared about what he'd seen. A few were just angry at me for telling someone who wasn't one of us. It was maybe worse that I'd brought him to the farm. But I stayed close to the area and I kept going back out. I tracked and I tracked. His scent disappeared into almost nothing. I figured he'd been put in a car. By the time I put it all together, I knew he was no longer alive."

Wade's story was hard for GJ to hear. She dealt with dead bodies, and occasionally, every once in a while, she dealt with the families of those who'd been murdered. That was the hardest part of her job. She always saw herself as granting closure, but it was something she wanted to hand out like a report, maybe pass it along with well wishes for whoever received it at the end. She did not like being face-to-face with the pain that prompted her work, but here she was.

"Once I realized he was dead," Wade said, as he looked around the table. "I just stayed gone. I'm sorry, I should have come in."

"Totally understandable," Eleri told him, her hand creeping across the tabletop to hold his again. "You just scared the shit out of us. And since he had your ID, we thought it was you on the table, Wade."

Wade nodded. Though learning that the dead body wasn't Wade had been a relief to Eleri, it wasn't much of one to Wade.

"So," Westerfield said to the table at large, "it appears someone was out hunting Wade's family. They found Randall, and maybe being human, not being prepared, not understanding what was going on, he got caught in the fray, and he got killed. They took him, probably because they thought he was one of them. Whether he looked like a human or not, they wouldn't know."

"No," GJ said, "not until they tested the bones."

"So the first thing we have to figure out," Westerfield said, "was how Randall's body ended up at your grandfather's lab."

17

"You're asking me to turn in my own family." GJ looked at Agent Westerfield.

No matter how good it had felt to be referred to as *Agent Arabella Jensen*, this assignment was for shit, and her boss knew it.

"I'm asking you to do your job," he said in monotone.

"Yes," she agreed. "Against my own family. This job ends up with my family losing our home, losing our inheritance, my trust fund, and being generally devastated."

He looked at her again. "Is your trust fund really more important than human lives?"

"Absolutely fucking not!" She almost yelled it. "However, it's going to destroy my family and *significantly* affect all our income planning. It might be a little nicer if I wasn't the architect of that."

Even as she said it, even as she looked at the expression on his face, she understood this was her job now. She'd signed up for this without having any idea what she'd truly agreed to when putting her signature on the dotted line at the bottom of the page. She looked again to Agent de Gottardi.

"I'm sorry," she said. She understood. It was his family that was already lost. When she thought about it—when she thought back to all the times she'd seen her grandfather bring the body of a wolf in and claim that he'd been hunting—she had to wonder if those were people he'd brought back.

"Fine." She looked at Westerfield, both her hands flat on the table, her spine ramrod straight as she made her decision. "Let's go tear apart my family."

"I'm sorry, Agent Janson," Wade told her, his heart in his eyes.

Ironic, wasn't it, that the one who lost the man he loved was the most sympathetic to her plight?

"GJ," she said, and tried not to grind the nickname out though gritted teeth. If he was *Wade*, she was *GJ*.

Eleri reached over, taking Wade's hand again. "Is Wade really involved in this? Is he officially on the case?" She looked back and forth between Wade and Westerfield as though the answer would come from both places.

"Technically, he's still on leave," said SAC Westerfield.

"Technically, so am I," Eleri replied sharply.

If GJ remembered correctly, Agent Eames had been looking for her sister. But this was a wild enough and personal enough case to pull them all back in.

"I'm on it," said Wade.

From everything GJ had learned at Quantico and everything she understood of US law, that was absolutely not okay. She looked to Westerfield. He had to know it was basically illegal for agents to investigate their own families. All evidence would be tainted. In fact, why was *she* being asked to do this? Westerfield seemed to understand the glance she had sent him.

He voiced his reply to her silent question. "This is what we do. We investigate no matter what. We're the only ones who can do it. I think it's time to say a little bit about ourselves around the table."

Oh, good, she thought, *say a little bit about ourselves*. What the fuck was that? This wasn't a boardroom ice-breaker meeting. She looked back and forth.

Westerfield opened with, "You understand what Donovan can do, and Wade is the same."

Randall, unfortunately, was not.

"Randall is just a regular human," Wade said. His use of the present tense, and the longing in his voice for that *regular human*, was almost more than GJ could take.

But Westerfield ignored it and turned next to Eleri. "Agent Eleri Eames. I stole her from the BAU. She's from our profilers pool. She was a little *too* good at it."

Eleri tipped her head. "It turned out I'm too good at it not because I had good hunches, but because I have a lineage of witches going back to Salem and beyond."

Holy shit! A real, live witch. Then she said it out loud. "A witch and a werewolf."

Her surprise was interrupted by Donovan's exasperated response, "There are no such thing as werewolves."

Clearly, there were. GJ didn't voice that reply. Instead, she turned and looked to Walter. "So, Walter Reed here—Special Agent Lucy Fisher—is *The Terminator.* And *me?* My special talent is that I'm a grad student?"

For a moment, they all laughed at her. Even GJ joined in. The fact of the matter was she truly had no idea. What Donovan and Wade could do was extraordinary. If Eleri had a background that went that far into witchcraft—and clearly Westerfield believed there was something to it, and apparently the Behavioral Analysis Unit did too—then why was GJ here?

Walter may not have those kind of skills, but Walter was the fucking Terminator. GJ had seen the woman in action. She had several tours of duty behind her as well as MARSOC Training. That shit was hard to come by. But what was GJ?

It was Agent Eleri Eames who looked at her and said, "You haven't figured it out, have you?"

GJ shrugged. No, she had not.

Eleri began explaining. "You are the granddaughter of Dr. Murray Marks. You're the daughter of a physicist and a lawyer. You were raised in science."

GJ shrugged it off. *So were a lot of people.*

Eleri was already shaking her head, "No, not like you. People did not cut their teeth on formal logic and common right triangles like you did."

Well, that much was true. She referred to it as "super-nerdy." Who knew it was a superpower?

Eleri shrugged. "I'm a scientist. Donovan's a scientist. Wade's a scientist. That's kind of how we all wind up here. It makes sense. When a person can do what we do, they start investigating it. But you ... You don't just have science degrees. You have it bred into your bones. When we were working on the Atlas Project, you thought of things that none of us did. You look at things in a way that the rest of us don't. I think that's why Westerfield recruited you."

Westerfield offered only a short nod in return. Then he was done with it. They were back to the matter at hand. "We need to find Marks," he said to the table at large.

GJ shrugged, musing on the fact that her nerdiness was a super-power. "Well, he's in France right now. And there's a tracking device on his car for when he gets home."

"I told you: he's not in France," Westerfield replied. The words short and sharp.

"He's at the Sorbonne lecturing," she returned, just as short and sharp, just because she wanted to believe it. Because it was her go-to answer.

"He's not lecturing at the Sorbonne. This may be what he *told* you, but that's not where he *is*. And you're absolutely right, the tracking device on his car currently does us no good because he's not using that car right now."

GJ was starting to put the pieces together. They'd told her he wasn't earning his money lecturing. So why would he actually be doing that now? What was there to prevent this trip from being a lie like so many others? For a super-nerd, she'd sure missed that connection.

"Here's what we know," Westerfield laid out. "Murray Marks came into possession of a body that was last seen three states over, thirteen days ago.

"Where exactly was Randall last seen?" GJ looked to Wade, trying to ask professional questions about a thoroughly unprofessional situation.

Wade answered in kind. "We were in Arkansas, in the Ozarks. At my family home."

Well, shit, she thought. *It turned out there were werewolves running loose in the Ozarks.* She shouldn't have asked. "That's where we start looking."

Westerfield looked at the table in general. "At some point GJ's grandfather got a hold of Randall's body and brought him back to the basement. He managed to get him there prior to GJ arriving."

"Could he have gone to the Sorbonne after that?" GJ pushed the issue. She wanted her grandfather to not be lying to her. It bothered her that he was lying to everyone, but mostly that he hadn't trusted her. "You said he's not there, but what evidence do you have? He could've made the trip after this incident."

"Nobody has seen him in France. We have people looking for him, and it's the first place we checked. There's also no record of his lecture at the museum. Nothing in public access nor at any associated university using the museum for space."

"Of course, he's not there," GJ muttered to herself. It would not be that easy. Westerfield wasn't going to let her off the hook, either.

"He wasn't in France. He was possibly in the Ozarks, participating in a hunt." Westerfield looked at everyone as though the words he was saying were not as thoroughly damaging as they were to all sides of the table. "He possibly bagged the body. He possibly brought it back. It's definitely there now. And he has definitely disappeared. His car remains untouched. There's no evidence he was seen at his own home, though we assume he at least made it into the lab." Westerfield looked to GJ. "The question is—and hopefully you know something—where did he go?"

18

G J was shocked to find herself in the Ozarks less than twelve hours after sitting around Donovan Heath's dining room table. She was in a family compound outside the small town of Bull Shoals. Her job now was to interview members of Wade's extended family. While doing that, she was trying to come to grips with the idea that these people—although she didn't know which ones—could truly shift form and become the large dogs or wolves that Wade and Donovan had told her about.

She saw and understood what bones with this series of anomalies could do, but she was still unsure whether it was a dominant or recessive trait. GJ desperately wanted to interview the family about it —but that was a job for another day. Right now, she had to follow the case and figure out what had happened to Randall Standish.

Westerfield divided them into two teams, sending Wade with Eleri and Donovan. This kept de Gottardi away from interviewing his own family and preferably away from the scene of the crime. The SAC then sent GJ and Walter here—into the Ozarks—to meet with the de Gottardi family.

He'd driven them to the airport with all of their unnecessary things from the dorm room pushed into the trunk and their go bags pushed into the footwell on the front seat of his SUV. GJ and Walter left much of what they had behind with Westerfield. And GJ had no idea where he'd taken it. They'd hauled their things into Donovan's dining room and repacked it all with an eye for what they guessed they would need as the case progressed.

Their belongings from their dorm room made it clear they were not prepared to go out and work a case. Though they had some non-khaki pants and some shirts that weren't the labeled, blue NAT pullovers, there weren't quite enough. They'd have to purchase more normal clothing along the way, and GJ was getting used to the idea that the FBI had a budget for these things.

Westerfield had told them to sleep in the car on the drive to the airport. Though Walter went out like a light—probably well trained to grab sleep whenever she could—GJ simply hadn't been able to. At the airport, they'd been put onto a plane with a degree of speed GJ had never before known and flown to another location, still three or four hours away from their final destination. Walter had driven that rental car, as this time, GJ found she was tired enough to sleep. Now, here she was, just outside of Bull Shoals, Arkansas. She wasn't even in the town, but she was up to her eyeballs in members of the de Gottardi family.

Extended members came and introduced themselves left and right. Although they were unsure what to make of the two FBI agents, they seemed to be willing to let them in and talk to them. She and Walter had begun by interviewing family members, splitting the group in half to go faster. They first tried to assess how the family members really felt about Randall. What did they think was happening to the family? Why would they be hunted?

GJ found the answers ranged from, "Little fucker shouldn't have been out there, he's not one of our kind," to "Oh dear God, I can't believe they shot a *guest.*"

It wasn't so much that Randall had been killed, it was that his murder made Pam into a bad hostess. Mostly though, GJ got the feeling that they were equally horrified that someone had been shot on their property as they were that someone was specifically coming after them. Wade's cousin, Burt, was an interesting interview and GJ, of course, had drawn him.

"Look," he said, "I've been hearing rumors about this for years. There's always talk about people hunting us. If you think about it, it goes all the way back to Red Riding Hood days—literally centuries. People don't like what we can do and we stay away. We try to keep to ourselves, but then this shit comes and finds us anyway."

Though GJ almost spit her drink out at his mention of his family's historical relationship with Red Riding Hood, she worked to keep her focus on his point. More bitterness came through his tone more than fear. GJ, drawing on all her Quantico training, nodded and agreed along with him. She made sure to respond as if clearly, things had happened exactly as he said they did. The more he felt at home, the more he would say. At least this kind of interview was something she was good at.

The weight of the gun on her hip comforted her, and it was still shocking that it did so. She found she was wearing a blazer to cover it up, and almost laughed at the idea that FBI agents didn't necessarily dress that way because they liked it or because it was protocol. She understood now; they did it more because it was the easiest way to get fast access to your gun without openly carrying it on your hip all the time. Though Burt had clearly seen the gun, he didn't seem to care that she was sporting firearms directly on her person inside his house. He was ready to talk.

"There were three of them. And one of those assholes shot me, too." GJ knew this. Burt had not been taken to a hospital—apparently a family rule—since he'd been in an altered form when he was shot. She'd also learned that three family members held degrees in various kinds of medicine. One was a veterinarian, one was an MD, and one had obtained a PhD in experimental medicine with an animal research focus. She'd seen some of that in the Comparative and Experimental Medicine Department where she had completed her own forensics master's. These people weren't just different, they were prepared.

Once Burt finished griping, GJ asked if she could inspect his bullet wound, even going so far as to let him pull up his shirt and gingerly remove the taped-on gauze. She noted what appeared to be surgical marks and clean, neat stitches made with Vicryl, all appropriate for the wound. Donovan would know more about it than she, but he wasn't here now, was he?

"They did a good job," she told Burt. "You're on antibiotics, right?"

Burt nodded. "We have a whole stash. We know what we're doing. We can't go to the hospital looking that way."

GJ had nodded along again, though this time she actually did agree with him, thinking that a wolf being wheeled into a human hospital was asking for far more trouble than help. She didn't want to contemplate what might happen if they took one of their men in as a big dog to the veterinary hospital. What if they opened him and found human organs?

She startled herself for a moment. Did these people *have* human organs? She assumed so, though she'd only seen the bones and the full, live humans that tended not to show their organs well. Another conversation for later. Right now, she needed to know about that gunshot wound. "How did you get it?" she asked. "Can you give me the details?"

Burt explained about the handful of his family members running through the woods. He told about Randall asking to go along and how they'd sent him back to change into old clothes. Burt had been surprised Randall came back so fast. Wade's boyfriend hadn't seemed like the type to have a dirty pair of khakis lying around.

GJ nodded. It seemed even Burt had picked up on that. She hadn't realized the distinction until she'd seen pictures of Randall. The body on the table—though she was certain now that it was Randall—wasn't dressed like Wade's boyfriend would dress. At least, not the way any of those pictures of Randall suggested. Though the ID on the victim hadn't been completely confirmed, Eleri wasn't holding her breath that Randall might have escaped.

"There were three of them," Burt said. "Two guys, older men, coming after us. One younger, smaller, might have been a woman. One white guy, one black guy, all dressed a little too nice for the woods. They were wearing camo though, and all carrying modified rifles. I didn't get a lot of chance to look. I mean, I got my own guns. I'm pretty good. So I can tell you, it was a single shot rifle, but they were reloading fast. They each had several firearms on them. My brother, Art, he's the one who dug the bullet out of me." The vet, GJ remembered. "He said it was a silver bullet. Fuckers shot us with silver bullets," Burt complained.

GJ only nodded again, as though everything the man said was gospel. The silver bullet part made a bizarre sort of sense. Werewolf legend was that they had to be killed with silver, and she couldn't help but ask, "Are the legends true? Obviously, you're still alive."

Burt just gave her a nasty look. "Yes, it's true. Silver bullets will kill us. So will wooden bullets and ice bullets, and just bullets in general. They kill us just like they do anybody else. This idea that it has to be silver is some mythological bullshit. The only consolation is that it costs them time and money making their stupid bullets to kill us. But homemade or not, it went through me like a son-of-a-bitch. Just like any other regular bullet would have."

GJ nodded. "That makes sense." She felt a little bit chastised, but had to go on with the interview. It was only after she agreed with him that Burt sighed and looked away.

"We let Randall come out with us. Wade's in love with the guy and Randall wanted to know more about how all this worked. So we let him tag along. We figured if he's going to be family, he should know. I mean, some of us change and some of us don't. Lots of times, we just don't know who will or won't until later—puberty, adulthood sometimes. So, we're all kind of in this together." He sighed deeply, though whether it was irritation or sadness, GJ couldn't quite tell. "We just thought Randall would be another addition to the group. At first, he was just out in the woods with us having a grand old time. And when those guys showed up and they started shooting at us, fuck, I got shot and I ran. I should have stayed and helped Randall."

19

Walter watched as the two large wolf-dogs emerged from the back room. GJ stood, stunned, beside her. As Walter cataloged her partner's O-shaped mouth and wide eyes, she realized for the first time that GJ's understanding had not been complete. Previously, her idea of what Donovan and Wade and the family members could do had been purely clinical. She'd seen the bones. She'd calculated how they fit and moved. She'd been told the sum of those parts, and it made logical sense to her, given what she understood of human physiology and the physiology of the specimens in her grandfather's lab. But now, watching two adult men walk into a room and two large wolves walk out—well, Walter saw that GJ hadn't truly been prepared.

Walter assessed the two. The easiest way to tell them apart was fur color. The hair on the grown men's heads matched the hair on their arms and matched the hair on their wolves. So the older, white one was Will Little, Wade's grandfather. The younger, more brown-red-colored wolf was Art de Gottardi, Wade's cousin and Burt's brother.

Interestingly enough, Wade was the odd man out in his family, not because he was a wolf, and not because he was gay, but because he was a physicist. As far as Walter could tell, most everyone in the family stayed in the area. She wanted to call the place "de Gottardi-ville," but her humor would likely not be appreciated. Besides, though they owned a lot of land, the de Gottardi/Little clan wasn't big enough to be a "ville"—just a family compound, nestled in the Ozarks, just south of the state line dividing Arkansas and Missouri.

Wade had not stayed and tended the farm, tended the relatives, or had kids. He'd left. He'd gone to the city, gotten degrees in things that weren't directly useful to the family. The man spoke in terms of quarks and spins rather than what it would take to grow a fruit tree or remove a silver bullet and stitch the wound up neatly.

Though Wade's decisions had taken him away, and though Walter couldn't tell if he had been tight in his family's embrace in the meantime, his loss now seemed to have ricocheted through all of them. Whether it was necessarily because it was Wade's boyfriend who was killed or because it was suddenly clear they were being hunted, all had rallied around him. That meant when Wade de Gottardi told his relatives that two FBI agents were coming to investigate, they happily opened their doors and began talking. That was something Walter had not expected.

She could only compare this extended family to her own insular communities. Having once been homeless and having also been a Marine, she understood those groups were tight-knit. They'd seen things and experienced things that others hadn't, thus tended not to talk freely. And they certainly didn't generally open their doors to outsiders. She was impressed that whatever Wade told these people had worked.

Now, she and GJ followed the two men—in their nonverbal wolf forms—out the back door. They were going tracking. Walter wished for a moment that Wade was here. He'd tracked Randall originally and could lead them directly back to the spot. Still, she understood from her investigation classes how important it was to get independent confirmations when possible, and they were trying to get that now. However, she also understood from her courses at Quantico it was equally important for family members not be involved in their own investigations, and for anyone with a known bias recuse themselves. To say those issues applied here would still be an understatement of epic proportions. Even GJ was completely involved with the other side of this case. In fact, Walter was apparently the least biased investigator. Ultimately, she'd been taught the idea was to present the case before a court of law. However, Walter could hardly imagine this case ever coming up on a docket or how she might lie on the stand if anyone asked her about werewolves.

Inside of five minutes, it became very clear that the wolves had a much faster natural pace than either Walter or GJ. Though Walter was fit and strong, the prosthetic leg did slow her down, and GJ... well, she was GJ. Walter turned to look at her and see if her smaller partner was keeping up. GJ stayed silent, offering a thumbs up, but not appearing to be out of breath. *Good.*

Quantico had made them both fitter than they had been, though Walter wouldn't have believed it. She'd been certain she was already as fit as possible and that nothing would make GJ any faster or stronger. She'd been wrong on both counts. Apparently, before this new training, she'd been working out only one set of muscles. Quantico taught her she was the proud owner of five or ten or five hundred different sets of muscles. She was sure GJ could enlighten her on the physiology if they ever got a chance.

They'd set up a series of signals ahead of time, given the wolves' lack of English skills. Nods, head shakes side to side, one bark or two barks, were now their only mode of communication. The men were dependent on GJ and Walter to understand what each sound or motion meant.

Walter hadn't been ready for this. She and Donovan had never gone running together, though she had seen him walk in and out of the house as a wolf. They hadn't communicated then, other than for her to wave and say, "Hi," and she expected nothing in return until he changed back. Here, a lack of communication was not an option. It was necessary, and wolves did not speak. Now, a series of grunts, followed by ground-sniffing, alerted her. Then both of the wolves took off in the same direction—an obvious signal they'd found something.

Walter called after them, "Stop. Will! Art! Is it Randall?" She needed confirmation that they were following the trail they specifically needed. Both men stopped, turned, and looked at her, their long faces and sharp eyes glowing as the light around them dimmed. Both heads nodded up and down once before they turned and took off. All she saw was the disappearing wolves in front of her. Walter took off after them.

GJ's body was ready to fall into bed and go to sleep, but her brain was nowhere near that happening. Her schedule wasn't helping either. She was in her fourth set of clothes since leaving the night before. Even her outfits had suffered a hectic twenty-four hours. Today alone —actually, late last night—she'd started off wearing her Quantico uniform. She'd then changed into her own personal clothing for the flight and she pulled out a business suit she had stashed away upon arrival in the Ozarks. Eventually, she'd found herself in hiking boots and gear. That outfit had gotten muddy on the knees as she collected soil samples from the spot where they believed Randall had disappeared.

Art and Will, in their wolf forms had encouraged her to inspect that particular position. Their dramatically changed shapes still astonished her, but she had to simply push her shock and curiosity out of the way to do the job.

Though the two men—*wolves*—had seemed insistent that this was the exact place where Randall had disappeared, it was GJ who'd insisted on collecting the soil. Later, in the dim light of the evening, sitting in the kitchen of Will Little's home, she could hold up the glass vial she had stuffed the dirt and muck into and see the coloration. It did not appear the body had been burned here. So that must have happened after he was taken away—probably after they discovered he wasn't what they'd thought.

GJ inspected her little sample. She had plenty of experience collecting soil, and she could practically see blood in this one. It was "fresh" as compared to weeks- or years-old blood. That usually couldn't be seen. There'd been no scent of decay when she sniffed at the ground nor when she opened the vial and put her nose close. There were none of the fluids a body might leak had it been left out to rot. So while she couldn't say the men had found Randall's site for certain, she could say it was not the site of an old body. In fact, it matched what she understood so far and further indicated Randall's head wound must have bled more than she'd initially assessed.

She had a thought she didn't like thinking. Though this was merely one case like so many others, she didn't like this one. She'd been at this a long time. Eleri was right: GJ had been raised on this stuff, even working some cases with her grandfather when she'd been far too young to sign confidentiality clauses or understand the losses the families suffered. She'd been his apprentice back then, soaking in knowledge on cases and digs. Even so, she'd never worked one so close to home.

"Wow. You're acting as if you don't need a microscope to see what's in there." Walter entered the room and slid wearily into the seat next to her.

"I almost can," GJ replied. "I can tell you this has blood in it. And because of the way it dug up, it was not fresh, but not old, either. It was beginning the clotting process."

"I didn't need to know that," Walter winced, and GJ laughed, pleasantly pleased to discover that Walter, the Terminator, the super soldier, was a little bit squeamish over blood.

"Compare notes?" Walter asked, and GJ simply nodded, setting the vial directly into her bag so it couldn't be forgotten. She had, of course, labeled it very carefully on the scene, much to the chagrin of Will and Art. They'd stood staring, vaguely bored, while she carefully dated, collected coordinates, and put more information on the small vial than most people carried on their driver's licenses.

"So," Walter asked, "did you get any information on the people who were out hunting?"

"Yeah," GJ answered, scratching at her knee. Only as she stuck her hand onto the wet fabric did she remember that she'd been kneeling in the dirt. She looked over at Walter's notes, finding that they agreed. There had been an older black man. Another man had been termed "middle-aged" by several interviewees—a white male. And lastly, the third hunter was a younger woman that people were fairly confident was of Asian descent.

"None of these is my grandfather," GJ said, both secretly pleased and yet also concerned, because ruling him out dramatically ruined their chances of easily figuring out who these people were. Until now, she'd believed it might have been her grandfather who'd killed Wade's boyfriend, and she was glad that he had not been the one to pull the trigger. Still, it was possible he was in this up to his eyeballs.

Will Little came up then and took the seat next to Walter, looking back and forth between the two women, still dirty from their run. He, of course, had taken the time to shower. This was his home, not theirs. Now that he was here, they couldn't keep their conversation private, a problem when you sat at someone else's dinner table discussing your case.

"I'm so glad," he offered up in a dry tone, "that the group of people hunting us is so diverse. If there was ever a time you *wanted* a cohesive group of racists, now would be it."

Were they racist? GJ wondered to herself. Perhaps they were species-ist. Although from the bone samples she'd studied in her grandfather's lab, she certainly hadn't found anything that demonstrated speciation.

"GJ." Walter's hand waved through her field of vision. Yup, she'd wandered off there for a minute.

"I'm sorry, what?"

"Will has something to tell us."

Apparently, Will had been talking while GJ contemplated species divergence and what kind of evolutionary pressures might have occurred to bring about men like Will Little. Instead, she should be listening to him. She could ponder the universe later.

"This woman—I think we may have seen her before. Did you talk to anybody else about this?" Again, Will looked back and forth between the two newly minted agents. It occurred to GJ for the first time that the de Gottardi-Little crew didn't know they were getting rookies.

"No. We did ask if people knew them, and everybody said no," GJ answered him. "Although, I have to admit, I thought there were a few odd ticks with answers. Why would that be? Why wouldn't they just say: I think I've seen her around before? And where do you think *you* saw her?"

She was pulling out her notepad, anxious to get these thoughts added to her notes as Walter reached for her phone to begin recording the conversation. Will Little was talking again, giving out valuable information rather than just shooting the breeze with the women who'd invaded his home.

"We tend not to say anything because we're constantly getting discriminated against. So we don't want to speak out against someone that we're not confident of, but I think I may have seen her at the grocery in town. You might want to go ask there. They'll know if this is somebody new, or if we're all being idiots and thinking that several different people are all the same woman."

That was a valid point, GJ thought. There were numerous studies that showed people often had difficulty distinguishing faces in races outside of their own. It didn't seem to matter what race you came from, but what you were exposed to. The problem was that different races used different distinguishing characteristics. So, it was entirely possible that this woman's Asian background might have caused all the white boys of the de Gottardi/Little family to not recognize that the woman in the store had been hunting them in the woods. Also, no one claimed to have gotten a solid look at any of the three assailants. Burt hadn't even been sure she was a woman. Not surprising. It was hard to commit a face to memory while running from bullets.

Being in a backwoods town in the Ozarks was another problem, from GJ's standpoint. There wasn't a lot of diversity here anyway, so who could say the grocer wouldn't make the same mistake? She didn't push it, though. Just nodded at Will Little, as she and Walter agreed they'd get on it.

"We're staying at the motel on Pinn Street," GJ volunteered, though she'd yet to check in, so "staying" a strong word for her relationship to the motel so far. "Is it the only one in town?"

Will nodded at her as Burt came into the room, deciding he, too, was going to join the conversation. He didn't move quite as easily as Will did, his side still stitched up, his right hand occasionally moving as though to cover the wound and hold the blood in, even though he'd been thoroughly taken care of.

"The closest place you can stay besides the motel is to go three towns over, way past Bull Shoals. So if somebody came here, that's where they would stay."

Will hit the nail on the head to what she was thinking. They had a lot of places to ask, and a lot of ground to cover before they would likely figure out who their three mysterious visitors to this little patch of family land in the Ozarks were.

20

Walter's stomach growled. The Egg McMuffin she had for breakfast was managing to both not sit well and not keep her from being hungry again. The sandwich was, sadly, the highest-end food she'd had access to that morning.

Bull Shoals was such a tiny town that it couldn't support much in the way of business, something Walter totally understood. The café would have taken too much time today, but if she was still here tomorrow, she was going to make the café happen, then hit up the grocery store. She would graciously forget motel rules about not having food in the room. Too bad.

Out here in the woods, she kicked up the dirt looking for clues and information in the same places she and GJ had come the night before. Once the two of them had rolled out of bed, they'd made a plan for the day. However, a good chunk of the morning was already gone, as they'd agreed to sleep in. They'd needed it after the twenty-five hour marathon they'd run since being pulled from their beds in Quantico with only three hours of sleep.

Walter had suggested she come back and check out this area. She'd been hopeful she might find more information in the daylight, and GJ, of course, said yes. In part, her partner only agreed because the evidence had already been trampled so many times. GJ had gotten her samples last night. It was fair game now for Walter to search out what she wanted.

One thing Walter still hoped to find—despite both Art and Will being unable to find any the night before—was spent casings. GJ might look for clues of blood and bone, but Walter looked for clues of cordite and firepower. Walter looked for evidence of arms.

Now, in the daylight, she was trying to figure out which location Randall had been killed from, where someone else might have stood to get a crushing hit to his head. Walter shone a flashlight in an attempt to illuminate any remaining footprints. She needed the extra light to get past the gray color of the day and the gloom that hung overhead, but as GJ had said, the site was so trampled, the signs were difficult to distinguish.

From what GJ and Eleri had deduced, and what she'd surmised herself, Randall had taken a blow to the upper right side of his skull, probably from behind. If she was the one doing it, that's how she would have made it happen.

That thought led her to conclude he'd likely been running away. Though the body was burned, she could easily guess that he would have marks on his hands and forearms from stumbling forward. Which then meant the blade—and the evidence of self-defense that Donovan had thought might cause the markings on his arms—might also have been an issue from him falling onto rocks when he was hit from behind.

She'd questioned GJ about this. Would the marks look any different? GJ had said if the rocks were sharp, no, so Walter came out and looked. She couldn't say for sure, but right near where Randall had been found and, according to Wade, dragged away into a car, she found several rocks that might have done the job. It was entirely possible Randall had not fought at all, but had simply been felled from behind as he ran in terror from the people who showed up and began shooting at his companions.

She disengaged, no longer thinking about Randall as belonging to Wade, as a family member. However, the disengagement could come back and bite her in the ass. She would have to remember to reengage before speaking to Eleri or Wade or even Donovan about it. They were all far more emotionally involved than she. She wasn't, but only because she'd made a conscious effort to do so. She hated this shit.

In the end, she found only one bullet casing, and she couldn't say for sure it had been used for the scenario at hand. She was standing in the woods in the Ozarks, at the foothills of the mountains. It's entirely possible anyone and everyone came out here and shot at any manner of prey. In fact, Will, Art, Burt, and several other members of Wade's extended family admitted to hunting deer though, apparently, sometimes they hunted as wolves. That was something Walter had not yet wrapped her head around, something she could absolutely not imagine Donovan doing. She simply couldn't see him going for the jugular, even of a deer, with fangs bared, chin dripping the blood of his kill. Though he ate his steaks relatively rare, he got them from a butcher and not the woods. Oh, the irony of Lucy Fisher—the Terminator—Walter Reed, having a relative pacifist for a boyfriend.

Though she wanted to simply slide the shell into her pocket for later examination, she'd learned instead to put it into an evidence bag. She used her GPS watch to note the exact location where she found it, and before she even picked it up, she took a handful of pictures from different angles. GJ would be proud. Only when she completed all the necessary steps to keep and maintain the evidence —evidence that was never going to see the light of day in a courtroom, because the family was freaking werewolves—did she put the bag into her pocket.

She'd found the shell casing a good distance away from where Randall had died. It would indicate there was a spot where somebody might have stood and shot at the group, not specifically where someone had gotten close enough to Randall to create the head wound. However, it was a good location to aim for the spot where Burt had been wounded.

Standing directly where the casing had been, she next looked for nearby areas that might offer cover—a tree to hide behind, branches to provide camouflage, an outcropping of rough rocks, something of the sort. Walter found herself able to stare directly to the path that the men claimed they had taken. They had also marked for her and GJ the location where Burt had been shot.

This spot was perfect for it, and though she couldn't tell by looking—and she didn't have Donovan's sense of smell, or GJ's innate sense of science—she believed this was the spot the shooter had chosen. She hoped that perhaps there would be a residue of silver in the casing, which would show that this one wasn't leftover from something the de Gottardi family had done, but definitely from their new visitors. She wouldn't know until after GJ or an analyst had tested it.

Walter scanned the area again from her new vantage point. She'd hiked out here, a good five miles. Sometimes she thought maybe she shouldn't do things like this. She had a prosthetic leg, after all. Things could go wrong, and there was no cell signal out here. But if she didn't do this, what was she? If she couldn't survive a night in the Ozarks, then what good was she? If she couldn't do what other agents didn't think twice about, then she wasn't fit to be an agent at all. She'd proved her value at Quantico, not only to her instructors and Westerfield, but also to herself.

So she hiked, her awkward gait making her maybe a little slower than some others. *Still faster than GJ*, she thought with a smirk. She had five miles to go to get back, and though the day wasn't overly hot, it was getting warmer. She needed food, and she didn't think she'd find anything else of value out here; she'd searched as hard as she could and was beginning to think the wolf hunters had picked up their casings for the exact purpose of covering their tracks.

She was about a quarter mile into her return journey, traipsing straight back toward the compound where the de Gottardi and Little families lived together—really all one big family—when she saw the movement. She was on family property. They owned hundreds, maybe even thousands, of acres up here. So at first she called out. "Hello? It's me, Walter. Who am I talking to?"

No response came back, so she called out again. It was only then that she heard the click of a rifle being cocked and felt the hair on the back of her neck rise.

Walter dropped immediately to the ground, a maneuver she'd had to relearn after getting a prosthetic leg. Rehabbing and getting out of the hospital wasn't enough; she discovered she still needed her tactical maneuvers, not just the ability to walk and jump like a normal girl. Even though she'd thought she was back up to speed, Quantico had put her efforts to the test. Right now, though, she was grateful for the obscene number of times she practiced it.

She didn't notice as her left hand hit the ground. She didn't feel the sensation of dirt in her fake fingers. She did feel the jarring sensation up into her upper arm that told her that her prosthetic hand was planted at her side for balance, exactly as she'd expected it to be.

What surprised her, maybe, was that as her left hand hit, her right hand was at the ready, her gun pulled from the holster on her hip. Though she'd thought earlier about maybe not bringing it, she told herself she was an FBI agent now. If Westerfield caught her out, in trouble, without her sidearm, that would be more trouble than being caught without it in a dangerous situation.

Yet, here she was. She scanned the area. Her ears had not been hurt in the war, a fact for which she was supremely grateful. She was also highly dependent on her ears for giving her more information from the environment. Though she had spent time in extremely high-decibel gunfire, she was able to use her hearing now to turn and try to place an auditory memory of where she'd heard that specific kind of snick that a rifle made as a person got ready to fire.

Walter wasn't one much for signs from the gods, but right then, the clouds moved enough for sunlight to come out. Her enemy was not as smart as she was. The sun glinted ever so slightly off the barrel of the rifle aimed toward her. Walter would have blackened it, but her enemy's error allowed her a moment. She used it to roll and come up behind a tree, popping upright and snapping her head to look around, just as she registered the sound of a shot and saw the ground puff up, the bullet hitting exactly where she'd been.

Well, shit, she thought. Thank God she'd been a fighter. Thank God she'd been shot at before, because she had not expected it out here. She had fully assumed that the people hunting the de Gottardi-Little Family would be long gone by now. They'd killed Randall and they'd clearly moved the body back to GJ's grandfather's house. They may have been upset that the person they'd sacked was not the kind they were looking for. Getting the body transported such a distance away was solid evidence that they were no longer here. At least, Walter would have thought that. Maybe they weren't *still* here. Maybe they'd come *back*.

Walter took a moment and peeked around the other side of the tree, hoping to see what she could. If she was lucky, she could catch a glimpse of the shooter slightly further up the ridgeline. It might save her life.

Walter held the low ground, a position she was not proud of. The trees and the rocks were her friends here, though she had no idea how well the other person knew the area they were traipsing. She'd paid attention on the walk out this way last night and today in the daylight on the way up. It was a lesson hard learned from losing the troops who stood next to you. One second they would be there, and in the next they would be gone in a flash of noise and blood.

While she carefully moved her head just far enough to see, trying to discern if the bulge she was seeing was actually part of the tree, or perhaps part of a camouflage outfit, the tree barked and cracked in front of her. She jumped back as a bullet hit almost directly opposite where she was.

Bad aim, she thought, but then, another shot spit up dirt too close to her feet for comfort. The problem was, the angles were wrong. Unless someone had side-swiped the tree, which didn't match where she'd seen the barrel glint just moments before, then another person was there, also shooting at her.

Son of a bitch, she thought, and crouched down low again. No more standing up straight, thinking the tree was adequate cover. Now, the question was, could it possibly be de Gottardi or Little family members? She had no evidence, but her gut told her in no uncertain terms that that wasn't it. Though not every family member had been happy to see them, she did not believe they'd follow her and shoot at her. These were the hunters returned. Did they think she was one of the wolves? It didn't really matter right now. If they killed her they might be disappointed with their find, but she would still be dead. She hadn't survived multiple tours in Afghanistan to die in the Ozarks.

Though her heart rate and her breathing accelerated with her fear, she now took active control of it. Slow deep breaths, in through her nose, out through her mouth. She let her eyes dart back and forth, scanning the area loosely, trying not to focus on anything specific. She hoped that as she scanned something odd would pop in her vision.

After a moment, she saw it, there on her right. Camouflage gear did its job and concealed him quite well. But her unfocused gaze had found him, an odd shape among the trees, a slightly older black male. Could he possibly be the one the de Gottardis reported?

Taking a moment, she tried to figure out if maybe these two were poachers, simply on the land committing illegal acts and not realizing they were shooting at a person.

There was no way, Walter thought. She was dressed in non-camouflage gear. Now, knowing these guys were back, and that they were doing their best to conceal themselves, she realized that giving them a pass was a dangerous mistake.

Slowly, she slid her head over, moving only far enough to reveal one eye. Anyone would have to have serious sharp-shooting skill to be able to take her out with just that small amount of her exposed. It was a trick she learned as a Marine, and one she'd taught to GJ at Quantico. *Play the angles.*

This time, with her gaze loose again and her heart rate now running lower, she saw a second person. It was possibly the one who'd first taken a shot at her, now slowly creeping around. Shorter than the black male in the distance, this person might be a woman or a small, thin man. Walter couldn't tell. The hat concealed her hair, which would have been a help identifying her, but not today.

Slowly, Walter slid back behind her own tree, though it seemed they already knew she was here. Still, she thought, no quick movements. If they didn't already know, she wasn't going to give it away. If they were coming closer, she was going to have to make a run for it. If she stayed put, they would be able to flank her and pin her in. As far as she could tell right now, they had no compunction about killing her first and asking questions later. If she ran, they might get a shot. If they took her down, they might converge upon her and kill her. If she ran, she might also get away. She might get away cleanly enough to be able to track back around and get to the de Gottardi-Little compound.

So many ifs to contemplate. Right now, however, these two stood in between her and where she needed to go. She did not think she would survive splitting them and making a run directly toward the homestead, so before she ran, she had something very important to do. Reaching down to the left side of her waist and using the pressure that she felt on her arm to operate the radio with her robotic fingers, she did what she could. She squeezed her muscles, pushing the fingers together and turned the knob.

21

G J was standing in the crappiest makeshift lab she'd ever been in when the signal came. Her new "lab" was merely the best lit corner of her motel room.

It did include a laboratory-grade microscope that Westerfield had practically thrown at her as he'd put them onto the plane. Now, GJ was convinced that the microscope, as well as the motel, had seen better days. One of the optics was scratched, leaving her unable to get a clear view of her magnification at forty times normal. While the microscope had a light in the base, the overhead light in the motel room to see how she was setting up her slides, was piss-poor. Even though she'd unplugged and moved several of the bedside lamps, they still gave off only the dullest of yellow glows.

She'd thrown open the curtains, grateful the view was at least pretty. Unfortunately, the day was a bit overcast, and while the quantity of light coming in certainly improved the weak light from the lamps, she couldn't say it helped a lot.

The radio crackling to life suddenly was a welcome change. Her head snapped up. Her eyes and ears turned automatically toward the sound where she'd left the walkie talkie sitting on the dresser top next to her, because of course, she didn't have an actual table or a desk in here. After the initial scratching sound, she waited for Walter to speak.

After another moment, when only static came, she decided it must be Eleri, or Donovan, or even Wade trying to get through to her. She picked up the radio, opened up the signal, and waited. When nothing came through, she frowned at it and wrote the noise off as a glitch. Or that someone unrelated to them was using radios on the same frequency. Cell reception out here was sporadic at best, so this wasn't an illogical conclusion. She was setting the piece aside when it began making static noises again.

This time she realized what she had missed the first time around. The static was the message. Three longer bursts, followed by three short rapid ones, followed by three longer ones, and *oh shit. SOS*. It couldn't be Eleri or Donovan or even Wade. It would be Walter, the only one who was really supposed to be close enough to come through on her radio signal. GJ knew Walter was out in the woods today having convinced everyone that she'd be fine out there by herself to retrace Randall's last steps and try to figure out if a car or a truck had taken him. Then maybe where they might have gone.

GJ abandoned her dresser top, leaving the microscope light on, and found her hand on the doorknob to the motel room before she even realized what she was doing. Her right hand had pulled the Glock from its holster of its own volition. She'd been wearing it and had even checked it to be sure she was loaded and ready, all without conscious planning.

Jesus, she thought. Her Quantico training had been even more thorough than she imagined, despite the fact that she and Walter were still a full month shy of actually graduating. Maybe Westerfield had known what he was doing.

She had keys in one hand, and a bag with extra weapons and ammunition for both her and Walter in the other. Luckily, she'd been wearing her hiking boots, as she'd originally thought maybe she would go along. But something had popped in the evidence and she'd stayed behind to examine it, though what she thought she might find the in dim light of the motel room was beyond her. Now she'd left her partner somewhere out in the Ozarks offering only a staticky SOS for communication.

GJ was in the car and wondering if she could be possibly fast enough to save Walter before she'd even realized she put the key in the ignition. *More training,* she thought as she took a hard left up toward the area where the de Gottardi-Little family lived. She considered calling the house but dismissed the idea as fast as it appeared. The last thing she needed was untrained civilians on scene.

As she raced along the paved roads, she prepped to flash her badge out the window if anyone with a siren came up behind her. She took a hard right onto gravel, fishtailing the tires and wishing that she could fly faster even though the car clearly didn't have the traction to do so. Finally, she was stymied further by turning onto two dirt ruts that they called a "road" up this way. Frustrated beyond measure, she worked to stay on the road as her speed crept lower and lower.

She'd bypassed the houses, going straight for the area closer to where they knew that Randall and the guys had gone for a run that first night. When she finally stopped the car and turned off the engine, she thought about the noise. *Crap.* Now fighting time, she opened the car door slowly to muffle the sounds she was making. All the while she looked around wondering if she'd alerted somebody of her presence with the sound of the engine as she approached, and already regretting that she hadn't run the last mile. She closed the door, holding the handle up and managing to almost completely cover the sound of the latch catching as she gently let the handle back into place.

Her right hand did this while her left patted herself down, checking. Gun, yes. Then she reached to touch her rifle with her other hand. Weapon holstered and ready for Walter, should she need to hand it off. She tried to remember how much ammo Walter had on her and was certain that her friend had carried her Glock fully loaded. *She also should have another two clips.*

While she was sure that Walter had a decent number of bullets on her, she couldn't be sure just how long they would last. When she heard the popping sounds in the distance, her head shot up and she turned to stalk that way. Though she wanted to run, she held back. That, too, had been drilled into her during months of training. You weren't any help if you were dead. You couldn't save your partner if you were incapacitated. And if you became a burden you not only weren't a benefit to your investigation, you were a detriment.

As she thought it through, she tried to reason a few positive points about the noises she'd heard. It was gunfire. It might be coming from Walter rather than toward her. GJ couldn't quite distinguish the sounds of the different guns. That was Walter's forte.

Gunfire meant that there was still active fighting going on, and she would only hope that meant that Walter was still in the mix. She didn't think any of the other men or women from the de Gottardi-Little family had come up with her. Walter had said she'd wanted to come alone, and GJ could only hope that was still the case.

When it came to Walter, anyone with her would likely only hold her back. While Eleri Eames might be some sort of witch, Walter was a magician.

GJ ducked into the trees, going from trunk to trunk, staying on the opposite side from where she'd heard the noise. Her eyes glazed and scanned as she looked for people in the distance. She saw movement but didn't catch what it meant. She first thought it might be a deer, but quickly dismissed the idea. With the gunfire, the animals would have scattered. If something was moving this close to the sound of bullets, it was likely a human.

GJ stopped, moved her head slightly out from behind the trunk, and looked again. This time, she found the form. Though it was merely an outline as though a tree had shifted over, she caught that it was human. A male, slightly tall, slightly portly, and definitely holding a rifle aimed to GJ's left.

Taking that as a clue, she followed the sight line of the barrel. At the other end, she spotted another hint of movement—just the slightest bit. She counted herself lucky for even catching that. Walter could disappear.

The man had been hard to find as he'd been in full camo gear with tree bark printing on it. Normally, it looked ridiculous when GJ saw it on people in the mall, but here in the woods, camouflage did its job. She was grateful she'd been able to spot him at all.

The rifle, on the other hand, wasn't his smartest move. Relatively shiny, the wood stock had been oiled. Even the clean metal made a statement. And once GJ saw it, she couldn't unsee it. That was good. Whoever this guy was, she'd be able to find him again.

Walter, on the other hand, was merely a flicker at the corner of her vision. As she saw the man with rifle lift the barrel slightly and take aim at Walter, GJ in turn pulled her own Glock and sighted down the barrel.

22

Walter rolled as the bullet pinged off a rock a little too close to her head for comfort. She had gotten into that eerie calm again, the one she was in when she was in theater in Afghanistan, when the bullets began flying and your life didn't matter anymore. You knew you could only dodge and weave, just like boxing. But with bullets, the hit was going to come a lot harder.

She hadn't expected to ever feel this way again. Despite the fact that she was becoming—or had become—a federal agent, the FBI warned them there weren't many gunfights. Just because of douchebags like Brian and Hank, who thought drawing their gun was the funnest thing ever, they'd all been given a lecture that being in the line of fire was absolutely shit-your-pants terrifying. Luckily, it didn't happen much. Even a stray shot or a gun on the scene rarely led to someone shooting at you. Though they'd practiced at Quantico, she still hadn't quite gotten the zing of adrenaline that accompanied real bullets and real danger. But here she was, of course, on her first case, drawing gunfire. She hadn't even *graduated* for real, for fuck's sake.

Walter rolled backward onto her butt and over her left shoulder. Coming up, she stayed low, head down, keeping her right arm free, her hand on her Glock the whole time. She did it without pulling the trigger, having practiced the maneuver many, many times, using her prosthetic left leg to jam into the ground and force herself back to a not-fully-upright position, but squatted just enough so she could see around.

As she came up, she spotted GJ off on her right. But suddenly drawing her focus, directly in front of her, was the man who'd pulled the trigger on her in the first place and he was the one she took aim at. Though as she lifted the gun, she saw him jerk, yelp, and fall back. The rifle fell out of his hands and he clutched at his elbow.

GJ had winged him.

Was it the result of bad aim? Walter didn't know. Her breathing was heavy now. Nothing could prepare you for the moment when someone actually wanted you dead and had the firepower to achieve it. Then again, GJ—though still not all that strong and still not stupendously fast—had become a crack shot. She wasn't a fast draw and she didn't do rapid fire well, but her aim had become deadly. *Maybe she'd meant to wing him.* As Walter thought about it, it made sense. They needed these people alive.

Forcing a breath, she swung around, looking to where she'd last seen the woman, and saw nothing. GJ took off in a run, chasing down the man she'd hit. Having dropped his rifle in favor of his freedom, he'd run in the opposite direction away from both of them.

Walter wanted to call out. GJ hopefully wouldn't turn at the sound of her voice, but if she shouted instructions it would leave both of them open to fire. The problem was GJ was running, and Walter knew there was still someone else out here who wanted to kill them —and maybe even a third person she hadn't yet seen. She couldn't tell. But she knew of at least two. GJ had only taken care of one.

Needing to distract from the open target her partner was making, Walter stood up to full height. Though GJ was doing a good job of staying low, and had the man been the only shooter, it would have been a wise decision, Walter felt the need to act. Gun at the ready, she mentally counted the bullets she'd spent. Since she'd reloaded the last time she'd ducked and covered, as well as once before, she was on her last magazine. She should have eight bullets left. It wasn't as many as she wanted, and she'd have to parse them out carefully.

Still, she called out to her partner, "There's one behind you. I've got her. Keep going."

GJ, bless her, did not turn, but clearly heard and began zigzagging her way through the trees. The man, who might still have a pistol on him, had at least dropped his rifle. With any luck, she would see some kind of movement as he grabbed for another weapon, which would protect her front. What she also needed to do was protect her back from where Walter had last seen the woman.

Still sweeping the area, Walter wondered what she might find. She found it. Her last turn and sweep had her pulling up short, staring directing into the deadly, dark eyes of a small woman glaring back at her. Two hands on a Glock, the woman took aim. Walter was looking right down the barrel.

With a deep breath, she made a decision.

"Hello. Nice to meet you," Walter offered as though they were in a park on a sunny day. She could only hope her tone masked the shaking deep inside her soul. She'd been here before. She had survived before. But having watched others not survive, she knew that any time you looked down the barrel of a gun, it was very likely your last day on earth.

"FBI," the woman hissed her recognition of them like a curse. Her dark hair was falling out from where it had been tucked up under her ball cap. With the cap knocked off and her roughed up look, she now seemed tiny and disheveled. This was the small Asian woman the runners had been talking about. For a moment, Walter wondered where old white dude was, and she was tempted to ask. If she was going to die from a bullet from this gun, she was going to get her questions answered first.

"You need to stay out of this, agent," the woman hissed again, and the words, if not the tone, gave Walter hope. If she was telling Walter to *stay out*, then maybe she believed that Walter could in fact do so. If she was trying to get rid of Walter, she probably would have pulled the trigger already. Walter was certainly close enough to make a target that would be hard to miss.

"What is it exactly that we're mixed up in?" Walter asked, as casual a tone as she could muster.

"You don't know, and you wouldn't understand." That was when Walter saw the gun begin to falter just a little bit.

She pressed harder. "Try me."

"No. It doesn't make any sense and it's evil. We're trying to clean it up. We don't need you in our way."

Oh, dear God, Walter thought. *A zealot. No wonder they were trying to kill Wade's family.* Quickly deciding on a conspiratorial tone and the idea that the FBI was on the same side as these people, Walter leaned in. She was giving the woman a better shot at her rapidly beating heart, but she hoped she was giving herself a better shot, too.

"I've seen them," she said. "And I think you're right...How do we kill them?"

The woman looked for a moment, eyes darting one way to another. Walter had to imagine that it was possible these hunters had seen Walter and GJ at the home of the de Gottardi-Little family. If that was the case, then it was likely nothing she said would be believed and Walter would soon be dead, surely shot for being a liar rather than taking her chance and getting out when she'd been offered.

"It's an old evil," the woman said grimly, the gun still aimed at Walter. Despite the conspiratorial tone Walter offered, the woman had not pulled her aim. "You don't know what they can do."

"Actually, I do," Walter said, her voice low, wondering if at this moment the old white dude wasn't creeping up behind her ready to put a gun to her head. Because she didn't know, she had to keep down this path. She spoke again. "I have seen it. I've seen the way the bones shift and pop, the way their muscles pull, and then there's something different. Something evil." She echoed the woman's words back to her and when the woman nodded, Walter took her chance.

23

Walter dove toward the woman, shoving her own gun down into the holster as she moved, needing her hands free for the move. Pushing her weight forward, she moved onto her right foot and ducked low. Should the woman fire off a shot, Walter wanted to be out of the way.

The woman gasped, clearly rattled by Walter's movements, which meant they'd worked exactly as intended. Using that dismay to her advantage, Walter shoved her left—fake—hand up under the woman's wrists. Exactly at the point where she was gripping the butt of the handgun. With the fingers and the thumb of her metal hand open to form a V-shape, Walter shoved hard upward, aiming the gun away from herself as she lunged. All of it happened in one smooth motion.

Even so, the woman squeezed off a shot, but it went wild, into the trees and away from Walter. She'd already calculated that even if she got hit, by having her left hand up at least the damage would be on the hand she could more easily replace. There had to be an upside to losing a body part in a war.

The left hand—while excellent for shoving the woman's arms out of the way—was nowhere near as capable for the tricky maneuvers needed to get the gun out of her grip. Standing now, Walter wrapped her own hands over the woman's and spun until her back was toward the woman's front. She had the gun and the hands around it contained. She thought about kicking back and dropping the woman, but not until she had control of the weapon.

With a squeeze of her arm into her own side, she applied pressure to the woman's trapped arms, making her drop her hold. The nine-millimeter fell into Walter's hands. Luckily, she'd practiced the crap out of this. Catching was hard when you couldn't feel the touch of the object as it hit your skin.

Within a second, it was Walter with both hands on the gun. Knowing she couldn't hold the woman with trapped arms and her back toward her for long, Walter moved out. From a distance, it would look like a dance. Until that last moment when Walter spun out and away, her stance wide, the gun in her hands. She stepped back twice, staying close enough to attack if need be, but far enough that she couldn't have the same maneuver pulled on her. Using the gun to motion, she waited as the woman dropped down on her knees, having been rapidly stripped of her dominant position.

Though her heart was beating fast, Walter knew how to cover it. "You have two options," she told the woman, "die now or come with me."

That was not FBI protocol, she knew, but she didn't really care right now. She figured she could be forgiven because she'd just been fucking shot at in the woods multiple times. The woman didn't answer. Walter pulled cuffs out of the back of her belt, shocked that she'd had the opportunity to use them. These were zip cuffs, light-weight and easy to carry. GJ had insisted that if Walter went out by herself, she had to come fully prepared. Who knew she'd be right? Walter had only had two pairs on her and she was hopeful that GJ had brought her own, but probably GJ had brought all that and more. The little nerd had everything.

When the woman's hands were securely zip tied behind her, Walter lifted her to her feet. She steered her prisoner along, using the bound hands as a lever. If the woman pulled too hard one way or the other, she'd pull her own shoulder out of the socket. Walter had no sympathy, so she simply steered and let the woman decide how much she wanted to resist.

In the distance, she heard GJ taking down the man they'd seen. She looked up just in time to catch the action. It was a tackle of epic proportions. GJ must have thrown herself at a high speed to get enough force for her small body to adequately smack the man and maneuver him to the ground. Though the two dropped out of sight, Walter heard the thud, meaning GJ had accomplished it.

She wanted to pick up her pace and help her partner in case things got hairy, but she found she was unable to push the woman any faster. Her prisoner was reluctant to move at all, and Walter did not look forward to dragging her across the ground. She was already late arriving to back up her partner—something she held against her prisoner. The list was getting longer.

When she finally got close enough to see what was going on, she spotted GJ practically straddling her perp, who was face down on the ground, hands behind his back.

"You have the right to remain silent," GJ said.

Good Lord, Walter thought, *she was Mirandizing him.* Walter, instead, had given her victim the chance to die, and didn't that just say it all?

24

GJ looked to Walter. "Where in the hell do we take them?" she asked.

They'd dragged their quarry across the distance and closed them into the car. No names had been volunteered yet, as both had remained stubbornly silent. Given that attitude, Walter and GJ had no issues force-marching the two out of the woods and ducking them into the back of the sedan. The third possible member of their little hunting party had not appeared, much to GJ and Walter's concern. They still had no idea if someone was going to pop up and open fire on them on any moment, or if he was already in another state.

Being careful not to give away their information or expose their very real fears, Walter and GJ stayed close to one side of the car, huddled low, and kept sharp watch in every direction as they spoke. They couldn't speak freely inside the car with the others in the back seat. It would mean giving away the major problem they were dealing with, which was that they had nowhere to take these two. The closest FBI branch was hours away.

"We can't take them to the compound. It's absolutely unsafe, and probably five kinds of illegal to walk them into the home of their victims," GJ pointed out.

Walter nodded easily in response. So at least that was decided.

GJ looked over her shoulder in time to see the small woman start to struggle against the bonds. GJ found she didn't really care if the bitch was uncomfortable. She shouldn't have taken shots at Walter.

Once they'd dragged their captives back to the rental car, they decided to put the two into the back seat. But that posed another problem. Being merely a rental, it didn't have any kind of safety divider, so the two needed to remain completely tied up, even more so than they'd been on the march. With a little ingenuity and luck, GJ found car seat safety latches embedded in the seats. The two, with wrists bound behind their backs, were now latched firmly down to those, much the same way an official police car worked. Only with zip ties.

Then Walter had taken one look and tied their feet together. It had taken a little more creativity to anchor their feet to their hands, so they were unable to kick the backs of the seats once they were in motion. But, though the four were finally ready, they couldn't go until they could decide where to go to.

"We have to call Westerfield," GJ said, already pulling out her phone. Once again, Walter nodded. GJ wasn't surprised that Walter wasn't speaking so much. She'd been in the direct line of fire. While GJ had hunted down a man who dropped his rifle, and tackled him to the ground in relative safety, Walter had faced the barrel of a gun. She was breathing steadily, but was clearly not yet back to her normal self.

GJ made the call.

Westerfield answered on the second ring. "Janson, what you got?"

She decided to go with exactly what it was. "Two perps."

"I'm sorry. What?" her boss responded, in a most unprofessional manner.

"We have detained two people who were shooting at us today. They match the description of those who fired at the family the other night, and are likely from the same hunting party that killed Randall Standish."

"You were supposed to collect evidence, not people," Westerfield said.

"Well, I guess you're right," GJ commented in a singsongy tone, as though she hadn't thought of this. "Should we just let them go?"

He didn't respond, the sarcasm in her voice plain as day, and GJ dialed it back a little before she continued. "Point is, we can't take them back to the family compound. We can't take them to the motel. I don't think it's very secure."

"Well, I suppose you could anchor them to something secure in your motel room," he offered in clear retaliation for her sarcastic tone.

Though the thought made GJ bristle with memories of being handcuffed to a hotel closet safe, she pointed out to Westerfield that it wasn't a likely option here. "It's the only motel in town. Everyone will see us coming. Everyone will see us going. Furthermore, I don't think there's anything in there we can cuff them to. There's not a safe at all, nothing anchored down."

"Exposed pipes?" he said.

"Not that I remember. Honestly, any pipe that's exposed in this place? One good yank and it would come right off the wall. It's not going to keep anybody safe. I'm guessing we're going to have to drive them somewhere, but we're looking to you for guidance on exactly where."

He gave them directions to a nearby small town that wasn't Bull Shoals. It was going to take well over an hour to get somewhere big enough to have multiple hotel options and a place they could stash these two. Westerfield would get himself on the next flight in, but it would still be a while before they could hand these two off.

In the meantime, she and Walter were expected to do some heavy-duty interrogation. GJ winced. Though she understood what this meant from her NAT courses, she didn't like the sound of it. If anyone overheard this call, they would be more concerned that it wasn't lessons from Quantico, but Guantanamo, that were being ordered.

Westerfield was ready to sign off, their assignment having been handed over and thoroughly described, but GJ stopped him. "Sir, there's one more problem."

"What's that, Janson?" he said, the tone in his voice indicating that he didn't want to hear it.

Well, too bad, she thought. They'd come out here. They'd caught two of the perpetrators, and they were bringing them in. He could suck it up. "Sir, we believe there's a third assailant. We're standing outside the car right now, where we have our two adequately tied up. We can make the trip and bring them in. However, if he's here, he could open fire on us at any moment. We have no clue where he is.

We haven't seen any evidence that he's here. We don't even know that there are only three of them. This could be it, or there could be a battalion in the woods. As soon as we can, we need to get somebody out here to search the area. See if they can find another car. I'd stay, but with these two, I wouldn't split Walter and me up."

"Hadn't intended to," he said, "but it's a valid point. I'll send Eames and Heath in to take a look. I'm bringing de Gottardi with me—"

"Sir, is that wise?" she interrupted. "Wade should not be interviewing the people who shot and probably killed his boyfriend."

"No shit, Sherlock," Westerfield replied. "I'm not going to let him run the investigation. However, I'm sure he'll have insights, and can help us phrase questions to get the maximum value out of our work. He wasn't there, but he was around, and he does know his family."

GJ conceded the validity of that, and also—as Walter had pointed out—how unlikely it was that this case was ever going to sit before a jury of her peers.

With everything settled, she and Walter climbed into the front of the car. Walter allowed her to take the steering wheel, even though she generally didn't like riding shotgun. GJ started the car and rolled them back along the dirt road, bumping in reverse along the rutted tracks until she found a point where she could turn around. Just as she got the car aimed forward, the air cracked and the back windshield blew out.

25

Walter leaned in as she tried to put a little more of a conspiratorial tone back into her voice. At this point, she couldn't tell if the woman was buying it or not. Though Walter had done this kind of interrogation before, Quantico hadn't quite prepared her to interrogate a prisoner whose gun she'd stolen and then aimed at her. Clearly, this woman wasn't forgetting that Walter had talked like a friend for a moment, but then forced her onto her knees and—at gunpoint—cuffed her and zip-tied her into the back of a car. So, this time around, the tactic might not work as well.

Walter was aiming for an *I know why I want them dead. Why do you want them dead?* kind of tactic. But it wasn't working. This time the woman only said two words: "They're evil."

Walter couldn't quite work with that. She wanted to know what *kind* of evil. She'd already admitted that she'd seen them pop and roll their muscles. That she'd seen them change. But she wasn't getting anywhere. Just the repeated phrase, "They're evil."

Before they'd given up and called Westerfield, Walter and GJ thought it might be best to go to a local police station, to interview these two there. As the FBI, they should be able to walk their perps in, use a room, and walk them out later. But the problem, as she and GJ had quickly seen, was that the interview rooms were hardwired, and there was no way they could have this conversation in front of the local cops without blowing the de Gottardi and Little families' secret wide open.

So, they were at the hotel Westerfield had set up for them. Having rearranged the furniture, they were now trying to interview two perpetrators in separate bedrooms on either end of the generic suite. As far as Walter could assess, it was not going well. She looked at the woman again and aimed for her best version of a sympathetic expression. She tried to summon her inner GJ.

"I get it. They shift, and they change, and that's not natural." She worked hard to keep a straight face as she thought of her own metal, wire, and rubberized limbs—things that were as *unnatural* as anything Donovan or Wade could do. But she looked to the woman, eyes sincere as she could make them, and waited.

The woman again only replied, "They're evil."

Walter gave up. This was a brick wall, and she was done hitting her head on it. "Who shot out the window of the car as we left?"

Though the urge to stay and fight had been strong, Walter and GJ had run. They already had two perpetrators in the back seat of the car with barely enough space between them to keep them separated. If they hadn't been tightly zip tied, they could have worked together and made trouble, caused an accident, or maybe even overturning the car while they were driving away. Knowing how to do that herself, Walter didn't put it past anyone else. Adding a third person into the back would have compounded the problems by tenfold.

GJ had displayed some excellent tactical driving while Walter had pulled out her phone and called Will Little, explaining to him that he needed to alert the entire family that at least one active shooter was up on the ridge. Walter had sent photos that she'd taken of the two they had in custody. Their faces were not smiling in those pictures.

Both Art and Burt agreed that these looked, as best they could tell, like the people they'd seen in the woods the night Randall had been killed. They also each agreed they couldn't put their finger on it for certain, given the darkness, the fear, the way everyone had scattered, and the fact that their perpetrators had been in the distance on the long end of a rifle.

So it might be a different woman. Walter wasn't getting much of anywhere as Ms. Huntress was not speaking right now. The forced mugshots and the perp walk into the back of a nice hotel hadn't done them any favors making friends. The woman continued to stubbornly refuse to answer questions, and Walter wondered if GJ was having any better luck than she.

If anyone could do this, it would be GJ. Her partner had rocked this at Quantico, and just as Walter felt the thought pass, a message pinged up on her phone, a silent low buzz that came directly from GJ. Two words flashed on Walter's screen where she had it slightly propped so Ms. Huntress could not see it: "No luck."

Well, shit.

"One moment please." Walter looked up at the woman sitting across from her, the scowl now permanently etched into her features. She tried to be polite and act like this was a casual interview. As though the woman across from her did not still have her hands zip tied behind her back and anchored to the chair; as though her ankles were not tied to each of the chair legs. The hotel chair, while padded, looked pretty but didn't come across as actually feeling very comfortable. Walter had ceased to care.

She tapped out a quick message back to GJ. "I'm invoking the name of Dr. Murray Marks."

Then she set the phone down and looked at Ms. Huntress. She was going to play a game now. She was going to pretend that she knew everything and hope that Ms. Huntress corrected her when she was wrong. *Ready? Set?*

"We have the body of the man you killed," she opened with. And for the first time, she saw a flicker of surprise, though the woman held it well before quickly resuming her sour expression.

"His name was Randall Standish. When you checked his—"

There it was. Walter tried not to pause as the flicker across the woman's face told her she found an error in Walter's reasoning. But Walter was ready to keep going. Time to prove she knew more than the bitch in front of her.

"His name was Randall Standish," she repeated. "I understand that when you checked his pockets, he had an FBI agent badge, and that you read his name differently. But you see, he'd borrowed another man's clothes because he didn't have the kind of clothing he needed to go out on a night run. And unfortunately, when he borrowed the clothes, he didn't realize he also got the wallet down in the pocket of the cargo pants. So, the problem right now is this: no matter what you and I may think of these guys and what they can do, you didn't kill one of them. You killed a human man."

Walter let the last sound linger and hang heavy between them, even though she didn't believe it. What she said insinuated that Wade and Donovan were not human, and not worthy of the respect that Randall was getting. However, she couldn't afford to stand on ceremony here. She couldn't afford to say what she really believed. That was one of the things both she and GJ had learned at Quantico: any means necessary to get the information. Anything that didn't violate the Geneva Convention, and maybe sometimes, a few things that did.

Walter was surprised all the lessons were still sticking. But here she was, staring at the woman who was staring back. Though the expression was still ugly and angry, it had changed. It was clear she was surprised by some of the information that Walter had.

"That's why the bones didn't work," Walter added. "You brought him back, and you thought you had one of them, and you even thought you had an FBI agent. But the fact of the matter is, you were wrong. You killed a human being. What are you going to do about it?"

Another small crack appeared in the façade, though Walter couldn't tell if the woman was thinking or growing angrier. It was right now when she thought about how quickly she'd taken the gun off this woman, and how long GJ had run to catch up with the man she had winged. She thought of how she had excelled at marksmanship and all the physical aspects of their job. But right now, she wished she had a little more of GJ's powers.

GJ, of course, had needed to interview the man. Given her superior medical skills and her ability to question people regardless of their demeanor—like, say, while they were in pain—this had been the natural solution. And Walter wasn't getting anything until the last moment when the woman looked at her and said, "It wasn't me. It was Harry."

26

"Which part?" GJ whispered to Walter where they sat in the center area of the suite, the bedroom doors pulled almost closed on their prisoners. It wasn't a good solution, just the only viable one.

She whispered again. "The part where I checked his wounds several times? Each time pressing my finger into it and causing him more pain. Well, I don't know if it worked, but he said another guy shot Randall."

Judging by the look on Walter's face, that wasn't a good answer. She thought that she'd achieve something by getting that out of the interview.

"What was the name?" Walter asked.

"Harry." She answered from memory even as she flipped through the little paper pad she'd written on. She'd been recording and copiously writing down everything she could.

"At least they both gave the same name. However, it's highly plausible that they simply gave the name of the one who got away. Blame it on the guy who isn't here to fight back."

"Or it might even be a fake name they're prepared to give," GJ lamented. "Either way, neither of them is taking the blame for the shot that killed a person."

She worked to keep her tone low, even as her irritation shot up. They were sitting in the central room of the suite, with one person tied to a chair in each room on either side of them. They'd pulled the doors mostly closed to block the sound, but it also blocked their vision. The concern was that anything their prisoners overheard would be like showing their cards in the middle of a poker game.

Westerfield was on his way and he was bringing Wade. The logistics of using Wade would be as bad as the issues of using a hotel suite for a police-style interrogation. They needed Wade to help with the interview, but neither of the perpetrators could be allowed to see him. If either one spotted a family member coming to the interview, they would know it was all over. Though GJ didn't believe either of their perps bought into the idea that the FBI was on their side, she still didn't want to just blow it wide open by admitting it.

They would have to wire Wade into the interviews with an ear piece. Let him listen and coach them on what to say and hope that he could stay calm throughout the process, while he listened to these two describe how they had killed his boyfriend.

GJ wasn't looking forward to any of this. As much as she was relieved Westerfield would arrive and take over the investigation, the whole thing was getting far too personal. The disregard for certain protocols was making her squirmy, but she kept her mouth shut because she had no rights there. She'd once stolen a skeleton from an FBI branch office and interfered with an investigation. Nope. No right to bitch about protocol. So she stuck to staying quiet and hoped her boss showed up soon to take responsibility for this clusterfuck.

Her wishes were granted by a ping on her phone.

Here. Her text message showed. *De Gottardi and I have arrived.*

She watched as Walter looked at her own screen, seeing the same message on the group text.

Sit rep. Westerfield demanded.

"Situation report," GJ thought how much she didn't like this one. While Walter watched, she tapped back an answer about how they had the perpetrators in separate rooms, how they were in the middle, and how Wade could not been seen, which meant he couldn't step foot into the suite. Though they hadn't heard anything, the doors were mostly closed, and they hadn't confirmed their perps weren't moving around.

That was probably just an unnecessary reminder for Westerfield, who figured out all of these things ahead of time. But GJ, still getting used to being called Agent Arabella Janson, wasn't taking any chances that she might miscommunicate and fuck things up. Not only was it her first case, it was Wade's boyfriend. It was her grandfather. And none of this was good.

While they waited, she and Walter stalked the suite and checked to be sure their prisoners were still tied up and sitting in the center of their rooms. Unsure what would greet her from the other side of the door, GJ slowly pushed it open. Though the man was a good two feet to the left of where GJ had originally placed him, she only looked down at the spot on the floor where he'd been and then glared at him. At least he knew that she knew he'd been scooting around. She closed the door on him, letting the adrenaline slowly fade.

Inside of fifteen minutes, Westerfield and Wade were ensconced in a second room directly across the hall. GJ headed over with her phone line open to Walter. Her partner stayed back in the suite, in between the other two, listening for noises and ready to tackle anyone who managed to get out of their zip ties or make any kind of a run for it.

Walter, unable to speak openly, was texting back answers as they spoke. GJ had no problem interrupting to read them out loud, but watching Westerfield pace in front of her was making her uptight. They all agreed they didn't like that both prisoners blamed "Harry."

"We don't know who Harry is and we don't yet have Harry's last name," GJ offered. "Mostly Walter's woman just repeated 'they're evil' over and over. My guy only stared at me. The fact of the matter is, we zip tied them and dragged them away while the third one shot at us. So I don't think playing the sympathy card is going to fly anymore." Then she thought of something. "Who's out there right now checking on the shooter we left behind? And on Will and the families?"

She'd said it like it was part of the case, and it was, but it was also the family of the man standing in front of her.

"I have another agent headed in," Westerfield said, scratching at the back of his head and scowling as though the case was ballooning out of control.

And it was. GJ didn't like this one bit. Why couldn't she have a neat, clean, money laundering case? But no such luck.

"Heath and Eames?" GJ asked.

Westerfield shook his head. "They're still trying to catch up with Marks. But as of yet, no one has figured out where he is."

GJ's heart constricted, but she kept her face flat. "Any leads?"

Though he was her grandfather, in this case, he was just another perpetrator in this case.

"Nothing yet." Westerfield shrugged with the smallest of empathy smiles. "But Will Little apparently grabbed a couple guys and headed up to the ridge thanks to your warning."

GJ couldn't tell if it was a sarcastic response or not. Nobody wanted the Littles or de Gottardis involved in today's mess. No one wanted them out shooting guns. To be fair, it was their land and they were the ones getting shot at. So she wasn't sure there was any way to stop them.

"We considered invoking my grandfather's name." GJ said, bringing the conversation around to the interviews again. "But neither of us ever got around to saying it. It's still on the table."

Westerfield nodded, scratched his head again, and said, "I've got a plan."

It was much later that same night when Walter sat across the table from Will Little again. She looked the man in the eyes and wondered what he might be hiding from her now. Westerfield and Wade had taken over back at the hotel with the two prisoners that GJ and Walter had brought in earlier.

Westerfield had GJ and Walter help implement the start of his "plan," and the two prisoners had been searched and fingerprinted to confirm what GJ and Walter found on their IDs. GJ and Walter didn't have a field kit well enough stocked for that kind of tech analysis, so they'd been stuck matching the names and photos on driver's licenses and doing a passable check to be sure the IDs weren't fake. They'd purposefully not looked until after the questions were done. They'd been aiming to come off as sympathetic interviewers—a weird, cross-purpose game when you had someone chained to a metal table or, in this case, zip-tied to a hotel chair.

With Westerfield and Wade on the case, they pulled up information quickly. They found the woman, Jean Ah, was in the system for petty violations and minor infractions. Because she'd been fingerprinted, Westerfield was able to pull her file up with relative ease. The man, John Kramer, was not, but a search of DMV records revealed that they actually had the right name there, too. Nothing between the two of them popped or linked to anything for the third man supposedly named Harry, and neither of them was giving up a last name. Both seemed chagrined that they'd given up their partner's first name already; now they were doubling down on silence.

With IDs confirmed, Westerfield had sent his newest agents away, despite the fact that both Walter and GJ had looked at him oddly. With only him and Wade left to further interview these people, it meant Westerfield was the only one who could interact with them. Wade would be left outside the room handling things from a distance. However, he didn't seem to care, and since they'd been ordered away, the best Walter and GJ could do was discuss it as they drove off. They weren't going to change any minds.

They'd headed immediately back toward Bull Shoals with only a stop for fast food to quell the growing crescendos from their stomachs. Walter knew the de Gottardi-Little family might be under attack and, despite the fact that it was a homestead and reasonably well armed, they would need help to protect everyone. There was still another person out there, most likely with a gun and a vendetta. The threat had not passed.

Now, Walter sat at the dining room table in the main house again. Across from Will, another agent joined them. She'd introduced herself as Christina Pines. Westerfield had told them that she was acting as a solo agent, having been pulled into the case from a leave she'd been granted. And for another moment, Walter contemplated the idea that Eleri also had been on leave, Wade had been on leave, and now Agent Pines, too. Was there something underlying the way Westerfield was building this group?

Though she longed to ask what it was about, Walter held her tongue. She figured if she waited, GJ would pipe up and ask for her. Instead, she'd arrived back at the homestead and was staring down Will Little.

"What did you do?" Christina asked.

"I texted several of my cousins and we took our guns to protect ourselves," he clarified, as though they might think he would go out shooting. "And we went out and checked the area. We found shell casings."

He'd put them on the table earlier. Walter inspected them briefly, not realizing quite what he'd intended them to be.

"You shouldn't have moved those," GJ chided. "They were evidence."

"They still are," he told her.

GJ was shaking her head at him, not in an angry way, but in the way of a parent finding a teachable moment. Walter still didn't think it was quite the right way to go.

"Now, once you've touched them," her partner continued to explain, "we can't guarantee that any fingerprints that are on them actually lead back to a crime."

"Well, if they're not mine, then they're theirs," he said.

"That does make logical sense," GJ started and Walter breathed a sigh of relief, but it was a moment too soon.

GJ began spouting the ethics and science of evidence contamination. This was not anything that the general populace enjoyed hearing about and she needed to be kinder. So Walter was grateful when the tone turned.

"So while it seems reasonable," GJ told him, "it's a set up for a court of law, we need chain of command."

"Are you really bringing a court of law in here?" He looked back and forth between the three agents sitting at his table, his expression suddenly on high alert.

At that moment, Art walked in. The last words he'd heard coming from his grandfather's lips were clearly deeply concerning. "You can't bring the courts into this. We'll have to lie on the stand, and some of us aren't very good at it. That's why we live out here like we do."

Walter held her hands up. "No one's bringing in the courts. However, as GJ said, just for the sheer issue of us being able to read the evidence, you have to leave it out there. If you'd like, you can mark it and tell us where to go find it."

"Well if we did that, then they'd have the opportunity to come back and collect it. Seems to me these guys have been cleaning up their casings as they go. They only leave them behind when we run them off scared."

Unfortunately, there was nothing Walter could say to argue. The shooters were doing a good job of cleaning up their tracks and she desperately wanted to get out there now to see what was left behind. There should be footprints and, hopefully, more casings. Surely Art and Will hadn't found them all. The hunters had to have arrived some way.

The acreage here was far too big. You couldn't get to the de Gottardi-Little property without driving in from somewhere. Even if they parked at the edge and managed the five-mile hike, she should be able to trace some level of foot print, hopefully in the right direction to figure out where the car was. Or had been. Perhaps there was another car waiting. They had two people in custody. If they came in two cars, that meant only one driver left. Then she paused.

"What do we know?" Agent Pines asked, fitting her words perfectly into the gap of Walter's thoughts.

"We know, GJ and I," and she looked at Pines then, who nodded for her to go on, "that there were two of them that we managed to get into custody. During that time, someone else took a shot at us. We believe it was another person associated with these two," She turned to Will. "But I have to be sure that it wasn't one of your people. Will?"

This time, Will looked back and forth between them. "My people wouldn't do that."

"I don't know that," Walter replied. She wasn't harsh or mean, but she wasn't pussyfooting around this, either. "To be honest, we received a little bit of open hostility when we got here. Some people weren't all that fond of Randall and Wade's relationship—"

"Look," Will interrupted her. "We're not in any position to judge." He glanced then at her robotic hand as though this—in some way—related her to them. She wondered if he'd been talking to Donovan. Maybe she got it: they all had some level of freak status. But the fact of the matter was, a prosthetic arm was nothing like being one of them. Nothing like having a pack of hunters on your tail and possibly letting a family member or a visitor get killed.

The second time he started, Will looked a little more put together. He was the grandfather of this family, and it was becoming clear that he was the leader, though he didn't seem to do that from out in front. While Walter appreciated his style, she wasn't sure she appreciated the clannishness of the de Gottardi-Little family and the doubts that raised in her mind.

"Y'all told us you were going out looking. So I made sure we were in." He looked to Walter then GJ. Christina Pines had not been here then, so he ignored her for the moment. "I called everyone. I gathered everyone. I made sure we had a head count. I don't normally keep that close of tabs on everyone, but this isn't normal. The last time several of us went out, someone died, and one of my guys took a bullet. So you can sure as hell bet we were holed up where we knew we were safe."

Walter wanted to believe him. She wasn't sure, but for a moment she watched as Christina Pines' fingers splayed across the table and clenched ever so slightly. When Will finished his sentence, Christina nodded at Walter and GJ as though to indicate the man could be believed.

Not knowing what to make of that, and certain now was not the time to ask, Walter asked her next question instead, aiming it again to Will. "You had eyes on everybody?"

"Not me, personally, but we did a head count. And I have to say, I've checked in today, specifically because this new agent comes in and says y'all are getting shot at. She wants to know where everybody is." As he got angrier about the questioning, his Arkansas accent deepened even more. "I've got several people who can vouch for each family member being present."

Walter looked back at him, her brows pulling together. "And do you trust them not to lie?" she asked. "Not to cover for each other?"

27

When everyone else was tucked in for the night, GJ found herself up late on the phone, dialing the number for Agent Eleri Eames. Normally, she'd never call someone at this hour—but normal had left the building a long time ago. There was nothing about this case that even approached regulation or reasonably sane. Now, they were suddenly working with a new agent, and it appeared nothing about *her* was normal, either.

GJ needed help. Westerfield had made it clear that they were to trust agent Pines. In fact, she was now the senior agent on the scene, though she seemed to be deferring to the two newbies. GJ found herself wishing Christina would just take over, would take the burden off their shoulders. But she hadn't stepped in with any orders yet, so GJ and Walter continued running the investigation to the best of their very new abilities.

In their first order of business, they'd brought the whole group together, and then split up the de Gottardi-Little family into three separate houses. Though there were many more places where the family lived—small houses along the sides of the property and nestled in various secluded spots on the land—they gathered everyone into the three biggest for now.

Their working theory was to not be one big target. The multiple locations might let them flank any attackers trying to get close. Though they expected a shooter—or possibly two or three—each house had more than enough fighters and firepower to handle it. No one said it, but they didn't want to put everyone in one building in case their missing perp decided to start a fire or throw smoke grenades and flashbangs.

Christina, Walter, and GJ each stood guard at one of the homes, waiting out the night in case something went horribly awry. As she sat there in the quiet dark and hoped their predictions were wrong, that no one would come, GJ had tried to imagine what might happen. She was grateful two of the three known members were in custody. But the fact of the matter was, her grandfather was not accounted for.

Given that Westerfield said Eames and Heath remained unable to find him, GJ had decided to do a little more recon on her own. She hadn't lied to anyone; she truly was not able to find her own grandfather at the time, but she hadn't mentioned something. In fact, she had hardly even thought of it. However, on the ride back to the compound, she'd scrolled through her contacts, and when they stopped again for a restroom break and drinks, she let Walter step into the convenience store and buy a few snacks for them while GJ stayed outside on the phone. She called up the number of her grandfather's longtime assistant and good friend, Shray Menon.

Shray wasn't answering his phone, either. He often traveled with Dr. Marks, though she had no idea if he'd gone along on this trip or not. No one knew, since her grandfather hadn't actually gone to lecture at the Sorbonne like he'd said. After leaving a message, all she could do was hope Shray would call her back, giving her some idea of where to start looking. But if her grandfather knew what she knew, and what she'd figured out, then Shray had been tipped off as well. It was a chance she felt she had to take. Her concern lay in the numbers, because the two they had in custody, as well as one more who had shot them, made three. Her grandfather made four. She had a hard time believing her grandfather was involved in anything that Shray didn't know about, let alone wasn't actively involved in. That made five.

Her next question was, just how big was this organization? It was a new thought that was worrying her, pecking at her brain. Three together was hard to swallow, but five? Two academics—who weren't present—and three hunters? It didn't add up. She sat up straight on her chair, searching as well as she could in the darkness outside the windows and hoping no one was sneaking up on the compound. If it was more than a couple people, she wasn't sure that she alone would be able to fend them off.

Then, there was the issue with Agent Pines. Later, after the impromptu questions when Walter and GJ had returned, the leaders of the de Gottardi-Little family and the FBI agents had dismissed the others and talked. They had themselves a reasonable discussion about where things stood and who could and couldn't touch the evidence. About what might happen and what had the family maybe seen before. Most of their trespassers had been presumed to be poachers. Now, they had to reassess what they remembered and figure out what those trespassers might actually have been doing...

The men had departed the meeting, leaving the three agents there to discuss amongst themselves.

In low tones, Christina Pine said, "Will was telling the truth."

GJ had picked that up from her subtle nods earlier. She and Walter both seemed to notice that Christina would stop, pause at odd times, and take a deep slow breath when the situation didn't really warrant it. A moment after that, she would usually nod. GJ had no idea what it meant. But later, when Pines had said, "He was telling the truth," both she and Walter had asked, "What do you mean?"

And that was when Christina Pines had told them what she could do. Christina believed she could influence people, make them think or see what she wanted them to. When she wanted Will Little to tell the truth, she pushed him to do just that.

"Do people know when you do this?" GJ asked, appalled beyond measure.

"No," Christina said. "I'm good at it. I've known I could do this since I was very young, and I've practiced for a long time."

GJ didn't say it, but she thought, *That doesn't sound like a very good skill.* The distress she knew she was showing on her face appeared reflected in Christina's own expression.

Unfortunately, along with Pines' skill came a sad level of acceptance. Maybe that's why Christina was an agent on her own these days. GJ did not appreciate Westerfield not letting them in on these "special powers" before he sent the agent to them. If GJ was right, she and Walter were actually the "freaks" in NightShade, because everybody else had some sort of supernatural talent. Everyone except the two of them. She understood about Heath. She understood about Eames. Wade was like Heath.

To a very solid point, the men—the wolves—made a kind of scientific sense. She hadn't had time to study them, but she'd known from seeing the bones that they moved in an unusual way. She'd intuitively understood their bone structures clicked or locked into place in a different position other than the standard human form. So while seeing what they could do had been a shock, it wasn't too much of a surprise.

Eleri, on the other hand, got seriously good hunches. Some people did that. GJ had always believed those people were simply better in tune with their subconscious minds. They remembered little bits and pieces that others didn't and their brains put the pieces together. GJ wasn't a neuroscientist, but what she'd seen of it made sense. Eleri's talents were legitimate.

But Christina Pines seemed to think that she could get inside the human mind and push it one way or another. That she could make a person think or say or see something that *she* decided. That was well beyond GJ's scope of science.

In her hand, GJ heard the phone in her hand ring through to the other side. A sleepy voice answered, "Agent Eames?" as though she were asking rather than stating. She'd woken up her superior agent, but she was in it now.

GJ didn't even allow the other woman to get an introduction or a brief hello. "This is GJ. I'm really sorry to bother you late at night."

"It's okay. What's going on?" The voice was stronger now, the brain behind it clearly coming around.

GJ appreciated that the other woman seemed to naturally assume that since she'd called late, it must be important. She explained that she was sitting watch at the de Gottardi-Little family compound, with an eye out for possible threats. But then she got to the heart of the matter and explained what she heard from Christina Pines.

"Oh, that." Eleri understood immediately.

So maybe she had been freaked out by Christina Pines as well or someone like her? GJ didn't know.

For a moment, Eleri stayed silent. "Look," she said. "Part of me believes that it's not my place to tell you this, because it's Christina's talent, but I've worked with her, and she's very good. I've seen her work."

"She can make people see things, right?"

"Yes," Eleri answered, no qualms, no hesitation, and that shocked GJ just a little more.

"I mean, come on, Eleri. That can't make sense. You may get hunches, but I'm a scientist. Christina seems to think she actually has some kind of psychic ability." Her incredulity must have come through.

"GJ, *that's what NightShade is*. It's why we're off the books. Everybody in the unit was called in from other places. Westerfield pulled me from the Behavioral Analysis Unit. He pulled Donovan from the medical examiner's office in a small region of South Carolina. Donovan wasn't even an agent until Westerfield got his hands on him, more like you and Walter. Some of us came from inside the bureau, already trained. Westerfield simply recognized what we could do."

"*What we could do?*" GJ interrupted. "I don't understand. Do you mean everybody in NightShade can...do something?"

"Yes," Eleri answered.

"But they're all like Donovan or like you, right?"

"No, not at all. I've seen things you wouldn't believe. We've solved cases that seem perfectly normal, and we've solved cases that we could never tell the world about." There was a slight pause. "GJ, Christina Pines is the real deal. You should listen to her. What did she tell you? Did she use her skills on you? Make you say or see anything?"

"Oh, good God, no," GJ said, suddenly growing wary. "Did she make *you* say or see anything?"

"Yes. We practiced so we would know what was an illusion and what wasn't." Another pause. "I don't see any reason why would she would ever have any need to use this skill on you, but she's there, and she can see things that nobody else can. She can keep other people safe by using those skills." Eleri finished her sentence, and GJ sat silent for a moment.

She figured she'd probably gone still more times and for a longer duration since she'd joined the NightShade division than at any other time in her life. After a moment, when Eleri didn't speak again, GJ asked, "Should I let her make me see something? Is it that important?"

"I don't know," Eleri shrugged. "If you ask, ask kindly. She appreciates being respected for what she can do and not being distrusted simply because she has a skill that you don't like."

"Well, shit." GJ felt like a bit of a heel now. That was a very good point. She was acting like those kids she hated in elementary school, the ones who were mean when she raised her hand all the time. She said she understood and thanked Eleri for helping her out. She was about to hang up when she was distracted by a faint rustling noise from beyond the walls.

28

W alter felt the hairs raise on her arms at about the exact same moment as the buzzing started on her phone. It was GJ chiming in on the open line that she and Christina and Walter had kept between themselves as they all stood guard at night. Though they had sent the men to their beds to sleep for the first shift, the women had all sat up, talking amongst themselves whenever they felt the need to, which hadn't been all that often.

The silence suited Walter just fine. She couldn't say she was really keen on this situation. They discussed the fact that they had no idea how many were out there, if any at all. In a private text, she and GJ discussed the fact that Christina Pines had some very unusual skills that Walter found creepy as all fuck. They discussed the fact that Eames and Heath had yet to find GJ's grandfather, despite searching left and right for him.

Walter didn't like any of it. She was supposed to be a junior agent on her first case. Well, she was *supposed* to still be a NAT at Quantico, but that option was over. But what she'd been taught—were she a normal agent—was that she would graduate and be placed with a more senior partner. However, she'd known that was not going to happen. She was GJ's partner before she went into the academy, and while she wished for a more senior partner to show her the way, she could not wish away the partner that she had. She merely would have liked it better if Westerfield had not so unceremoniously dumped them here. They'd been told to solve the problem when they had little to no idea what was going on.

She was slowly standing from her seat. She'd been in the chair between rounds, tipping it back on the hind legs to help her stay awake. She faced a window in the corner of a room, able to just turn her head and look ninety degrees; and when her alarm on her watch went off every five minutes, she made a slow and complete rotation around the house. She peeked out the windows without moving the curtains. She checked the trees, the sheds, the open hills in the distance. She stopped and let her eyes dark adapt, and simply watched. She had seen nothing.

But sitting here now, something had raised the hair on her arms. Her phone had lit up, and she smacked her hand over it, trying to hide the light, just in case it showed through to the outside.

Though she couldn't exactly see anything, she didn't want anyone out there to know people in here were paying attention. Torn between GJ's message and keeping her eyes focused beyond the window, she very carefully pulled the phone off the table, covered it, and snuck a peek at the message.

It said only what she was already confirming with her own eyes: "Someone is here. Alert everyone."

GJ had already done that, Walter saw, as her phone buzzed again, the light beginning to glow. Again, she smothered the light, this time holding it to the front of her shirt, hoping no one outside saw. This message was not on the line between GJ, Christina, and Walter. This was the line that went to Will, to Art, to Burt—who shouldn't be up defending anyone as he was still recovering from his own bullet wound—and several others between the three houses.

They were all sleeping with their guns. They were ready. The appearance they gave was that it didn't bother them that much, and Walter had to wonder how a family like this lived out here in the woods—if they were truly ready for these hunters. Could it be because they'd seen them before? Their calm reactions, though, didn't fully mask their anger and fear. They were mad about Burt, about Randall, and more. They acted like fighters, not like family. Walter knew; she'd seen it before.

She could only believe that GJ's alert would rouse the men in her own house. Given that, she made it her mission to make sure that she saw where these insurgents were coming from and to have a headcount ready when the others appeared behind her. With a slow, small motion of her hand, she created just the tiniest sliver of space at the edge of the curtain. She moved her face ever-so-slightly into the opening while keeping her body behind the wall. She knew how to do this; she'd known this for a long time. It was just part of who she was.

Waiting for her one eye to adjust, she scanned the area, watching for movement among the trees. She knew she wasn't going to see human forms sneaking down the hillside, like in the movies. If she was lucky, she would spot anomalies, things that her brain told her weren't right. She let her eyes glaze over and waited until she saw it: a rock that moved, a tree that skipped a little bit from one heartbeat to the next, then another moment where she actually saw movement between one tree and the next. That was at least three.

Turning the brightness dial down on her phone, which she should have done earlier if she'd had any sense at all that this would actually happen, she texted GJ and Christina. Her message was only the number three. That was when she heard the footsteps behind her. She knew those footsteps—knowing such things was a matter of survival where she came from.

Burt de Gottardi had a hitch in his step these days. He was easy to see and hear. Art was at the house to her left close by, Will further out, at the third home. Coming up behind Burt was the woman Walter had met earlier, Alicia.

As Walter listened, she heard the sounds of a gun in Alicia's hands.

"Do. Not. Cock. It." She barely moved her lips with the order as she kept her eye out the window.

Though she'd seen people moving about outside, and thought they were heading inward toward the house, she had no idea what kind of equipment they had. She'd not seen the glint that would indicate that they had night-vision goggles, nor had she seen any shapes indicating they had listening devices. But it was entirely plausible that one person was sitting up in the tree with the dish, unseen, waiting, while the others moved forward slowly, armed to the hilt, getting their instructions from the person in the know. If they had heat-imagers, they might know exactly where she, Burt, and Alicia were standing right now. Where to aim.

Behind her, others slowly trickled into the room on stealthy feet. GJ's alert had brought them and told them of the danger. Some of the men and women in the house weren't here; they'd been told not to come, to stay back with the children. They were sleeping down in the root cellar and in some of the central rooms, trying to pull off the idea of a slumber party with the children. They'd fooled no one. The kids had been scared, soothed only by the presence of the FBI agents and the calm reassurance of their parents. But they knew. They knew Randall had been killed, they knew Uncle Burt had been shot, and they knew this was not going the right way.

"I want to be ready," Alicia whispered back.

"They might hear it. Wait. Cock it at the last second," Walter advised.

"Don't shoot until I can see the whites of their eyes?" Alicia asked, her snarky undertone lifting Walter's spirits. Alicia might be ready to fight, she might be ready to blow some motherfucker's head off, but she was keeping it together.

"If you can see the whites of their eyes before I give the order to fire on them, then yes, go for it."

"Thank you, ma'am," Alicia replied, and she stepped up to stand ready beside Walter. Hopefully, the woman was safe in her position behind the wall. So Walter let her stay there, back to the pretty wainscoting, shotgun lifted.

It was Walter who scanned the dark room that they stood in, looking at the five people who'd joined her.

"We need proper positions. We need to be ready in all directions around the house. We need to be at the windows, but stay down and out of sight. If they have thermal imagers ..." Even as she said, it she watched as they caught on and all of them dropped to the floor or moved to the spaces behind the walls, just as she had showed them. Walter nodded at them. "A good thermal imager will find us. Even here, even low. But at least in the meantime, we can make ourselves smaller targets."

Walter looked out the window again, this time when she texted a different number.

She sent the number eight.

She got a number back from GJ: 14; and a number from Christina: 10.

29

G J opened the phone line. They'd been communicating amongst themselves via text to stay mostly silent as the figures crept down the hillside. The numbers were adding up, now totaling well over 30.

They had many people inside the houses. Too many?

Though the de Gottardi-Little family had armed everyone to the teeth and though they appeared well-trained, GJ still didn't like this situation. They were now stuck inside. Whoever was coming down the hill had control of the outside, and the outside was bigger. They were capable of surrounding. They could blockade the cars, the roads, any open path. If they decided to use firepower, they could concentrate it into the middle of the house. If they decided to use something worse than firepower, well, the family was all clustered together making three solid targets. They'd known that would be a problem when they'd set up, but they had not expected numbers like this.

Turning the brightness down on her phone and moving back from the window, GJ stayed where she could watch the changing movement and see how close these others were getting. She whispered over the line to Walter, "Is it possible that these are not our hunters?"

"I don't think so," Walter replied almost immediately. "Who else would be here? Who else would be casing the house? We know it's not the FBI. Could be the CIA. Could be local police force, except..."

"Yeah," GJ cut her off. Walter was right. It was only then, in the gap as they both took a breath, that Christina stepped in. "These are the hunters."

That was it. Four simple words. *These are our guys.* GJ understood. "What does that mean we should do, Christina?"

"It means open fire when you get a chance," Christina said. "Do not be afraid of killing them. They are here to kill these people."

"They're evil," she heard Walter say. Because GJ had seen the notes from Walter's interview at the hotel earlier, she understood that perhaps Walter wasn't making comments about the people outside but repeating to herself what the people outside were saying about them.

GJ, ever the student, was thinking of her training. They weren't allowed to open fire. They couldn't fire until fired upon. They weren't allowed to kill someone simply because they felt threatened. But here, what would happen if they waited until fired upon? And just what kind of fire was coming down the hillside?

What if Christina was right? Eleri had told her to trust the senior agent. That meant firing on these people if she had the chance.

Then there was the issue of Walter. Could her partner suffer PTSD? It was a legitimate concern. Walter had been a solider, after all. She had lost limbs to an IED. She had lost friends to the same IED. Surely, there'd been some kind of lasting effect from that. Though she'd signed up for the FBI and she passed all the tests, as Walter had often said, "You don't know what you'll do with live gunfire until you're in it." And GJ wondered if you didn't know PTSD until you were in it, either. Hogan's Alley had been solid training, but they had all known it was training. They had known they couldn't die. GJ did not know that now, and her heart raced.

She was wondering what Christina might be able to do about the situation outside. Her mouth opened before she thought it through and said, "Christina, can you make the house disappear? Can you make them see—"

That was when the bull horn came on from outside. No lights accompanied it. Just the sound of rough, male voice, "Send the dogs out."

Dogs? GJ thought. That was hardly what these people were. They didn't even look like dogs, more like wolves. Her scientific mind was taking over, and she wondered for a moment if she was actually so scared she couldn't feel it or if she was just angry because this man had first insulted the homeowners.

The voice boomed over the bull horn again. "We don't want the people. We know some of you in there aren't afflicted. We only need the dogs. Send the dogs out, and the rest of you will be safe."

GJ noticed where he was swaying back and forth, pointing the bullhorn alternately between the three main homes. This meant he knew where the people were, and where they weren't. Her heart rate kicked up another notch. The homes weren't that close together, but they were close enough that all would be able to hear him. GJ wondered if maybe there weren't enough people out there to surround all three houses quite thoroughly. *Shit.*

"How do we respond?" she asked softly into the open phone line.

Walter answered right away, "I want to say with firepower, but I think it's not right."

Christina replied, "With nothing. We wait them out. We make them ramp up their demands. We see what they're going to do. If they fire one shot on us, do not hesitate to take all of them out."

Though Christina had come in and quietly done her part—held down the fort, helped the men and the women set up their ammunition and find safe rooms for the children, all before GJ and Walter had come back—she had not really played the part of senior partner until now. Christina Pines was an experienced agent. Perhaps she'd been in a firefight like this before. She certainly sounded like she had. So GJ waited with them, with the people in her house standing silent and armed at various points. For a few moments, there was an eerie silence. As she looked out the window, she saw that none of the figures moved this time. Where they'd been slowly creeping closer, and one by one coming in tight around the house, now they stayed still and quiet.

She could see the occasional glint of moonlight off a rifle barrel or some other equipment. Given the shapes she could discern as her eyes adjusted more to the night, it appeared they must be wearing some kind of black or camouflage. They were very hard to find. That was going to make it very hard for her to return fire, but she was willing.

This was so far from what she had gotten her education for. She'd thought she was a scholarly student. She'd thought she was studying the behaviors of ancient human societies and current killers. Now, she was getting a more up close and personal look at those killers than she'd ever intended. Her work was no longer academic.

The voice cut once again through the eerie silence. "We know what you are. Send out the dogs. If you don't, we'll be forced to kill you all. It's not something we wish to do."

This time he gave a timeline. Five minutes. All dogs.

On the open line, Christina's voice came through, "He doesn't know how many there are. He has a good idea how many people are in here, but he doesn't know how many are what he thinks they are."

"This is the stupidest thing!" GJ blurted out. "I think it's a recessive gene. So it doesn't even matter if he takes these guys out, he's leaving it in the population." As she said it, as her voice trailed off, she realized she had just made a case for the people outside to kill them all. She shut up. She wanted to say she was sorry, but the voice boomed. "Four minutes."

Behind her, the members of the de Gottardi and Little families looked to each other as if to ask, *Do we go out?*

"My kids aren't changers," one of the women said.

The man next to her agreed. "Our kids don't have it. And neither of us do. If it's recessive, it isn't even in us."

GJ didn't bother to correct his bad science. Beside them, another man looked at the two who'd spoken as though they disgusted him.

GJ understood. They'd come here to the Ozarks and brought their families to live in the compound. Were they not going to stand together? Were they going to attempt to push people out the door in an effort to save themselves? GJ did not want to be in the middle of this kind of family affair. Not while their lives depended on all of them sticking together.

"Three minutes," the voice boomed.

Christina's voice immediately followed over the open phone line again. "Hold. He hasn't said what they're doing at the end of the five minutes. We're not doing anything until they initiate. Don't send anyone out."

Walter echoed the sentiments right on her heels. "We have a few here who wish to go....No! You stay put!" Walter barked into the distance, her voice coming through the phone as she issued orders to those in her house.

"Two minutes."

GJ pulled her weapon, checked her clip, checked the chamber to be sure she had one loaded. She did. She'd been ready five minutes ago, but she was more than ready now.

"One minute!"

The voice filtered through her bones and she felt every muscle in her body tense. She raised the gun, looking to aim where the bullhorn was. It was tempting to shoot in that direction. If she could shut up the voice, maybe she could shut up the instructions the voice was giving.

"Christina, I've got the bullhorn," she said.

"Excellent. If they fire, take him out first." That wasn't exactly what GJ was thinking, but it was close enough.

Then the bullhorn voice came loud and clear through the air again. "Time's up."

30

Walter waited. Though her entire body was tense, and though the situation had her on the highest alert possible, she kept her heart rate low and her breathing steady. Her weapon was raised and aimed. The man with the bullhorn had told them their time was up, but so far, nothing had happened. There were no bullets coming through the windows or doors. They had not lobbed grenades or bombs, or lit anything on fire. So Walter waited. Empty threats were no good, and she knew how to be patient. She simply had to keep the people behind her waiting as well. She saw herself as the commander of a small, fairly well-trained unit, and there was no mistake that she was in charge now.

She stood at the front of the small formation, closest to the window, ready to take the brunt of whatever came through. That's what a commander did. For the briefest second, she imagined GJ in a very similar position, in her own special corner of another house.

She had no idea if Christina had raised a weapon or a bare palm. Perhaps she was going to work some kind of voodoo on the people outside. If she could do that to thirty or forty or fifty people at once, that would be a godsend. And Walter wished the other agent would, but she heard nothing through the open phone line and saw no evidence of it in the people outside.

Walter breathed in slowly through her nose, then out through her mouth. She did it as she waited, carefully counting her breath a fifth time, a sixth, a seventh...And, on the eighth, it happened.

Movement started in a wave outside. They came down from the trees into the yard, moving as a unit. They stayed low, almost like trained troops, weapons against their shoulders, aimed and ready. Though they still didn't open fire, they came in with force. Walter was waiting for flashbangs, for noise, OC or CS gas. She could handle any of those, but that wasn't what happened. This was not a crowd trained tactically like she'd expected, and it threw her a little off-guard.

They moved with a lightning speed. Not inhuman, not like the wolves, but coming through the yard with steady determination. As they got closer, she saw their formation was odd and unsteady. But they were together enough, ready to fight if they had to, ready to have each other's backs.

Walter slowly shifted her aim from one intruder to the other, ready to pull the trigger if anyone out there did it first. But they didn't. They just came closer and closer.

"What do we do, Christina? Do we fire?" GJ's voice came through the phone, and—though Walter would have expected it just five months ago—there was no waver in the sound.

"No, they haven't fired on us. We don't yet know what they want."

"They want the men and women and children who change!" GJ hollered back.

No longer were they trying to be quiet on the phones. No longer was there any thought that they might remain hidden. They didn't.

As Walter watched the shadows get closer and closer, she counted them. The numbers were even higher than the latest estimate. She whispered it into the phone. Unfortunately, she got confirmation back from both Christina and GJ of the same thing.

The shapes in the dark outside began to take fully human forms as they blocked out some of the moonlight. Some of the shapes hovered between the house and the trees. Some came right up to the pretty flower boxes on the windows, stood in the shrubs along the front. One stood on the front porch. Then, their guns came through the windows, smashing out the panes. The knobs rattled, and what sounded like battering rams or very heavy shoulders, started knocking against the heavy wood.

Through the shattered window panes, long bore barrels of rifles swept back and forth, searching for aim at the people inside. As she heard the first growl behind her, Walter wondered how she had missed several people changing while she stood right here in front. She now led an army of armed humans and angry wolves.

"Hold your fire," Christina ordered.

"The rifles are through the windows here," Walter ground out through her teeth.

These people were much too close now. Even though she was backing away, they might be able to hear what she said into the phone. It was a massive tactical mistake on her own part, but they had no other communication between the houses.

There was no single building on the land that was big enough to put the family all in one place. They didn't want to do it either. They hadn't wanted to hunker down for a war they didn't believe could happen. They also hadn't wanted to create a single target. Though Walter agreed wholeheartedly and tactically with that decision at the time, having three fortresses spread the agents thin. She regretted it now.

"Hold your fire," Christina whispered back, steel behind the soft command.

Was Christina going to do something? Walter wanted to ask as she retreated. Right foot, left foot, right foot, left foot, she never crossed her feet, shuffling so she didn't trip or fall or run into anything. All of it unconscious training from what felt like many years ago. She watched the rifle sweep back and forth, as though looking for something. She couldn't see the person on the other end of it, just some hands on the weapon because the raised foundation of the house made the height awkward. But she knew as well as anyone that you didn't have to see your killer to die.

The bullhorn came again, "Send out the dogs!"

This time, Walter yelled back, "No!" as loud and long as possible.

Even as she hollered it at the top of her lungs, she heard another bullhorn. This time, the voice was higher pitched; it wasn't as sharp or heavy, but it was angry. The mechanical twist of the system obscured the speaker for only a moment. It was GJ's voice coming from the house maybe fifty meters away.

"You are on private property," her partner's voice boomed through the device. "You are trespassing. You have put barrels of rifles through the windows of our homes. Arkansas law states that we can fight anyone who comes into our home, and you have done so now. You are battering down our doors. We have the right to fire upon you at will. You need to leave now! You will all be arrested on multiple counts of assault!"

The first voice, the man's voice, boomed again. "Send out the dogs!"

This time, it followed with a brief explanation, as though someone was having a conversation with GJ, and Walter wondered what this meant. If they could keep him talking—if GJ could employ the hostage negotiation skills she'd excelled at in Quantico—they might be able to get the hunters to go away.

Walter took the moment to turn and make eye contact with the woman behind her. "Alicia, go. Tell me what's happening on the other side. How many are back there, or are they all on this side of us? I think they might be. You might be able to get out the back and go out into the woods."

Alicia turned, disappearing quickly, staying low and stealthy. Walter liked the woman's style. She had five kids, and Walter never would have picked her out for the soldier type, but by God, Alicia was good.

The voice on the bullhorn began explaining again. "They're an ancient evil. You've heard of them in the myths. Humankind has never been able to eradicate them, and they kill us. We have to eradicate them. It's time for a species extinction if humanity wants to continue."

Through the phone, Walter heard GJ's muttered swearing. "Oh my God, this man is mentally deficient." Next she heard the same voice come through the bullhorn, venting her scientific frustration. "It's a genetic mutation, you fuckhead!"

Walter couldn't help but laugh. Though she was about to die, God bless GJ Janson—she'd made Walter smile.

"It's not a genetic mutation. I understand you want to defend it that way, but that's not what it is."

"Bullshit!" GJ yelled back, and Walter laughed again as the eyes in the room looked at her sideways, wondering how she could find such humor at a time like this, and all she could think was, *how could she not?* Though GJ had completely lost her "hostage negotiation class" cool.

"Hand over the dogs." The bullhorn came again, and once again

Walter—at the top of her own lungs, having no bullhorn of her own —yelled back, "No!"

Though Walter's voice roared in her own head, she caught the sound of GJ's voice as she talked through the bullhorn again, "I am a Federal Agent!" God, that sounded good to Walter's ears. "There are Federal agents here. Three of us are coming out. One from each home."

Well, shit. She was getting put on the spot. It was Walter's cue, and Christina's too. She only hoped Christina was in a place to follow GJ's instructions. It would look bad if they didn't act as a unit.

Turning, she nodded to Art. "You're in charge here." She passed him control of their small unit as she started following GJ's instructions right out the front door of this little house.

Alicia popped back in then. "They aren't on the other side. If they are, we're not seeing them."

Walter stopped with her hand on the knob. "Wait until you know it's clear. Take flashlights," Walter told her, "Be ready to shine them in their eyes if you encounter any of them. Blind them. Kill them if you have to."

"I'm staying here," Alicia said.

"No." Walter responded immediately, ignoring the request and overriding it with a clear order. "If someone has to take the non-fighters, and someone has to take the kids, they need fighters to protect them. I want you in charge of it. Take five other fighters from this house. Clear the other houses if you can get in around the back."

"Yes, ma'am," Alicia replied. This time her resolve firm with the instructions she'd been given.

GJ was talking up a storm. "We are wearing tracking devices. These devices send our heart rate and vital signs back to our home office. If anything happens to us, the wrath of the entire FBI will come down upon you. We have two of your members in custody already. You'd be foolish to think they won't sing like canaries when charged with murder of federal agents. We're coming out now."

To her side, Walter saw and heard as GJ opened the door to the other small house. Walter stepped out onto the porch where the hunters had been battering the door just moments ago. She believed there were at least three of them just beyond where she could see, maybe down in the bushes now. But she was following the orders, because clearly GJ had a plan, and Walter didn't.

As of yet, no bullets had been fired, an outcome she had to admit was better than expected at this stage of the game. Besides, those inside had guns and knew how to fire them. She came out with her weapon in her hands directed low at the ground in front of her. Ready to fire, but not immediately aiming at anyone. GJ emerged and motioned Walter to her side. Up the hill Walter saw movement and could only assume it was Christina.

She was sweeping the landscape, trying to get another good head count of the attackers around her when she heard a shocked yell from GJ. "*Shray?*"

31

G J stared at the man she'd known almost all her life.

"GJ?" he asked, but given that she'd already spouted his name, he knew who she was. "What are you doing here?" His whisper was low and harsh.

It suddenly occurred to her, *he didn't know.* She hadn't announced that *she* was the FBI. To her, it had been obvious, but clearly not to him. *No*, she searched her memory and recalled she had said only that he would *kill a federal agent.* Maybe he hadn't put it together that the federal agent was her. He sure seemed confused.

GJ played on it, putting one hand behind her back and signaling to Walter to stay silent. She could only hope Christina would catch the same sign and understand.

"Shray, what's going on? Can you explain?" Then, she rephrased it. She didn't really want him explaining. She didn't want to have to tell him why she was here. "Is this your group? Is my grandfather here?"

She tried to sound like her old self. Like GJ before she'd been to Quantico. The GJ who was merely an academic.

He looked at her, still frowning. "No, he's elsewhere. He went back."

To the lab? She wondered, but then dismissed it. She didn't care where he'd gone. If he wasn't here, Donovan and Eleri should be able to find him. In fact, they'd probably already located him if he'd gone back home. She pushed her weapon back into the holster. Shray had to have seen it. He had to be close to figuring it out, but maybe he simply wasn't putting the pieces together yet. It was a common psychological flaw of adversity and trauma, to see things as you expected them to be rather than how they actually were. Now, she was banking on it.

"Shray," she said again, "I don't understand."

"I don't either." He grabbed her by the wrist and began to pull. She could see now that he and these people were dressed like swat team members. The only difference was they wore no official insignia, just the black of night with Kevlar and helmets protecting them as they went and committed their bad deeds.

He tugged her further away and she walked with him, only resisting the slightest amount. Again acting like old GJ, she faced him as she worked to signal Walter from behind her back.

"Why are you here?" she asked.

He spoke over her. demanding, "Do you know who lives in that house?"

"Well, yeah. I was visiting a friend, and then all these people came out of the woodwork."

"Those aren't your friends," he said, looking at her with a stern fatherly reprimand. GJ took it and his scolding. "Do you know what they can do?"

"What are you talking about? What can they do? I mean, they're kind of like preppers: they live off the land." She let her speech slip from the command she'd learned at the academy. "But they're not stockpiling water and being all Branch Davidian. So, what do you mean?"

She stared at him as though she truly didn't comprehend his issue. She wasn't going to be the one to say what these people could do. She wouldn't say that she had seen it, or that she knew he was responsible for killing Randall Standish. She wasn't going to utter the word *werewolf* first.

"Do you really not know where you are?" He looked at her.

His eyes were dark in the night and it was difficult to discern his expression, but she shook her head, looking up at him. She worked to recall the girl she'd once been on her grandfather's knee on an archeological dig. Shray Menon had often run information back and forth to the campsite.

It occurred to her she'd been stupid. She'd texted him earlier in the day to find out where her grandfather was. She thought she'd given nothing away at the time. But now, as she put pieces together, she realized her grandfather could never have done this without Shray. Shray was in it up to his eyeballs.

He handed the bullhorn to another man as he passed. "Take over. I'm getting her out of here. You—kill them all," he commanded, and GJ felt herself stiffen at the words, but forcibly relaxed her muscles.

"Wait!" she cried. "You're going to kill my friends?"

"They're not your friends," he repeated. "You don't know what they can do. They're dangerous".

"They can't be dangerous. They grow vegetables!" GJ protested, yanking her hand back, and purposefully bumping into him. With her voice, she aimed for a petulant tone. With her hand, she aimed to drop a very small GPS tracker into his pocket.

He turned then and stared at her. "They're *werewolves*, GJ. Haven't you been down in your grandfather's lab? We were pretty sure you've been throwing the power out and going down there"

Well, shit, she wasn't as sneaky as she thought she was. "Of course, I went down and looked. He has the best bone collection this side of Johns Hopkins. The skeletons down there, they all have a genetic anomaly," she threw it all out there, wondering how he would reply to that.

He would know; he knew she was smart. He'd helped train her. He had to have already figured out that she'd seen it.

"Yes," he uttered again, the word harsh though his lips. "The anomaly is that they're *werewolves*. They're tainted by an ancient evil, GJ. We have to get you out of here."

Good old Shray, *saving* her. Babysitting her. Giving her lessons when her grandfather was busy, and now pulling her away from the very work she'd come to do.

Tough choices, she thought. She'd known it would come to this even when Westerfield first assigned them this case. As she got further and further from the de Gottardi-Little compound, she thought about what her options were. Luckily, she still didn't hear any shots, but as she moved into the trees she realized the tough choices were here. Right now.

She could no longer ignore the people she was passing as she walked with Shray. Though they were hard to see—which was the point—she could make out their uniforms of Kevlar vests, tactical pants, and helmets with chin straps. It was going to take a carefully placed shot to take one of them out, and GJ desperately wanted to warn Walter. They couldn't waste bullets shooting at tactical vests. At least Walter would already be aiming that way—for the head, the neck, the thigh. Exposed places. GJ needed to let everyone else know, too. If it came to gunfire, this fight would be up close and personal. Shotgun to the face where possible. She fought the shudder and found she was able to repress it, think about the options in cold terms.

She was thinking it through like an FBI agent in a deadly situation. She was also thinking of bone fragments, and D-MORT—the team that came out and cleaned up after mass casualties. Quickly on the heels of the first thought was the one that D-MORT wouldn't come here. It was too much risk to the secrets these families kept. Still, a forensic scientist would need to examine the bodies, and return them to their next of kin. Perhaps Westerfield would come up with an individual story for each of them and how they died, so that nothing would be officially investigated here. GJ didn't know; she also hoped they could avoid the shootout she saw coming. What she did know was that if she needed a shot, she needed a *clean* shot, and that she didn't want to shoot Shray Menon. She was well aware she might just have to.

Stopping suddenly, GJ realized they'd moved beyond the loosely formed wall of his people. She was now a traitor behind enemy lines and she could only hope he didn't know that. She was banking on it. Shray had at least gotten her out of the line of gunfire.

"Shray," she said, hearing her own voice sharpen with the words. "You can't do this. You can't come in here and you can't kill these people."

"They're not people," he argued back, quickly and fiercely.

"They *are* people and you will get arrested when you do this."

"No, I won't." Though his expression was stern, it was also confident. "Who even knows these people are here? They don't have Social Security numbers and some of the kids don't attend public school. They don't go on census, because they know what they are."

"No," she replied, just as confident as he'd been. "They don't go on census, because they know people like you are going to do head counts and try to come kill them." There she was again, offering up a little bit of education, instead of the aggression the situation so clearly required. She'd also subtly played the hand that she did know what they were and what they could do. Though she hadn't revealed how. "You cannot kill them. I am warning you now."

"You said there were FBI agents in there, but it was a bluff, right?" Though he asked it like a legitimate question, he talked himself out of it before she could answer. "It has to be. There's no way the FBI got involved in this, and word would get out if the Feds know what these people can do."

"The FBI already knows," GJ said. "Some of them even work for the FBI!"

Shit, she should not have said it. She was trying to talk Shray down, and now this gambit only worked if she made it work.

She now had to bring him in. In handcuffs.

"Shray," she said, "I'm one of the FBI agents".

32

He stared at her hard, his eyes unblinking for all of ten full seconds while she waited. Then he laughed.

"That's very funny, GJ. You may like these people. You may have thought some of them were your friends, but they're not. You don't know what they can do."

"Yes, I do know," she argued back. "I've been studying them as long as you and grandfather have, I just didn't fully understand until recently." That first part was bullshit and she knew it, but she didn't correct it. She hadn't been alive as long as Shray and grandfather had been studying these people, but she wasn't going to waste breath over a simple error like that. "I do know what they can do. I've seen it, and if you wondered where I was for the past five months, I was at Quantico training to become an FBI agent."

As she said it, she pulled the badge out of her back pocket, and felt the very satisfying feeling of flicking it open with a practiced wrist. Shray stared again, but this time he didn't laugh.

"You've have got to be fucking kidding me," he responded when at last he found his voice. Then, he thought about it for a moment, pointed at the badge, and said, "That's fake."

"No, it's not. I got recruited. I went to Quantico, and I trained. I am agent Arabella Jade Janson, and you are under arrest."

"No," he said in simple but firm protest. He held his hands up, palms out, backing away from her. He'd holstered his own weapon.

He'd come here to kill, and he'd gotten the shock of a lifetime. She was glad she could deliver it and hoped she could make it work in her favor. "When your grandfather finds out ...He's not going to—"

She interrupted. "You can bet I'm going to tell him. You can also bet you're not going anywhere."

She held up the zip-tie handcuffs she'd pulled out of her back pocket. She'd come prepared for this. She had twenty sets of zip-cuffs tucked at various points around her person, ready to tie up any of these motherfuckers she could get.

Though she'd initially only been interviewing Will Little, Burt de Gottardi, and his cousin Art, she'd grown to like them. They probably didn't think of her as a friend, merely as the FBI agent who invaded their property to help save them from people poaching on their land. But she was starting to think of them as friends. She was not letting anybody come in and run a raid on their compound, including her own family.

"Shray, you're under arrest," she repeated. "Put your hands behind your back. I'm going to cuff you."

"No, you're not," he repeated firmly as though he still didn't believe she was licensed or capable or both. He continued backing slowly away.

GJ inched forward, matching him step for step, not letting the distance between them grow. She knew this from Quantico. She didn't want to rush, didn't want to make him run. She wanted this to go down as simply as possible, but she already knew, it wasn't going to be simple.

"GJ, you can't do this. You can't let this plague fester. We've been working for decades to eradicate these people."

"I know," she said. "They are people. You've been killing *human beings* for decades, Shray."

"They aren't human."

"They are," she replied, as adamant as he. "And you're under arrest for the murder of Randall Standish."

"I didn't murder anyone."

"Well, his body was found in your laboratory. If you want to get nitpicky about it, you *know* he wasn't even like them. He was human, even by your twisted definition. He wasn't related to this family. He couldn't have carried the genetics. You killed a plain, normal man, Shray."

"I'm not the one who shot him."

"Oh, so that makes it okay? It's fine to go out and shoot at people if you're bad at it? Because you missed," she asked, slowly inching her way forward. By millimeters, she was closing the gap between them. Though she wanted him to initiate this final showdown, though she wanted him to make the first move, she knew she would have to.

That was when she heard the first bullet fired. Having no idea who fired it, she kept her training and stayed calm. It was time. "Three, two, one," she counted to herself. Then, she jumped, tackling Shray to the ground.

33

Walter had fired every bullet in every magazine she had. She'd had six packed completely full, plus a round in the chamber, ready to go.

She'd been trading them out as needed, the slick movements returning easily from her Marine days, despite the mechanical hand. She'd dropped to the ground and rolled backward into the foliage by the house. The bushes were crappy at stopping bullets but excellent at concealing her location. She shot at the figures who passed her as they attempted to get through the front door. She aimed at the ones who climbed through the windows with their rifles aimed. And she shot at them a handful of times before she saw their Kevlar and understood she was bruising but not even stopping them.

When the first shot had been fired, she didn't know who fired it, but she knew—as a fighter always did—that the first shot was an "open fire" signal for everyone, and so she did. She took out several of their people and felt not one bit guilty about it. They'd come here hunting humans. She was fighting back.

Burt, who'd come around the side of the small home to crouch beside her, had made not one noise. He'd simply appeared next to her with the butt of his rifle tucked into his shoulder, as he too had carefully taken aim and fired alongside her. She expected him to grunt from the pain of his bullet wound, but he didn't make a sound other than high speed bullets leaving the bore of his gun. As she looked more closely in the dark, she saw he was bleeding.

Understanding the question she asked with her eyes, he only shook his head and mouthed three words. "Ripped the stitches."

She nodded, and they kept going. It was what Marines did. What concerned her was that GJ was out there, and Walter didn't know where. Walter and Christina had been in the open on the front lawns, and they had dropped immediately to their knees, quickly firing and finding cover. Burt had come out just a moment behind her, not seeming to remember or act as if he was already injured. She guessed he figured he already had one hole, so what was another? He was an amazing soldier, though, staying low, and managing to avoid fire.

Luckily, his task wasn't too difficult, given that many of the hunters had put their rifles through the windows, leaving them trapped with Walter's gunmen now outside and behind them able to fire on them before they could turn around.

However, Walter was still meeting the fire in front of her. Despite the greenery they crouched in, they were sitting ducks. It wasn't long though before she saw something that was going to end this gunfight.

She almost dropped her jaw open at the sight, but then decided it was not a good look. GJ was heading back with someone in front of her. She was steering him by his hands, which were cuffed behind him, pushing him along as he purposefully stumbled in front of her. All the while, she managed to use the man as a human shield. She shouted over the sound of bullets, Walter was not sure how she managed it.

GJ yelled to the cuffed man. It was the man GJ had first spotted then run after. Walter had gotten the distinct impression GJ knew him, but now she was returning with him clearly handcuffed. Walter would need to get the story later, but right now, she holstered her handgun and picked up the shotgun Burt had brought. She cocked it, aimed at the intruder, and squeezed off a shot. All she was doing was protecting herself and Burt now. Burt had distance covered with his rifle, she was blasting at anyone who came close, and they'd finally gotten some of the others running scared. She was just starting to think they might come out of this alive.

"Hold your fire," GJ yelled, her voice somehow booming from that tiny body. "I've got your guy."

But they didn't stop. The rate of fire slowed a little, but it seemed that, in the dark, when no one could see what GJ had done, nobody decided to follow the firm command and actually stop firing. Walter cocked the shotgun again and blew away another person standing near her.

Unfortunately, she watched as he twitched on the ground. She hadn't gotten a good enough shot. Maybe he'd gotten close enough but his Kevlar still protected his vital organs. She'd likely busted him backward without enough damage to kill. She would need to keep an eye on him. Walter cocked the gun as GJ yelled again.

"I have Shray Menon."

GJ knew the man's full name. *Interesting.*

"I have my gun aimed at his head, and I will take out your leader if you do not stop firing now."

The words didn't work until Shray yelled, "Do as she says!"

At that point, the gunfire slowly died down. One last shot echoed in the distance at the other house as they seemed to get the message over there, too.

"I'm holding him here at the house," GJ said. Then she commanded them all. "The rest of you need to turn yourself in to the FBI agents on the property."

But it was too late. Walter already heard the sounds of rapid footfalls. As they turned and ran away, Walter pulled the rifle from Burt's hands and took her own aim, watching as one of them fell as he ran. It was shamefully satisfying.

GJ turned sharply then, aiming a shot loosely behind her as she yanked on Shray, keeping him off balance, keeping him from striking out and taking advantage of her altered attention.

Good move, Walter thought, and quickly GJ—whether she'd hit her target or not—was back in place with her gun at the man's temple. He jerked away from the heat of it, but GJ didn't seem to care.

She said something to him, but from this distance, Walter couldn't hear it. She probably wouldn't have been able to even if her ears weren't ringing with the unshed sounds of gunfire still singing in her head. She could only sit and watch as the remaining people on foot did not turn themselves in. They, too, took off, running into the distance or disappearing between the trees.

GJ force-marched the man, who was almost a foot taller than her. Though thin and wiry, she looked strong. Walter was proud of GJ for commanding the situation as she came closer and closer to the front of the house.

Moving the gun, GJ jammed it into the middle of his back. Now near enough for Walter to hear, the words were crisp and mean.

"I know anatomy better than you do, Shray. This is going straight through your heart." GJ threatened him like a champ. "If you like, I'll go straight through your lungs. I'll take them out without hitting anything else vital, and you can die suffering. So you're going to walk into this house without any fuss, and you're going to call your people off."

"They're already gone," he said. "You won't find them."

GJ didn't respond. She just pushed him up the three short, wooden steps, and through the door, bringing the enemy right into the de Gottardi- Little home.

34

Walter followed GJ back, watching as she pushed the zip-tied man through the front door and into the house. Walter, right on her heels, noted the expressions of the de Gottardi and Little family members as this killer entered their home.

"GJ," she whispered harshly, "what are you doing?"

GJ stopped for a moment, her hands still on the zip tie cuff, still controlling her perp—just the way they'd been taught. "Where else am I going to take him, Walter?"

It was a good point. They couldn't leave him outside. The hills were crawling with his own people. There was no way that leaving him outside would not get him rescued. They couldn't even leave him on the front steps, as there was every possibility one of his own people might just take a shot at him to keep him from talking. Walter knew; she'd paid attention that day in class—and she understood as a Marine—the need for protecting people whether you like them or not.

Once through the doorway, GJ turned away from her and looked to Will Little without removing her gun from the man's back. "Where can I put him?"

With only a small nod and a point, Will directed them back into the dining room. This room was relatively centrally located, and with the curtains pulled and the lights off, hopefully no one outside would be able to see in and take a head shot at Shray Menon.

When asked, GJ replied she wasn't too sure how likely it was that that would happen. Given that this man was her grandfather's assistant, he was likely relatively high up in the organization. Hopefully it meant they wouldn't try, but he wouldn't be any less dead if she and GJ were wrong. Walter voted to protect him while they tried to figure out just what information they might get out of him.

With GJ's hostage still standing there, they were only able to communicate through simple sentences and motions behind his back. GJ set him roughly at the table and pushed the chair under him. In tandem, she and Walter, without a word, began zip tying his ankles to the legs of the chair. These chairs were not made for this. Unlike the hotel chairs, these weren't designed to withstand rough use. This was a family's home, not a war zone, although it had become one.

When he was secured, Walter didn't even try to count the number of zip ties they'd used in the last 24 hours. Walter looked at GJ with her eyebrows up.

"This," GJ said, "is Shray Menon. He's my grandfather's assistant. And the one on the bull horn."

He only scowled at them, but Walter had another idea. Before they dove into this, they needed a plan. She motioned to Will and Art, but not to Burt, as he was already injured. She suggested that the two keep tabs on the man at the table. Several others stepped up to join them, and they circled Menon cautiously. Though guns raised initially to aim at the man, Walter motioned for them to keep their barrels down, and they did. Guns kept in firm grips, they left their fingers resting on the trigger guards. That was the right way, Walter knew. If Shray made any sudden moves, these people wouldn't hesitate to kill him. And though GJ and Walter might lose their star witness, Walter figured that was likely the way it had to be.

With their suspect covered, Walter motioned GJ away. Christina came through the door to join them from her position at the other home and Walter beckoned her as well.

Eyebrows up, Walter looked to the senior FBI agent. "You left people on guard?"

"Absolutely," Christina replied firmly, clearly not offended that she'd been asked. Without hesitation she added, "We need to get back to our posts if we can."

It wasn't safe here. It wasn't safe inside or outside, and there was nowhere left to go. Walter thought of those she'd sent out. "Somebody has to get Alicia and bring the children back. I don't know where they are and I don't know how many went with her," she commented.

Though they had two items already on their plan, they hadn't yet begun to talk about Shray.

"We need more guards," GJ said. "There were even more people out there than we thought and since we've got *him*, it's entirely possible they'll be coming back for a rescue. This may not be the end of it, not even for tonight."

Walter nodded. GJ was right.

Number three on the agenda, more guards. Number four, "What do we do with him?"

"I don't know, really," GJ shrugged. "I can't shoot him. He's the leader, so hopefully this helps call off the dogs." She was keeping her voice low. Her quarry was in the other room and they did not want him to hear what they had to say.

"We should take advantage and question him," Walter said.

GJ nodded. "About my grandfather most likely, as clearly there's some level of organization here and it's bigger than three people poaching humans with some guns."

"Do you want to do it?" Walter asked.

Christina was hanging back, staying out of it as the two newest agents batted ideas back and forth about who should ask what and how. A few moments later, Christina inserted herself into the conversation. "I can make him tell you."

———

Walter turned and looked at the other woman. "I'm sorry. I didn't get much of a chance to catch up on what it was that you could do. I thought you could make people see or do things. But now you're saying you can be, like, a truth serum?"

"Almost," Christina replied, the lack of emotion in her voice disturbing. But Walter let her go on. "I could make him believe he's talking to your grandfather, GJ."

"What?" Walter watched as GJ's face exploded in a surprised expression and Walter was sure hers did the same. It only lasted a moment until she put it together that making people see things should include the ability to make them see specific people.

Christina offered a half smile. "I can make him believe that he's sitting at the table with your grandfather. Is there any reason he wouldn't tell your grandfather the truth?" She sighed as she clearly thought through logistics Walter and GJ knew nothing about. "It's easier if I have something to work with, if I'm not trying to create a person out of thin air."

"Don't you have to know what my grandfather looks like?" GJ frowned.

"No. *He* does, but *I* don't. As long as he knows what your grandfather looks like and as long as he believes your grandfather is sitting across the table from him, then that's what he'll see. It helps if you know your grandfather too, so that when you ask a question—when he hears your grandfather's voice—he doesn't hear things that take him out of the moment. Like things that wouldn't make sense or things your grandfather would never say. Any of those things might make him question what he was seeing. It's best to avoid that."

Christina looked around, a little left, a little right, and Walter looked, too. There were none of the de Gottardi-Little family members present. Although why Christina might be worried about werewolves listening in, understanding that she was apparently relatively psychic—and a disturbing level of psychic at that—Walter didn't know.

"So GJ needs to go sit across from him and when GJ walks into the room, Shray will see Murray Marks," Walter clarified. Christina nodded. "So you, GJ—" Walter was beginning to pick up on what needed to happen, "—should ask questions and talk to him as though you are your grandfather."

"Exactly." Christina nodded. "You'll probably make minor errors, but he'll excuse that because he sees your grandfather. He'll think everything is okay and hopefully he'll answer accordingly."

"Unless he's figured out what you can do, Christina," GJ said.

That was something Walter hadn't considered. "Why would he? It never even occurred to me this kind of talent existed."

"Me either," GJ offered, looking to both of them. "But it also never occurred to me that my grandfather was a werewolf hunter, so let's just say my world's a little upside-down these days, and I'm trying to anticipate their next moves."

"Valid," Walter commented. "Assuming he hasn't figured it out, you go in. So, next question, what do we want to get out of him?"

"We need to know the size and scope of his organization first," Christina said, nodding to both of them as if to ensure their agreement. Only in these moments did she seem to be the senior officer running the scene. The rest of the time, there was something about her that made Walter think she was sad, alone, and not wanting to be at the front lines. Yet here she was. Was it because she agreed to it? Or maybe Westerfield had threatened her job? Walter didn't know, and she wouldn't likely find out tonight.

"So, let's say when we have GJ walk in as Murray Marks, Dr. Marks says to Shray that GJ called him and he just arrived."

GJ nodded. "That works. I'm not sure how to get him to describe their organization to somebody he thinks already knows about the organization."

Shit. Walter thought for another moment, "How about you tell him that GJ called and you have no idea what's going on. You came because GJ said she was staying with friends and she ran into Shray. She told him—Dr. Marks—exactly what happened. So he would need his assistant's full side of the story." Walter was still trying to sort it all out, herself. "That way, he could ask what exactly happened. Like, would Menon believe that you simply hadn't wanted to tattle on him?"

"It's plausible," GJ said. "That's how I got him handcuffed out there. I caught him completely off guard. He said I didn't know who I was staying with, whom my quote 'friends' were. It didn't even occur to him that I was the FBI agent I was talking about."

"Really?" Walter asked. "Doesn't your family know? You told them, right? So, wouldn't your grandfather's assistant also have heard this?"

And that was when she saw it: The expression on GJ's face changed. Slowly, her partner shook her head. "I haven't managed to actually tell anyone."

Well, shit, Walter thought again, that was news. Walter would have told everyone. She hadn't told anyone she'd graduated Quantico only because she didn't really have anyone to tell. "All that aside, we have to figure out the timing," she said.

They then discussed how long to wait, how long it might have taken for Dr. Marks to get there. Deciding an hour was good, they went back to their houses, organized the troops, and sent a party out for Alicia and the children. With everything as organized as it could be—which Walter was now certain still wasn't enough against these hunters—they reconvened. Then GJ straightened her back and walked into the room where Shray Menon waited.

35

G J felt her nerves ratcheting up as she talked with Walter and Christina one last time. They'd checked everything out and then waited another thirty minutes before GJ walked into the dining room where Shray still waited.

He'd been sitting, zip-tied to the seat the whole time. As far as the de Gottardis reported, he'd asked for nothing. With a deep breath, she walked in holding her back straight and lengthening her stride. Letting her hand hang stiffly at her sides, she mimicked the stance she'd often seen on her grandfather. She had no idea if all of this was necessary, and it felt more than a little bit weird.

According to Christina, Shray was watching Dr. Murray Marks, her grandfather, come stalking into the room. If that was the case, then what he was seeing clearly didn't exist, and GJ's mannerisms probably made no difference.

Nevertheless, she couldn't afford to break stride, so she kept it up. Shray's eyes got large, but he didn't say anything. She had no idea if he was wondering why she was strutting in here like a fool or if he was actually seeing her grandfather. Her answer came only a moment later.

Still tied to the chair, hands behind his back in a supremely uncomfortable position, he managed to lean forward just a little bit as GJ settled across the table from him, her hands flattened against the smooth surface.

"Murray!" His face held restrained excitement.

Holy shit, GJ thought. He really believed she was her grandfather. *Go, Christina.* Even though it still made her feel odd that the other agent could do such a thing, she mentally praised the woman.

Pausing for a moment, GJ realized she was under-prepared. Though she'd had thirty minutes, and though she'd thought this all through, she'd missed the mark on the very first piece. How did her grandfather address Shray? She didn't know, so she threw it out there with some irritation to mask her lack of knowledge. "Shray, what's going on here?"

"Why are *you* here?" He was asking it even before she got the question out of her mouth.

"GJ called me. She said she'd run into you while she was out visiting her friends." It was hard to speak of herself in the third person. In response, she tried to lay it on thick, as though she didn't understand anything.

"Well," Shray said, looking furtively back and forth. *Ah, he didn't want to be overheard.* A lesson from hostage negotiations popped into her head: overcome objections.

"I told them we needed our space," GJ replied. "They left." Though Shray had watched his guards walk out of the room as the fake Murray Marks had walked in, it appeared it was only her grandfather's word that made him believe he could speak freely. But— because Murray and GJ were supposedly on excellent terms—this should work. The problem came if Shray and Murray already knew that GJ knew about them.

Luckily, in the next blink, GJ realized they didn't. They knew she'd been in the basement; Shray had admitted as much to her when they were outside, but it didn't seem they had known, until she told Shray, that she'd thrown in with the FBI, that she was hired and on the payroll. She used that to her advantage, hoping that maybe he still didn't quite believe her, or that he wouldn't out her. "Well, she said that you had talked to her about something she found in the lab."

Shray nodded, his head moving up and down quickly, his agreement measurable by quick jolts of his chin. "Yes, I told her we knew. I don't know if I was supposed to. I mean, she's been sneaking in for months now."

So, they'd known about that all along. *Well, crap,* she thought. She tried not to let the flat line of her mouth falter. It was a common expression her grandfather wore when irritated or confused, and she aimed to keep this up as best she could.

"Who's out here? Who came tonight?" GJ asked, as her grandfather. The slight affectation of an English accent wound through her tone because he swore he had picked it up from so much world travel.

"Exactly who you said."

Another *oh, shit* crossed through her mind, this one sharper and darker than the one before. Not only was her grandfather involved, he had apparently ordered a mass genocide on non-random members of the de Gottardi-Little family tonight. *Son of a bitch.* She wanted to arrest him right there on the spot, but she couldn't, because she suddenly realized another flaw in their plan.

What happened when Shray wanted to see Murray and GJ together? It wouldn't happen, *couldn't* happen. She pushed on, aiming to collect the information they'd all agreed upon. Walter and Christina were just beyond the door. Though she had promised that no one was listening, they were listening hard.

"What was our final head count?" she asked, thinking that might be something her grandfather would say, though she had no idea what the protocol was, or what lingo they used for a situation like this. Did they talk in terms of *werewolves*? Did they just say *dogs*, as Shray had done before? She'd have to remember to use that.

Her grandfather's assistant shook his head. "Zero. We got none of them and they got me."

Mortified, GJ covered for her natural expression. She'd been asking how many of his own people had showed up. Shray had taken the question to indicate a body count. She had to assume that was because they'd spoken in terms of body counts before. Without showing it, she swallowed her revulsion and continued.

"Well, it's kind of your own fault," GJ said as Murray. Her grandfather didn't suffer fools and he didn't seem to ever believe that the fates were against you. If anything bad happened, it was your own fault. It was a lesson he'd taught GJ early on in life, and she intended to reiterate it to Shray now as well. "How many of our people?" she asked.

"They didn't get any."

"How many showed?" She asked again, thinking that an organization like this probably didn't all live together on a plantation or a military base or even a farm like the one she was currently sitting in the main house of. Chances were, they had come from all over.

"Fifty-eight," he said, his head count fast and sure. She had to believe it was accurate. It was more than they'd seen, more than they'd counted, GJ thought. Even while she was out there in the woods tackling Shray, handcuffing him and bringing him in, she had probably been surrounded. It was plausible the only reason nobody took her down was because they saw her with Shray, and they saw the way Shray interacted with her.

Just then, another thought crashed through her mind. Maybe they knew her—or at least knew of her. If her grandfather was so high up in this organization, maybe he'd spoken of his granddaughter. Maybe they knew the name "GJ," and when Shray had said it out there in the woods—loud enough for everyone to hear—maybe they'd instinctively backed off knowing that they shouldn't get themselves tangled with Murray Marks' granddaughter. Another breath. *Short and sweet*, she reminded herself. *Get in, get out.*

"Are they still out there?" she asked, this time keeping her voice low, signaling to Shray that she understood.

He shook his head, the negative coming through small and tight. He was pissed about that, unable to even look up from the table surface. GJ understood that this was what the man believed, but that didn't mean there weren't wanna-be heroes out there, waiting to come back and break him out. Or kill his captors. Or take down the whole compound. She couldn't cover the disturbed sigh that worked its way out of her lungs. Thinking about what her grandfather would do, she tried to make it work.

She looked Shray in the eye and asked, "You really pissed the bed, didn't you?"

36

As Walter stood beyond the doorway listening in on the conversation that GJ was holding with her grandfather's assistant, she felt her blood run colder and colder. It appeared whatever mojo Christina Pines was using was working, and working well. Next to her, Christina stood listening, but Walter could see the tension in the woman's muscles. She noticed the way her hands occasionally pressed flat against the drywall and clasped at it, almost the exact same way she'd seen the woman do to the surface of the table the other night. It indicated she was doing something even if Walter couldn't see it.

But Walter could hear it. From the other room with no eyes on the situation, she could hear GJ's voice come through clear as a bell, but it was obvious that Shray Menon was hearing the voice of Dr. Murray Marks, his mentor, long-time friend, and boss.

Next to her, Christina let out a slow breath as Walter stayed close to the wall. The wire from the listening device was not long enough to allow more than a single step back from where she held the receiver against the wall. The other piece went into her ear, keeping anyone around from hearing what she and Christina were listening in on.

The solid nature of the wall transferred the sound relatively well. It was a physics issue that she'd had to have GJ teach her several times to pass the test in class. Now she heard every word even though she found she didn't want to. The number of hunters was higher than those they'd seen. There had been people out there that she hadn't known about at all, and that wasn't the most disturbing thing.

What was most disturbing to Walter was that this was the "local unit." These were the people they'd been able to assemble in just a matter of a few hours. It almost stopped her heart to think there were nearly sixty people available who believed in the need to kill others unlike themselves. And that these were just the ones who felt they could get here and meet up on time. Not only that, they were prepared. These people each came with their own uniform, safety gear, rifles, and ammunition. They had gone so far—believed in the myths deeply enough—to cast silver bullets themselves.

It was stupid. Walter understood. Even so, she was more than a bit grateful for the mythology they embraced. There was every possibility the ridiculousness of that silver bullet had saved Burt de Gottardi's life. Silver was lighter in weight than lead. It flew slower, and it didn't warp quite as badly as, say, a hollow point could upon entering the body. The very thing they had planned on using to kill him had likely saved him.

Still, casting your own bullets spoke of dedication, of hours of work, of the long-term gathering of resources. This was no longer a group of hunters. It was well beyond *load up your guns and get 'em, boys*. This was an organized plan. It was a militia, and as she listened Walter came to understand it was actually worse. This wasn't even a militia. It was only *part* of a militia.

She heard GJ's voice from the other side. "All right, Shray. Let me talk to GJ. See what I can do about getting you out of here."

Walter heard the steps as her partner stood and walked through the door. As it opened, GJ didn't make eye contact with Walter or Christina on either side in hopes that Shray wouldn't notice that she was talking to people who'd been hanging out just beyond the door, making her promise that no one was listening into a blatant lie.

She closed the door on him for the briefest of moments, and Walter saw that she shook with small shudders of anger, fear, and more. That's also when Walter noticed the breach in protocol. GJ should have let Art, Will, and others with guns rush back into the room and surround Menon. Instead, she'd given him a momentary chance to break his bonds and make a move.

As Christina pulled GJ aside, holding her hands, Walter calmly opened the door and ushered the others in. To her trained eye, she didn't see anything amiss. With a small nod she motioned Art aside and whispered, "Check his bonds. He had a moment alone. Be thorough."

Art nodded, and the group resumed their positions. Again, barrels of the rifles aimed down. Handguns pointed more toward Shray's feet than his heart, but the fingers were on the trigger guards, and these people were ready. Shray Menon needed to worry about vengeful de Gottardi-Little family members mistakenly firing on him when they shouldn't. Walter, on the other hand, didn't really worry about that at all.

It was Christina who led the trio a good distance away, back to the room on the other side of the house where they'd first discussed this interview. The room where they'd spent their half hour planning and acted as though it was the time taken for Dr. Murray Marks to arrive at the distant compound.

GJ's breathing was noticeably evening out as they walked further and further from the room. Walter could only surmise that GJ had been forced to hold it together in front of a man she knew well as she heard the same chilling details that Walter had.

"You okay?" Walter asked in low tones. It wasn't a question she asked often. Not of her troops, not of her partners. But right now, she understood. She hadn't been around for the Civil War. She hadn't had to watch people kill their own family members, and in essence, that's where GJ was headed.

When GJ nodded, Walter believed her. The words that followed gave Walter a little more insight into just how tough GJ Janson was. "I'd say I'm losing my family, but the problem is I lost them a long time ago. What I'm doing now is learning that I lost them."

That was something Walter had never encountered, growing up the way she did—being at loose ends until she joined the military, and then on active duty. People woke up with you. They went out with you. They either came back, or they didn't. There was none of this sense of long-term loss and need to keep secrets. There had been no time or place for that in her life, yet here she was.

It was Christina who pulled them into the room, closed the door, and made sure that their voices didn't get back to Shray Menon. Normally, they would have been more cautious with the family members nearby, but if there was anything Walter believed right now, it was that none of them were going to help this man. So at least, no leaks from this room would reach his ears.

"We have maybe one more shot at him," Christina said. "One more time that GJ can go in there and be convincing as Dr. Murray Marks and get more information out of him. After that, he's going to wonder why he hasn't been released, or why he hasn't seen GJ again. If we take it too far, he'll likely become more belligerent."

As Christina explained this, Walter had to wonder: did Christina just push people? Or could she go digging into their minds too? Was she reading something from the man? Walter didn't know, and there wasn't time to ask or figure it out. They had to keep going. She would have gladly done the work and taken this hit for her partner. The emotional effort it cost GJ wouldn't have happened to Walter. But she couldn't pull off pretending to be Murray Marks. GJ had to think on her feet and know what her grandfather would have said in the same situation. Walter simply couldn't run the assignment. So she said something she knew would hurt her friend. "We have to send her back in."

37

GJ was about to go back in and run her second stint posing as
her grandfather when her phone buzzed. Though they'd
alerted Westerfield to everything that had happened and updated him
on the path they'd taken and the results they'd gotten, he hadn't yet
answered the phone. GJ could only assume that he and Wade were up
to their necks interviewing the two in the hotel. Maybe they were
letting the captured hunters in on what had gone down at the farm
tonight now that he had information. But he hadn't returned their
calls yet, so when the phone buzzed she picked it up immediately,
thinking it must be Westerfield.

As she held it in her hand though, she realized her first thought
had been incorrect. One, only her phone was buzzing. Had it been
Westerfield, he would have likely called all three of them on the same
line to begin with. Walter and Christina looked at her oddly and that
was when GJ saw the second thing: the name and picture on the front
of her phone indicated it was her grandfather.

With wide eyes and a stunned heart, she held it up showing the
other two. "What do I do?"

"You talk to him," Christina said. "Shray Menon doesn't know your
grandfather's on the phone and he can't hear out here. You can have
an entirely separate conversation with Dr. Marks." Christina said it as
though she understood that what she did would mess with people's

minds. That they wouldn't necessarily remember things correctly even if they'd been told what happened in the end. But GJ was shaking her head.

"No. I mean, why don't Eleri and Donovan have him? Shray said he went back. I assumed that was to the lab. How did they miss him?" She took a breath and watched as Walter and Christina realized that she couldn't answer the phone. Why wasn't her grandfather already in custody? She wasn't supposed to have to deal with this, too.

Suddenly it hit her. She didn't want to be the one to bring him in. She didn't want to be the one who trapped him so someone else could. It was already killing her to have Shray strapped to a chair in the other room. Sure, he was apparently a killer, and that changed everything. It twisted her memories of being out on digs with her grandfather, with Shray at their side. More than once, when she was small, he'd carried her when she was too tired to walk. He patiently answered her questions when she was too young to realize she was being a pest.

If her superpower was science, then her grandfather and Shray were the reason NightShade had recruited her in the first place. That —for her very first assignment—she should have to lock them both up was the ultimate stab in the back. To them, and to her. She didn't want to do it.

But she couldn't *not* do it. No matter how she loved them both— and she did—she couldn't leave them out there. They were killers. They believed in genocide. And she didn't want to face it. It was now, as her phone rang, that she realized she'd at least believed she was off the hook with her grandfather. She'd truly believed Eleri and Donovan would find and arrest him and all she'd have to do was acknowledge that he'd gotten himself caught. Instead, she was going to have to play the bait in the trap. It was her *grandfather*. This was going to break her.

"So what do I say?" she asked them, pointing at the phone as her spirit started to crack and peel.

"Shit, shit, shit." She muttered it under her breath. She'd been ready to walk in, she'd been prepared to have another go at Shray. She had a list of information that she intended to get. Now, at the last moment, she was screwed.

The phone rang one last time and went silent as it went to voicemail. GJ let her arm fall slack as though she'd messed it all up and missed it, but it was Christina who shook her head as though reassuring her there were other opportunities.

"What does your grandfather know?" Christina asked. As always, once again, she was taking the role of senior partner, but only for a moment. "He doesn't know we have his assistant, right?"

"Right," GJ and Walter both answered at the same time.

Then GJ filled it in. It was getting more complex by the second and she didn't like any of it. "He knows that I've been in the basement. He knows that I've been in his lab, and apparently he's known for months now and he's let me do it. What he doesn't know is that I know he knows."

Good God, she sounded like one of the corny old western spoofs, but Walter and Christina didn't seem to get the joke. They only nodded at her and agreed. It was important to keep straight who knew what when she spoke to them. That was a Quantico lesson—week three.

"We'll take a minute, we'll figure this out, and then we'll have you call him back. Because if he can give us information we can use with that man in there, that's going to help us wrap all of it up. What do we need to do on the phone call with your grandfather?"

"We need to know more about the network," Walter offered. Her tone flat, though her pace sounded a little like she was excited.

They'd intended to get that information out of Shray and GJ didn't know what she could possibly say to her grandfather to ask for that.

"How? He doesn't know that I understand what these people can do, let alone that I'm here. He doesn't know that I'm with the FBI." She saw the looks on their faces. She hadn't told her family and that was strange, she understood, but people didn't understand her family. She'd been born and raised a scientist. In their eyes, joining the FBI was only one step better than becoming a beat cop or an accountant or a day trader. There was nothing wrong with it, but it didn't fit in. She might as well have wandered off into an artist colony and lived at a commune making lint sculptures for all this was worth to them.

Even her forays earlier into forensic science had been a strange version of following her grandfather. He'd always been the pure scientist, in it for the academics, and she could see that discipline in the traces of what he was doing now, if she looked for it. For herself, GJ had been in forensics in large part for justice. The FBI had already turned out to be a better fit than she intended, but she had yet to figure out how to explain it to those she loved.

Christina and Walter took a moment to absorb that fact then offered small nods. They went forward, trying to pretend this was perfectly normal. GJ almost laughed again. There was absolutely nothing about her life right now that was anything even approaching normal.

Once they'd decided together on the best information they could get from her grandfather, GJ made a motion to call him back, but Walter offered her flat palm for a moment, making her stop. Then her partner opened the door, made soft comments just beyond it, and suddenly GJ heard the mild noise in the background come to a stop.

Good idea, Walter, she thought but didn't say as she once more wiped her palms down her pants legs. No point in giving her grandfather any clues by way of background noise. This time when Walter nodded, GJ didn't even think, she just pushed the button before she lost her nerve. In a moment the line rang through. A second ring, and then he was there.

"GJ, my love!"

"Grandpa!" she said back. The relief in her voice was something she didn't have to fake. Still, she launched into the script they'd decided on.

"Where are you? How was the Sorbonne?" She threw it in there as though she was just curious and giddy to know about his grand lifestyle. In truth, she had to sound like herself and yet ferret information out of him.

"The Sorbonne was great," he told her. "One of their best-attended lecture series. I did three days."

She forced a smile to her face as she wondered what else he'd been blatantly lying to her about. "That's fantastic, Grandpa. I can't wait to go with you next time."

She wasn't sure if she was laying it on too thick or not, but the way she and her grandfather normally communicated, she didn't think so. Invitations to academic speeches were something he had intended for her to be getting these days, or at least sometime soon. It was just another bubble that was about to burst in her family.

"Are you home?" she asked. "I have another weekend off from my internship coming up. I'd love to come out and be there when you're actually there."

"Oh, I was. You just missed me," he said, sounding sad that they'd passed again. Was it genuine? She no longer knew. And she fought a little harder, wishing this could all be easier, wishing she'd caught him while he was in the lab. She'd already known that was unlikely since Donovan and Eleri had not yet checked in to say that they'd arrested him—or even that they'd found him.

"Well, when are you going back?" she asked. "I'm sure I can rearrange a few things with my friends and my classmates. I should be able to skip a day here or there. It's just been so long since I was in when you were home." She didn't bother to comment that she had carefully arranged her own planning to make sure that she could get into the basement lab without interference—although ultimately, what good had it done? Her grandfather had known.

He finally offered her something they could use, told her he was one state over, and she felt herself pause and stutter. Was he *here*? Had he been with Shray before the raid? Or had he possibly been one of the people outside? Could he have been in the trees and heard her on the bullhorn? Did he know she was flat out lying to him now?

Hear heart stuttered a little as she asked, "Grandpa, where? Where are you? Which state?"

"West Virginia. Police officers up here caught a case and I'm consulting. But we found the body this evening. I'm going to be doing a dry autopsy—they want a full forensic workup—tomorrow. I expect to be heading home by tomorrow night. Don't worry, I'll wait for you this time." She could hear the smile in his voice. It might be because he was getting to see her. It might be that he had an autopsy on the table waiting for him. It might all be a lie.

She felt her own forced smile slip. "That would be great, Grandpa."

GJ sighed out the words, knowing that her intention behind the sound was not the one he would likely be reading. West Virginia was safe, if it was real. It was far away. He might know that Shray was here and he might know what Shray had planned to do. He might even know that Shray had failed to check in or someone might have told him what had gone down. But it was also possible he didn't know any of it. Unless someone here had reached out and specifically told him, he had no reason to believe that GJ was here. No reason to know she was FBI.

She thanked him, told him she'd see him in a few days, and clicked off just moments before a howl of several wolves, all at once, rose up in the yard behind her.

38

W alter heard the howl of the wolves outside as she watched GJ's expressions change in rapid succession.

"What the fuck are they doing?" she asked GJ and Christina, as though the other two might have the answer. She knew they didn't. With a slight movement of her hand, Walter pushed back the edge of the curtain ever so slightly and slowly slid her head over to get one eye staged for a look.

Nothing. She couldn't see anything. It was dark, and she wasn't sure what she expected to find. She also didn't think she could stand there long enough to let her gaze adapt. She was a target, even though most of her *should* be protected behind the wall.

Letting the curtain fall shut, she turned to GJ and Christina again. "I told them not to go out like this." As she shook her head at being disobeyed, both the other women looked at her.

"I said it, too." Christina shrugged as though to ask, *What were they going to do?*

Though Walter wanted the people in the house to run like a military machine, following commands as issued, she knew that was not going to happen. This just confirmed it.

She held her FBI-issue Glock in her right hand, and had only noticed that she was doing it as she racked the slide and chambered a bullet. She was ready. But why were members of the family out there...like that?

Unable to help herself, Walter once again pushed back the edge of the curtain and tipped her head in an attempt to get a glimpse. Again, she saw nothing. Though why she'd hoped for a better outcome, she had no idea.

This time when the howl went up, she paid attention, trying to scope out distance and direction, since there was nothing for her to see. Again, she let the curtain fall and looked to the other two, desperately wanting to ask, *What do we do?* but not quite having it in her DNA to utter the words.

"Okay," GJ said, the tone indicating that she was thinking, finished with wondering and returning to logic. "Why would they do this? None of them are dumb. Why would they go out like this?"

"I don't know," Walter said. "They can't use any weapons. They have no opposable thumbs." She almost laughed but couldn't.

Christina chimed in next. "They're supremely recognizable. The people out there will have absolutely no qualms about shooting to kill if they see a dog in the woods. It doesn't matter if it's an actual dog or wolf, or if it's one of the family members. They'll shoot first and drag the carcass home later."

Walter nodded in acknowledgement. "The hunters out there are locked and loaded with silver bullets and ready to shoot to kill. They won't hesitate." This was why GJ had started a conversation about what none of them could figure out. Just saying that gave Walter pause and she thought for a moment about it.

"Do you think the hunters are still out there?" GJ asked.

Walter answered without hesitation. "Of course, they are." She would never have left her own commander in a situation similar to this one. If anyone else on her team was held hostage, the furthest away the team got was however far away they needed to be to regroup. Once that happened, they would surge again. Walter was fully expecting a second attack tonight.

"So," GJ offered again, the flat calmness back in her voice, "what are their advantages?"

Again, the idea gave Walter pause. She judged them harshly. She'd told them not to go and they disobeyed, but they weren't her troops. She wasn't even technically in charge. She supposed she could pull rank, as the three of them were federal agents, but seriously, what could they do? This wasn't an arrestable offense. These people were on their own land. And it wasn't as if she could take them to court and say, "I told them to stay in the house, but they turned into dogs and ran outside."

She didn't let her grip on the gun go lax. She clutched it in her right hand ready to aim and fire faster than a cowboy in the old west. Her finger rested on the trigger guard, just as she'd noticed so many of the de Gottardi-Little family members doing earlier in the day. At least they were well-trained. Walter was ready but she was thinking. Turning to GJ, she said, "Fangs. They have fangs."

"True," GJ said, nodding. "They're powerful fighters. The problem is they have to get close enough for hand-to-hand, or fang-to-hand, and that's no match for a bullet. Go on."

"Speed," Walter added. These guys were fast. She'd clocked Donovan at more than forty miles an hour. It was a short-burst run, but he told her he could keep the speed for quite some time. Hours if necessary. Walter didn't doubt him. Donovan wasn't prone to exaggeration. He was more prone to clocking himself and calculating averages to collect data in different seasons.

GJ nodded. "Speed's good, but they can't outrun a bullet. What else?"

"Fear," Walter replied. "This militia or organization seems to think the dog shapes are demonic in some way."

"Maybe," GJ offered. "Maybe if they truly believe that, they'll want to not tangle with them. Except they came out here tonight specifically for the purpose of killing them."

"Still..." Walter let her thoughts trail off.

The more she turned it over, the more she realized maybe changing form wasn't the worst decision. Humans walked through the woods carefully placing feet, slow and steady, and eventually, it almost always happened that a twig snapped. Trolling her memories, she realized she couldn't find a time that she'd ever heard Donovan approach. The dark color of his coat meant he could remain virtually unseen. Though his eyes often reflected light, everything else on him blended into the night seamlessly. Maybe they were on to something.

"Okay," Christina hopped in then. "Let's assume they're not idiots. Let's assume they're out there in some kind of formation and doing something reasonable. Let's assume they're not just going to get themselves killed, or create a scenario in which we have to rescue them. All right, that assumption already on the table, why are they out there howling? What's out there right now?"

"People," Walter said. "The hunters. The militia didn't leave. At least not all of them." The howling had died down in the distance, but it had tapered off, the way wolves do when they'd finished their cry, not as though they'd been interrupted by bullets or fighting. Walter had to believe that that was a valuable piece of knowledge, that the wolves were doing okay.

It was GJ who posed the next question. "We also have to ask something entirely different. We have to think about the hunters. 'Why here?' 'Why now?'"

"What do you mean?" Walter asked. It was clear to her then that she still often thought like a Marine. She was thinking that way now, in terms of defense and offense, strategy and evasion. GJ was looking at a bigger picture, and Walter needed to do that, too. But it still felt obvious to her. "They came here and they killed Randall. And we're here because they started that."

"Exactly," GJ said. "But why did they start it? And why here? Aren't there families like this all over the US? My grandfather has bones from India and China and Europe, some of them thousands of years old. Families like this have existed forever, at least as far back as we can count, it seems." Walter frowned as GJ launched into what appeared to be an anthropology lesson. They didn't have time for this. Maybe it was better to think about defense, offense, strategy, and evasion right now.

But GJ seemed to already sense Walter's thoughts and she shook her head. "Are they currently mounting attacks on families all over the US? Just all over the Midwest? The Ozarks? What? Why the de Gottardi-Little family? Were they just an easy target? Because I don't buy that. I never knew that these people existed, and I've seen their bones since I was a child. I'm one of the few people who's constantly been exposed to evidence of them, and I have the background to figure out on my own that their bones went together and slid against each other in a way not like a standard, wild-type human build. Yet I still had no idea this existed until, *God*, three days ago."

It gave Walter pause, how quickly this had all gone down, how quickly it had all gone to hell.

"Call Westerfield," Christina said. "Ring and ring until he answers. See if he knows anything."

It hadn't occurred to Walter that she was allowed to pester her boss. She was used to being sent out on a mission and accomplishing it. She had a set of rules. She followed them. Sometimes she came back with a no answer, sometimes she came back with a yes. But she didn't simply dial up her boss and pester him in the middle of the night.

Christina raised her eyebrow and brooked no opposition. Walter transferred her gun into her prosthetic hand and reached for her phone.

On the fifth ring, he answered. "Fisher."

Though it still sounded odd to her, hearing her true name, and while it made her feel even more like she was back in the military, Walter told him everything they had. Then she asked their questions. The problem was, Westerfield didn't know any of the most important answers.

39

GJ watched Walter move her thumb casually over the disconnect button and put the phone away. Walter had put Westerfield on speakerphone. Though he'd gotten their previous messages, she'd been right earlier and he was up to his eyeballs in his own crap.

The two hunters he and Wade had been interrogating had given up basically zero information. Though why it had taken the agents so long to determine that, GJ didn't know. When she thought about it for half a second, she discovered she didn't want to. She was beginning to develop some additional questions, and these were about Westerfield. What kind of Special Agent in Charge pulled his trainees out before they completed their training?

She and Walter had been sent into the middle of the Ozarks alone, and one of them—her—had no idea what she was walking into. Westerfield had known, but he'd given her no professional briefing and no personal heads up. She wanted to be flattered that he simply trusted her to figure it out, but the flattery only went so far. Her growing list of questions reached further.

Though Westerfield ultimately knew nothing of the answers to their questions, he wasn't completely devoid of information.

GJ had asked over Walter's speaker, and he had answered, "No, there weren't similar raids going on against other families like the de Gottardis and Littles in the US."

So the answer to "Why here?" wasn't just that the family was here. Families like theirs were everywhere. No, there was definitely something special about *this one*. He'd managed to confirm at least that he'd always suspected that the hunters organization existed across the entire US. Though he, too, was surprised by the high numbers they'd counted, not having thought it was so big. Their intel had not come back with that kind of record-breaking size before.

As for "Why now?" Westerfield had no clue. GJ didn't either.

She looked once to Walter and Christina and then turned. Heading into the other room, she looked only once at Shray, still zip-tied to his chair, wondering if he saw her grandfather again as she walked by.

She grabbed Art by his arm and tugged him along. She pulled him out of the room, into the kitchen, through to the back bedroom that had thankfully been vacated in an effort of getting all the family members toward a central location.

She just looked at him, deciding that he might answer what they couldn't. So she asked point blank. "Why are they here Art? What do you know?"

He hesitated, and it bothered the shit out of her.

"Art?" she pressed, almost growing angry, but fighting the urge to let it show. It wasn't a good negotiation tactic.

He shook his head, still not speaking.

GJ had to fill in the spaces. "So you know. You know why they're here, and you didn't tell us? You didn't give us what we needed to help fight them off? We're here to help you. We're here to save your family members. You do understand that they're trying to kill you?"

Art nodded, and that bothered her even more. He understood what was at stake, and yet he still wasn't giving her the information she needed.

Oh, fuck. After staring at him for a moment, she wouldn't say he cracked. He simply made a decision.

"You have to talk to Will. Will is the only one who can make this decision, and maybe not Will alone."

She didn't even think about it, just took his arm, dragged him back in to the room where they were guarding Shray, and traded him out for Will. Will followed along calmly, seeming to understand that something had cracked, and he waited calmly for GJ to say the right words. She didn't have them.

"Will." She looked at him dead in the eyes, "What the fuck is going on here?"

"These people came to our home. They came onto our land. They shot and killed our guest and then aimed at family members as well. You know this."

"No, Will, I don't know this," GJ responded, trying to keep her voice from rising to a crescendo. She was trained better than this, she reminded herself. Yelling at him would yield her nothing. She understood the psychology behind it. However, she also understood the psychology that made her want to yell and hit things. And she definitely wanted to yell and hit things.

Unable to throw punches, she started throwing questions out into the dark. Thinking along the lines of police interrogation. If he lied, she might see when he flinched. It would maybe, *hopefully*, send her down the right path. "Who is it here that they want, Will? They came for someone in particular. Did they want Wade? Because they killed Randall, and he was wearing Wade's clothing and his ID."

No flinch from the head of the household. "Is it the house? Is there something special on the land? Like a mineral reserve?" she asked him. Money was a powerful motivator. But again, no flinch. "What is it, Will? What's here that they want?"

There! Just the slightest twitch showed on the lower eyelid of his right eye.

"What is it, Will?" she demanded again through clenched teeth, fighting to keep her ire down, to keep the tone out of her voice, when she was frustrated enough to draw her gun and aim it at this man she was supposed to protect.

"It's not mine to say," he said on a sad sigh, echoing Art's words from earlier.

"Well then who the fuck's is it?"

"None of us alone. It belongs to all of us."

"Is it bigger than a breadbox?" she quipped, thinking now was not the time for Twenty Questions. The questions were stupid, but as soon as it was out of her mouth, she saw it was at least useful. Were they protecting the entire house? An underground cave? Or maybe a magical amulet? She had no fucking idea.

Again, a twitch flashed at the corner of his right eye. She was glad that despite her anger and her stupid question, she'd still been watching. "So, it's bigger than a breadbox. Is it smaller than a house?"

Twitch. *Yes.*

"Animal, vegetable, or mineral?" She tried again, slower. "Animal, vegetable, or mineral?"

Son of a bitch.

"Mineral," she said. "Give it up, Will, because I can play this all day."

Still, he didn't speak, and GJ grew more and more irritated as she stood there trying to question this man who was trying equally hard to stare her down. Hadn't he figured out that she'd figured him out? She was done. "Do whatever you have to. Convene a tribunal. Draw straws. Flip a coin. I don't give a flying fuck, but, Will, we cannot protect you. We can't call in more agents if we don't know what's going on. We can't protect whatever this thing is that you think they're coming for, if we don't know what or where it is. Or even why they want it. You have five minutes."

40

Their little tribunal took more than a solid fifteen minutes. Walter kept looking at her watch and counting the time, waiting for the signal. In the meantime, Christina had walked back to the other house. GJ had headed to the third building, and together they checked in on everybody, as best they could.

It was rough, Walter thought, standing on the porch, holding guard over them. There was one pair of night vision goggles between the three of them. Though they thought they had come prepared—GJ had many things in her go-bag—she did not have enough equipment for them to feel safe during a full assault on the compound.

They'd alerted Westerfeld that they needed back up, but he was unable to pull agents in from other cases. Also, he was unable to reach out to the FBI in general, because as it stood right now, they had family members walking around in the shape of wolves. He couldn't and wouldn't risk a standard FBI agent, fully trained and valuable to the bureau, seeing something like that. In fact, Walter got the distinct impression that the "normies" were not allowed in Nightshade at all—and she began to wonder again just what she and GJ were doing here.

She'd watched over her two partners as they walked in two nearly opposite directions. That was a tactical mistake, she knew. Luckily, each was heavily armed and doing their best. No shots were fired, and with each passing, silent minute Walter wondered if it was a trap.

It's what she would have done if she'd been on the other side of this. Let them get in different houses, let them get split up. Then come at them when they were separated and weaker. It hadn't happened, though. Despite her tension and her extra-high state of alert, the other two women had returned completely unharmed.

The wolves were still off in the distance; she'd heard them baying once more but further away, and then nothing. Again, she'd strained her ears, making certain the sounds had trailed off in a natural fashion and weren't cut short. She listened for gunfire, both up close and in the distance, and heard nothing. Though she forced control of her body, she relaxed noticeably when Christina stepped through the door behind GJ. Then she let another layer of tension go when she was able to close and lock the door behind her partners, keeping all of them in.

The other houses were reported back as safe. Alicia had been located in the woods with the kids after another cousin had been sent to find them and check in. They decided to stay there for the night and move further off the property in the morning.

GJ came straight through the door bearing more scientific information. She didn't greet her partner, but said, "Wolves bay for communication."

Well, it was another advantage, but they could have used a damn radio, Walter thought.

"I asked the others at the house. I wanted to know why they thought they might have gone out and done it. So, it's okay. I mean, I guess, it's an advantage."

They're not dead yet, Walter thought. She knew because she kept hearing them, and she'd started to recognize some individual voices in the sounds, at least she wanted to believe she had.

With the three of them back it had taken only a few more minutes —though time seemed to drag on forever—before Will came out and motioned the agents to join them in the back room. They'd left junior members of the family guarding Shray Menon and now there were no feds in sight or sound of the captive either. Walter didn't like it but, given the look on Will and Art's face, there was something here. She felt she needed to be present for it. She felt they all did.

They went into the back bedroom and stood in a loose formation around a queen-size, four-poster bed. Walter figured it was the most awkward board meeting she'd ever attended.

Will started with, "We took a vote." And Walter decided she didn't give a flying fuck. She didn't care how they arrived at it, she only cared what they'd arrived at.

"They're here for our records," he said, voice flat—concerned, but not overly upset. Maybe he'd been through this before. That was an important question, Walter thought, for she was still trying to wrap her mind around the idea of such a valuable record collection.

"Records of what?" GJ asked, always on top of it, always ready for more information for that greedy little brain of hers.

Not *records* in vinyl, Walter thought, records of happenings. Duh. She must be tired.

Will waited out his own heavy sigh, then said, "They're here because we're the oldest family like us in the US. We can trace our ancestry back to the Egyptians."

"The Egyptians had wolves?" GJ asked. Walter thought about all the places her partner had listed where her grandfather had found skeletons. Egypt had not been on the list.

It was Will who gave her a smirk and raised an eyebrow, "You've seen the hieroglyphs, right? They worship the dogs."

Holy shit. Walter almost physically felt the realization smack her in the face.

But it was GJ who voiced it. "And you can trace your lineage that far, or is this another myth, like werewolves?"

Leave it to GJ to look these people in the eye and tell them their family history was absolutely, plausibly, incorrect. Still, Walter found herself waiting.

"Yes," Will declared, no uncertainly in his tone.

Though she was no GJ, Walter had learned to listen to the under-tones. She wasn't quite a human lie detector, but if Will Little's records were incomplete or possibly faulty, he didn't know about it. He didn't believe in the possibility either. He was sure of this to the marrow of his bones. His weird, shape-shifting bones.

"We have ancestry and recorded births and deaths on every known American family with our genetics." He looked back and forth between the women as he spoke, stating his points as though these were standard scientific observations on par with any research or genealogy GJ might have dug up in her past life as an academic.

"How many families are there?" Walter asked, wondering for a moment what Donovan might belong to. What group, what family, what branch.

"There are fifteen family groups, and numerous individual families mixed in with society. They're scattered all over the States. Mostly, the groups land in places with fertile farmland and open spaces. We do seem to get more and more crowded at times."

"Why now?" Walter probed, repeating GJ's question from earlier. "If these records date back to the Egyptians, then they've been here for how long?"

"I think it's because of the Littles," Will said, and Walter stopped, hoping everyone else would, too, giving him time to expound on what he meant. Sure enough, he did. "My family—the Littles—were outside of Billings, Montana. The city expanded and basically got too close. They decided to move. I and my immediate family had already relocated here—my wife's the de Gottardi. The rest of the group came down here and joined this farm. Overall, our family units have gotten a little smaller—with technology being what it is, more were able to leave and live solitary lives, but still stay in touch."

"People like Wade?" Walter asked, wondering why the words had tumbled out her mouth. Will almost laughed.

"You think the FBI recruited him just because he's a brilliant scientist? I mean, he is," and as she watched, his chest puffed up with pride for his grandson. "But honestly, he's in your division in part because he belongs to the oldest family in the US. He's in because he knows or is related to most every faction here on the continent."

Bullshit, Walter thought. Unassuming Wade, who liked to talk about quarks, spin, and all kinds of things she couldn't pronounce, let alone understand, was actually some kind of *ambassador for the werewolves?*

But Will wasn't done. "About two months after the rest of the Littles cleared out of the Billings place, their compound was raided and burned to the ground."

41

G J listened, almost too fascinated to do her job and protect these people. She wondered if maybe people dressed in black, carrying rifles and wearing Kevlar, were sneaking up on the house right now as she listened to the story Will told. The compound outside of Billings had apparently shown no evidence of the records.

"What kind of evidence would you have left behind? What kind of records are they?" she asked.

"They vary quite a bit," Will told her. "We actually have stone tablets for some of them, old bibles, probably worth millions in their own right."

"Like people do with births and deaths recorded in the front?"

"Very much like that. Some of this is on scrolls, written on ancient papyrus. Some on early paper that's falling apart. We've been working to document it digitally where we can."

For a moment, her brain flashed back to a few small pieces of paper, documents she'd seen in her grandfather's lab. She had a brief moment to wonder if her grandfather had managed to steal some of the family archives. But she didn't say anything.

"So they came now because the documents are all here suddenly?" GJ asked, noting from her partner's expression that Walter was about to ask an identical question.

"Almost," Will offered. "Previously we've kept them in a number of locations. We decided it was time to consolidate. We've lost several pieces over the years and the various moves. Our goal, like I said, was to digitize as much as we could so that, should an original artifact be lost, the information wouldn't be. We thought we were being very good about it. No strange changes, no big packages, just small quantities of the documents moved at a time, and it's taken us about ten years to gather them here. We wanted them in one central location, where we felt we could protect them well."

Walter raised an eyebrow. *Small wooden homes? Farmers?* Her partner didn't say anything out loud, but GJ could practically hear the words coming from Walter's brain.

Will must have psychically heard them, too. "You've seen how well-trained my family is."

Walter offered a slow, careful nod, acknowledging his point. And GJ understood. They grew tomatoes and potatoes to eat, and they practiced firing with sharp aim to keep their documents and their history safe. "So how did this group, this anti-wolf militia, figure out that you had all the documents here? Did somebody leak something on social media?" Once again, she'd meant it as a joke, and once again, she saw Will Little's eyeball twitch.

He sighed, because by this time, he knew she could read him. He'd already been given permission to tell, so he didn't hesitate. "I don't think anybody tweeted anything out," he offered with a wry tone, "But one of the reasons for consolidating was too many people who knew too much. We wanted to keep the archives safe in a small number of hands. In fact, probably about seventy percent of the people here don't know that they're here. It's part of the goal. We have a council and we voted on it."

Of course, GJ thought. *Naturally, there was a werewolf council.* She wondered if they had to be able change in order to get in the door, or if simply being a family member was enough.

She was tempted to get the genetics figured out and then test herself, curious if she might now give birth to a werewolf baby one of these days. *Better that than Bat Boy*, she thought absently. And there she was, getting snarkier from stress and lack of sleep. Her brain was going off the rails. Will Little's brain wasn't, though, and GJ tuned herself in again by sheer force of will.

"It's entirely possible someone from their organization has infiltrated us. When the family outside of Billings got out, there was evidence that someone had come and searched the place within days, maybe hours."

GJ looked up at Walter, their eyes connecting. Everything they heard told them more and more about how well-organized and well-informed this militia was. What had started as three zealots out acting crazy—or maybe just drunk—one night, had turned into a terrifyingly organized attack.

"We've also had some infighting lately," Will offered, and GJ couldn't help it, she desperately wanted to roll her eyes, because the last thing they needed right now was trouble from the inside.

However, she kept her voice steady. "What kind of infighting?"

Walter, too, was leaning forward. Only Christina was staying back, and as GJ watched, the woman's hands, already flat on the table, clenched just a little bit. And she had to wonder what the hell Christina was doing.

"It goes in cycles." Will said, and GJ wanted to throttle him. But she didn't ask, *what goes in cycles?* Instead, she smiled and stayed still, and waited.

"We have a roaming pack of Lobomau. In fact, it's part of the reason our group has gotten smaller. Some of the wolves are more aggressive."

"*Lobo mau?*" GJ asked.

Will shrugged. "An old term—it's Portuguese. The Lobomau are gangs of roving wolves who go out causing problems."

Good to know. Werewolves had street gangs.

"Needless to say," Will offered, "the Lobomau don't like having their information recorded."

"These aren't Lobomau," GJ said, already incorporating the term. These were humans. Or at least, she'd seen no evidence otherwise.

"No," Will offered, "but I wouldn't be surprised if one of them gave up some useful information to the hunters. The Lobomau? They'll turn on you if they get the chance."

42

G J found herself sitting at a table with Walter, Christina, and Will Little. They all stared at each other for a moment, having been left alone, finally, to figure out what the ever-loving fuck to do about this situation.

"If this organization gets their hands on your records, that means they can find every single person like you in the U.S., or at least most all of them?" GJ asked. She was pretty sure that's what she'd gathered from Will's earlier comments about the documents. However, she wanted to be sure before she proceeded, and the majority of what she was hearing was blowing her tiny little mind.

Will nodded. "All of us here in the US, as well as a handful of families in Europe and many in India."

As GJ watched, Walter startled a little bit. Turning her head ever so slightly, she asked, "What?"

It was an odd reaction for Walter to have, but Walter looked at her and said, "Donovan's part Indian. His mother grew up in Calcutta."

Oh, GJ found herself once again startled by Donovan's heritage and background. How had she missed all this? When she thought about it in light of the new information, realized she had noticed his bone structure indicating Asian descent. She wondered if the backs of his teeth were shoveled and decided that they probably were before she realized she needed to keep her head in the game. And the game was here, at this table.

"It's not just this organization, these people," Will said. "It's the Lobomau, as well. They've been coming for the documents, too. It's a big part of the reason we moved them to a central location. The Lobomau actually managed to successfully get some of them from us. Luckily, the family that had them stolen managed to digitize the records first. So the Lobomau have the originals, but we at least retained the records."

"That's good," GJ chimed.

"Not really. Not in the end. The Lobomau slaughtered the family that they stole records from. That incident was part of our decision to reconcile all the various documentations we had and put them into a single, safe location."

From the look on Walter's face, she was thinking the same thing GJ was. It wasn't looking very safe.

Will sounded very certain in his idea that this was a safe place. She wondered again how to defend against a relentless enemy that had numbers far larger than expected, especially when her own SAC wasn't doing a very good job of sending them backup.

It was Walter who said, "We can safely assume these guys are coming back as soon as they're capable. We've got their leader, or one of them, in custody. We haven't killed him, so there's a chance they can get him back. If they've got any kind of communication or tracking device on him, they may not have to take much risk. GJ bullshitted about us sending our vitals back to the bureau, and that may be the only thing keeping us alive. But as I said, it was complete bullshit. We don't have anything."

Will Little twisted his head a little to the side and offered up words in a more comfortable tone than GJ was willing to believe. "Actually, we have a lot."

"We need backup. We need an army," Walter said.

"It's coming," Will assured them, which left GJ once again wondering what the hell he was talking about. All the family members had been gathered into the three houses. Some of the children had been sent away with Alicia and a couple of other guardians. Word was they were okay, but she didn't know how long that could hold, because she didn't know where they were. That was for safety, but it also made her nervous.

That was when Will turned and looked over his shoulder. Coming up from the cellar was a wolf. By himself he padded up the steps, nudging the wooden trap door slowly upward.

She heard him before she saw him, and when she saw him, he looked somewhat familiar. GJ frowned at the brown hair and hazel eyes and the feeling of vague recognition faded into dust as Will turned and said, "Hey, Wade."

Wade, apparently as a wolf, simply nodded back to his grandfather and trotted into another room, disappearing into the home, right before GJ's eyes.

That was Wade, she told herself. Then she mentally repeated it several more times, trying to wrap her head around it. If she had to deal with one more bout of cognitive dissonance tonight, her brain was going to explode inside her skull, and explosions in contained spaces were very, very bad.

Then she turned back to the table, her warped mind processing things slowly. "Army? Backup?" she asked.

Wade had been out there. The wolf howls. It was dumb to go out. But Wade hadn't gone out. This was the first time she'd seen him *here*. She looked then at Will. Maybe the wolves hadn't simply gone out hunting themselves. Maybe there were wolves coming in. "How many?"

"I don't know," he said. "We'll ask Wade when he can talk. He should have rounded up a handful before he came."

It was mere moments later that Wade turned up in an outfit of khaki pants and a t-shirt. It was a little off for standard Wade, but probably the most Wade-like thing he was able to find in the closet. Even in the short time that GJ had been around him, she didn't think she'd ever seen him wear anything other than khakis and a white t-shirt with a plaid shirt buttoned down over it.

He barely said hello and then walked to the other side of the house. It was Will who said, "Glasses," and GJ remembered Wade wore them. He wouldn't have carried them in—not in that form. Will saw her confusion and answered her question before she asked. "For everyone who has glasses, we keep a spare prescription in each of the houses."

Of course they did, she thought. Sure, if she shape-shifted and ran through the woods looking like a wolf, she'd want her prescription available wherever she wound up. She was wondering if he had poor eyesight as a wolf when he came back into the room still wiping the glasses off as if it was part of the habit before settling them on his nose.

Without a word, and without waiting for an invitation, he pulled out the last seat and joined the group at the table. Walter held out her hand and Wade leaned out to clasp hers across the short distance. That was probably as close to a hug as Walter got for anyone who maybe wasn't Donovan, GJ thought.

"Did Westerfield send you?" GJ asked. She was hoping her boss had finally sent them the backup they so desperately needed.

"Somewhat," Wade said. "I told him I was leaving and he let me go. There aren't enough agents to cover this. This requires Nightshade agents, or my family members."

GJ tried to think it through as she was interrupted by Will.

"How many?"

"Twenty-five," said Wade.

43

Walter finally felt better. Numbers were important. She was finally starting to feel more comfortable considering family members as troops. She appreciated the skills she kept seeing, both for her own safety and the work of the group, and for their skill in running a mission. "So, you left the hotel this morning, and you rounded up other family members nearby and came in?"

Wade said, "I left early yesterday. I've been traveling, gathering people. We came in as close as we could. We changed, and we snuck in through the back paths. They're changing now, getting situated between the houses. Some have visited here before, but some haven't. Others are still out in the woods holding spots that we know are well fortified."

"How are they with arms?" Walter asked, realizing that when she said it, she meant weaponry, and when others said it, they might be thinking about the thing that she had a prosthetic version of. She might have also inadvertently asked how well these wolves handled guns...

Wade didn't question her. "They're good. I brought the fighters. We've made sure that the remaining family was safe and off their land, because, honestly, I'm concerned. If we bring the strongest to gather here, the vulnerable ones left behind can be attacked."

"Good thinking," Walter told him. It was what she would've done. Then again, maybe it was just what Wade would have done. He'd been in this a lot longer than she. They tried to sketch out a plan, and though Walter worked at finding out, Will refused to tell anyone where the documents were kept. But Walter pushed back. "How can we protect them if we don't where they are?"

"How can you protect them if someone can torture you and you tell them where they are? We've managed to keep these safe for thousands of years. Give me a shot at this, honey."

Well, fuck. Walter wasn't ready to concede that they actually had kept the documents safe. By Will's own words some had been stolen. Worse, some of their people had been murdered trying to protect them. In addition to that, Walter did not like being referred to as *honey,* and it had been a long time since someone had had the balls to do it. She did think she had to admire him for trying. Even so, on the outside, she glared, letting him know that word would not be acceptable again. Though they'd probably outnumbered their attackers from the beginning, it had been a difficult fight. Some of their numbers had been children; many had been untrained. As far as fighters went, they were underscored. Now, however, their forces were bigger than the ones coming.

She was about to say so to the table when GJ voiced exactly the point Walter wanted to make. "We have a greater number now than they had when they came last time, but we have that because of reinforcements we just brought in. What if they do it, too?"

Walter nodded, and looked to Wade. "Did anyone see you coming in? I think the big question is: do they know that we have reinforcements?"

"I can't imagine they did see us," Wade said. "We know this land, and so many of us went out. I sent signals. Will sent a handful of scouts out to find the incoming, so we could lead them in along the paths we know that are silent, dark, and as stealthy as possible. I didn't encounter anyone, and I didn't hear any gunfire. I have a hard time imagining that anyone out there in the woods wouldn't have fired on us if they'd seen us."

Walter thought it was pretty plausible, unless one lone person was sitting there in the dark, watching. In that case, firing on a pack of wolves could easily go badly then. They might get a couple, but in the end, the pack would turn and the shooter would likely be dead, so she wasn't quite as confident of Wade's assessment of their stealth.

As she watched, though, another long and pointed face nudged up the door to the cellar. Ears perked up as the lithe body wriggled out from under the door. Walter wondered why no one was helping them through, and then she decided it was none of her business. She was the interloper. The FBI wasn't sending backup. She, GJ, and Christina were the ones who didn't belong, and maybe these people knew exactly what they were doing. Even as she thought it, Wade reached out to her right hand and gave it a quick squeeze. "It's good that you're here," he said. "We need some tactical experience."

Walter then asked the question that she needed to know, but had dreaded asking. She didn't want to see the looks on their faces. "What is it that we are protecting?" They all looked at her like she was nuts, as though the answer was obvious, and she wanted to point out that it wasn't.

"We're protecting the people."

"Do we have any people who need more protection than others?"

"The women and children," Will said immediately. Wade was nodding.

Unsure if she could talk about the documents now that the crowd had been added to, she took what she could get. "Women and children" was a pretty standard answer, and she'd partly expected it, but she wouldn't have been surprised if one of these people here—one of these family members—didn't turn out to be some kind of Egyptian deity, and maybe needed more protection than the others. So she was glad that the initial answer had been simple, but it wasn't enough. "What about the property?"

"What do you mean?" Will asked.

"How valuable is the property to you? Can we light it up? Can we burn the house to the ground to make them think that we're gone?"

That made the old man sit back and run his fingers through what was left of the hair on his head. It still looked pretty good, but was thinning just a little, and she had to wonder how it would look in wolf form. She didn't ask, though.

"We have to save the property," he said. "This is our home. This is where we live. I mean, obviously, if it comes down to people or property, then ..."

"But that's the problem," Walter protested. She'd been in this situation before, and she knew people under-predicted the damage. "It almost definitely will. I can't say it will come down to all the property, or one life. It could be chairs, it could be walls, it could be all the buildings. It could be that your well is poisoned. I don't know," she shrugged. "I can't tell you what those ratios will be. But you have to go into this willing to give up a lot—probably even things that you love—to save the people. Too many people wind up trapped or dead trying to save property because they don't believe their lives are truly in danger, or they don't understand how far their enemy is willing to go.

"I want to know ahead of time what we can and can't do. If I see an opportunity, and I can—I don't know—start a fire and save a handful of lives, should I just do it? Or do I wait until the very last moment, because the property itself is valuable and worth saving? Is there anything in here that is worth more than the human lives?" Then she quit trying to hide it and just blurted it out. "Like, say, these documents you're talking about?"

44

GJ felt her head snap up as Walter started asking her questions. What was here that was more valuable than human life? GJ would've said *nothing*. It was a snap response, and something they'd specifically been trained for at the FBI.

But Walter understood *war*. However, as GJ thought about it, she recognized the value of the question. It didn't matter what *she* thought was most valuable. It mattered what these people thought was the most valuable. That would be the way they made their snap judgments when they were fighting. Their snap judgements, their sacrifices, even their statistical maneuvers would be based on the thing that they most wanted to protect—and if it wasn't themselves, that changed everything.

The answer came back from Will. "We have to protect the documentation. We have to protect enough of us to keep going, and we must keep the documents. If they find it, they can see that we know of every wolf in the US and on many other continents. It won't matter if we survive here if they get their hands on our genealogy."

That was the issue, GJ thought. *Too many points to protect, too many things and too many different places.* If they were thinking about it, they would likely protect their women. Childbearing was much harder and more time-consuming than child siring. They were protecting their genetic pool. Though it sounded from the way Will Little said it that no individual was more important than the documents.

That idea—protecting a statistical outcome—was probably the hardest thing of all. Again, GJ found herself looking to Walter. She raised her eyebrows, as if to say, *You're the expert. What do we do?* Then again, Wade was here, too.

He was not only an FBI agent with seniority to either of them. This was his family and his home compound. He probably knew the area like the back of his hand. Actually, she could say for certain that he did. He had managed to sneak in here without getting shot or even detected.

Just then, in the background, she heard another series of howls. They went up, one after another, until an entire chorus echoed between the hills. In half a second after that, she heard gunshots as well. They couldn't be too far away. She understood from her training what a gunshot sounded like—up close, at a hundred meters, at a mile. She was starting to be able to place them. Walter was likely much better at that than she was, but now was not the time to ask.

One of the howls cut abruptly, and everyone at the table jerked to their feet. It was Will Little who held his hands out to everyone, asking them to wait. To not act yet.

"They'll signal us. That's not the signal, so we have to wait. Those should be incoming. One of my guys is there to meet them and help guide them in. But until he gives the signal that they're under fire and they need help, we don't move."

The howls went up again in the distance, and GJ listened closely. Though she heard absolutely nothing different, several faces around the table visibly relaxed. She could only assume that they were hearing something she wasn't, some sort of signaling. Even as she thought it, Wade nodded.

"They're good. All is well."

"It sounds like someone got shot," GJ said, no longer able to hide the concern racing through her brain. They were acting as though the abrupt cut-off of one of the howls was no big deal.

"It's plausible that they did," Wade said, "but it's either a completely fatal shot or not too damaging. Either way, any survivors can come in on their own two feet—or their own four feet."

The thought passed through GJ's brain again about the physiology of the people. She pushed it aside. Though all of this was scientifically fascinating, there was no time now to linger in her curiosity. In the strictest sense of it, if she didn't protect these people, she would have no science to study.

Around the table, they talked, hashed out options, and made a plan. The number of weapons in the arsenal at each home was discussed. And again, the thought shot through her brain: not only was there a militia outside, but there was one inside as well. The numbers were looking better and better. Though the people outside were armed and protected, the people inside had something those outside didn't: a serious survival instinct. They also had something to protect, something that appeared to be sacred to the heart of each of them.

That helped, she understood. It meant they would hopefully each make similar decisions. Though Walter might be, GJ was not ready to command a unit of thirty, each of whom had a different agenda.

The group at the table hammered out the best places to stash guns and to set shooters. Who should hold grenades, smoke bombs, flash bangs, and the other things GJ had never expected to find in a family farming compound in the middle of the Ozarks. But after her training, after the cases she'd seen at Quantico, she probably should have. It was fifteen tactical minutes later before the cellar door shuddered again.

Another furry nose nudged it open, and another wolf slipped through as the door tried to push him down. He made it anyway, yanking his leg up quickly at the last moment to avoid getting it slammed as the door fell shut. It was another four or five minutes before the human emerged from the bedroom that the wolf had ducked into. And again, Will looked at his newcomer.

GJ had been wrong. He was a she. Will greeted Cherie by name and asked her, "How many?"

Cherie offered a prompt, "Eighteen."

Mentally, GJ was tallying the numbers when the tinkling of glass, once again, brought her sharply to her feet. Gunfire followed. Only this time, it was close, too close. This time the sound came from the next room.

45

W alter watched as GJ sprang to her feet, her own feet not far behind. They ran for the room where the others were guarding Shray Menon. He was their most valuable asset, and Walter was pulling her gun from its holster, racking the slide, and getting ready to aim.

Even as she made her way through the short distance of the house, it was GJ who held her arm out, as if to hold Walter back.

"They're losing him," GJ said calmly of the people in the room who were supposed to be guarding their find.

Walter nodded angrily, "Yes, they are." They didn't need Shray Menon enough to fight for him. None of them felt their own lives were worth his, and so when it came down to it, those coming in would have the advantage, and they would win by sheer force and determination. They wanted their leader back.

But GJ shook her head at Walter. "No, they're losing him *on purpose*. It's okay."

Walter wasn't sure how in the ever-loving hell that was okay. They'd brought Shray here on purpose. So why lose him? GJ had tackled him, hauled him back, and they'd interrogated him. He was likely still useful for information. They would have already gotten it if they'd not been so rudely interrupted by arriving wolves, distant gunshots, howls, and new army members coming in to plan out tactical maneuvers.

"I tagged him," GJ whispered. "Out in the woods, before I tackled him, I put a tag in his pocket. He's trackable. I didn't tell you. We didn't have time. I meant to."

"Oh," Walter stuttered as the idea took root. "Good thinking." It sounded like something she or Eleri or Donovan would have done. And yet, here GJ was, already picking up on the standards in Nightshade, tracking her victims. They heard the window break again. There were shouts, a few random shots. As far as Walter could tell, no one had been hit. There were no yelps, screams, or cries of pain so it sounded like they were doing exactly as GJ said. They were putting up a good show, but letting Shray get away.

The others from the table crowded the hallway behind Walter. GJ turned and looked at all of them, very carefully in a very low voice, explaining a plan that she hoped would not carry into the other room. If Shray knew he'd been tagged, then the whole thing was useless.

If they sweep him, if he figures it out, Walter thought, *if he puts his hand in his pocket and discovers the bug, it's all useless.* But she didn't think he would. He seemed to barely believe that GJ was a real, card-carrying FBI agent. To carry the thought out further—that she might be using spy tech against him—was something Walter didn't think would happen quickly.

She turned to the others and whispered, "You, stay here. You are defending the house. Wade and Christina are in charge."

Looking between the two of them as though she had the authority to do so, she pretended she did and issued the command. "It's up to the two of you to figure out who the most senior officer is. GJ and I are going to track Shray. I have the skills, and GJ knows the quarry. If he loses his GPS tracker for any reason, then we need to be there so that we can follow him all the way to the end. We need to see where he goes and who he meets up with."

She was thinking about cars—for Shray, for them—but GJ asked her first, "Are there any vehicles? Any keys that we need? Anything that we need to know if they hop into a car?"

Walter had several tracking devices in a small pouch on the back of her belt. It was almost like one of the tactical belts cops wore, but not quite as bulky, and nowhere near as obvious. So she had them if she needed them, but they weren't useful unless one of them could get close enough. "If they get to a car, we may not be able to follow any further. If we can at least touch the car before they drive away, we can track it. If we can get something sticky on the tracker, then we might be able to throw it at the car from a short distance and still trace it."

"Won't they hear it hit?" Will asked.

"Maybe," GJ said. "Hopefully they'll think it's gravel. Worst case scenario, they have to stop to get the tracker off, which buys us a little more time."

Walter couldn't find any flaws with the plan, and they asked around the house if there was anything sticky they could use. This was not what she'd imagined when she joined the Nightshade Division.

Sure enough, one of the men hopped up from the table and came back quickly, bearing some kind of putty that actually had a good, tacky feel to it. Probably for hanging posters or something. Walter didn't ask—she was just grateful. She added it to the small pouch at the back of her belt. With weapon in hand, she turned to GJ. "We have to go now. If we're tracking him on foot, we have to get out of here."

"Back door," Will said. "Wade, show them."

And like a shot, they were off. Out the back door, quietly down the steps, following the instructions Wade gave them to get around to the side of the house. Walter caught a glimpse of a man she believed was Shray Menon heading deeper into the woods and just out of sight. GJ had pulled up her phone, dimming the screen and turning on the blue light shade.

They used every advantage they could to hide themselves as they walked through the night. Over GJ's shoulder, Walter watched Shray's tracker aiming away through the trees. Thankful for the information the device provided, they took advantage of the opportunity to stay safe and hidden. Now they headed straight out from the side of the house, at a ninety-degree angle from where they would have gone if they'd followed the man's footsteps.

Cutting wide afforded them cover, but it meant they would have to be fast and silent. Walter knew the drill. She only hoped GJ could remember her training well enough. She worried that her younger partner hadn't had quite enough practice at it.

The man walked for thirty minutes with the two of them trailing along at an angle. If he had food, he didn't stop to eat it.

If they had food, Walter thought, she would have eaten some of it.

But they didn't. There'd been no time. The strike had come at the window unexpectedly, suddenly, and they'd been out the door just as quickly with no time to prepare. GJ hadn't even told her that she'd smacked a tracker on the man. It was a brilliant plan, but they could've done with some extra help. Extra readiness. They stayed to the west of him, and after tracking him for about forty-five minutes, Walter noticed a form in the distance ahead.

The man sat, small and silent, directly between them and the path Shray Mennon was cutting through the woods. Their quarry walked with purpose, confident of exactly where he was going. Walter was bothered by this. It meant these people knew the grounds, and that they'd been here many times before today.

Though it was tempting to ignore the form crouched and trying to hide from them, Walter found they couldn't just take a wide berth and ignore him. She watched as the shape in the woods shifted slightly. The man's rifle swept slowly from side to side, almost like sprinkler watering a garden. They were going to have to take this one out.

Sighing quietly, Walter examined her options. She didn't enjoy knowing she was going to jump this person, and would likely wind up killing them. For a moment she tried out alternate scenarios as they crept ever slowly closer. The first goal was to get as close as possible without being detected. What she wanted was to tie him up. Zip-tie his hands and feet, bind him, gag him, leave him in the woods. But there was no scenario she could come up with to make that plausible. In every outcome she thought of, his friends would find him.

Chances were there was a check-in system. She knew she would have it if she were leading this operation, so she had to assume they had it, too. She had to assume they were three steps ahead. It was the only way for her to always know that she could win. Which meant, bound, gagged and zip tied, her quarry would be detected as missing. He wouldn't answer his call and someone would come and check on him. Any reasonable person in the woods at night would have some kind of a knife, and that would be it. He'd be free again.

Her quarry would be back up on his feet, as dangerous as before— except, now with information. He would know there were two women following Shray Menon. Information of what they looked like, what their sizes were. And Walter didn't doubt for one second that she was highly recognizable with her prosthetic hand. The leg could be hidden. At this stage of her recovery, it would take someone who knew well what kind of limp or movement a prosthetic leg would make to detect that with the pants on. But the arm—the hand especially—could not be hidden. It meant that, as soon as this person uttered anything about her prosthetic hand, she was completely identified. She was likely already a target. Possibly GJ was, too.

The one thing she hoped was that GJ's grandfather's involvement made GJ the kind of target that they would bind, gag, and zip-tie—not the kind they would kill. Still Walter harbored no illusions about her own uselessness to them. They would kill her on sight.

She didn't want to kill the person in the woods. She'd seen several of them face-to-face so far, and she didn't like what she saw. They came from all walks of life. Young, old, Asian, black, white, southern accents, and those who sounded like they came from a distance. If it hadn't been for their uniform style of dress and expensive gear, they would've been quite the motley crew. So, she and GJ snuck ever closer. This was going to be a sniper situation. One shot, one kill, and she wasn't going to make GJ do it.

She motioned to her partner, hands and mouth moving in sync to convey the message with zero sound. "You, lookout. Cover my back."

GJ nodded and held up her fingers showing off the number six, indicating that she had Walter's. Closer, Walter settled in, barely seven meters away from her quarry and she waited for her eyes to adjust.

Though she could see well enough now in the moonlight, the shadows under the tree were harder to pick through. She stared at them until they became just a little clearer. Just enough to see the strap under the chin. The edges that the Kevlar vest made, where it bulked up the wearer. She lined up her gun. A nine millimeter was not the ideal sniper weapon, but it was what she had, and she was plenty close enough. She wasn't shooting soft, silver bullets.

She sighted her target with a trained eye. Deep breath in, out through her nose, slow her heart rate.

Pull the trigger.

With a silent jerk at the sound of her gunfire, he fell over.

46

Walter stayed still where she was, keeping her breath slow. Behind her, GJ still scanned the area, weapon up and ready. Her partner had not seen the man fall, and in fact, as he toppled backward Walter had changed her assessment. It was a woman.

This was merely a piece of information. She made no gender distinction when she killed. It was an insult to women everywhere to think they were somehow more delicate. They weren't. She wasn't. GJ sure as hell wasn't. GJ's vulnerabilities were all her own and had nothing to do with gender.

After they'd crouched, unmoving, counting out the full thirty seconds, Walter slowly inched them forward. She waited for the sound of a shot out of nowhere. They had no Kevlar. They should have. For all the cool toys they had, they had no tactical vests, no helmets.

Again, she was three steps behind, but protective gear was big and bulky and she had yet to find a way to transport what she needed in her pockets. She could carry five trackers, a gun, zip-tie handcuffs, and all her other tools for the space cost of one tactical vest. So now she waited for a sting and fire of a bullet to rip through her side. It was a feeling she'd felt before, so she knew when it didn't happen.

They inched forward, again and again. All the while, GJ watched her phone. Walter pointed to it and GJ nodded, giving a small thumps-up in the very, very light glow. *Good*, they still had a tracker on Shray Menon. This had been a time-consuming stop, but Walter wanted to leave no eyewitnesses behind.

In the end, she realized she was going to have to risk moving faster, so they could maintain their tail—even though it would give someone who'd been lurking and waiting for them the opportunity to make a sudden move, it had to be done.

Walter leapt forward, covering the body and getting her fingers jammed into the pulse point. The body didn't so much as jerk as she laid on top of it. Whoever she'd been, she was gone now. Dead.

Motioning to GJ, Walter started forward and they picked up their pace. They didn't know, but they had to assume that this one person was the station for an entire area, and with any luck they'd just cleared it. Without luck, they'd feel the sting of bullets. But again, if they were going to follow Shray it was a tactical decision they had to make.

GJ picked up her pace, impressing Walter with the quietness of her footsteps. She even managed to get a slight bit ahead of Walter. Following the tracking device, looking up ahead, and trying to get a good visual on one of the men who'd helped raise her.

They watched as the little bead on the phone screen followed what wasn't a map, but only an open green space in front of them. There were no roads or any marked spaces via GPS, so the dot that was Shray's tracker just moved and moved and moved.

They slowly crept behind it trying to close the distance as they went. They'd lost a lot of ground taking out the person in the woods, but Walter couldn't regret it. It had needed to be done.

Their brisk pace brought them closer and closer to the advancing dot, but then it stopped. GJ motioned to Walter and, though they moved quickly, they understood. They would be coming to a halt soon.

Shray had reached either his destination or an important point along the way. Maybe he'd run into somebody. Walter could only hope that they would get a visual. As they got closer she got her wish. He'd run into another person, one of his own. And they were speaking. The other person wore no tactical gear.

Next to her in the silence, GJ gasped.

GJ felt the hit as hard as the time she'd been shot dead in the middle of Hogan's Alley, a simunition taking her straight to her heart—or straight to her tactical vest. Either way, it had knocked her backwards. Though they were simulated ammunition, they still packed a wallop. So did this.

Shray Menon was in the woods in front of her and speaking to her grandfather. She ducked and tried to hide, not ready for the sensation she felt. Luckily, Walter was also tugging her down to keep them both out of sight, to keep the two men from turning in their direction.

Her grandfather wasn't supposed to be out here, she thought. Actually, none of them were. All of this was *wrong*, and GJ was working hard to wrap her brain around it.

On some level, she'd been denying this to herself for quite some time. She'd known what was in her grandfather's basement. She'd known the lab existed. It had taken a while to come to grips with the fact that his artifacts, his bones, his human skeletons, had no appropriate provenance. That could only mean they were stolen. But she'd ignored the possibility that the remains belonged to somebody, some family, some human being that her grandfather had completely disregarded, and now he was *here*. In these woods. With the people who'd been hunting a fellow NightShade agent's family.

Shray's very presence was almost absolute proof of her grandfather being involved, but still, until she'd seen him, she'd shaken it off. She'd twisted her thoughts into pretzels, trying to figure a way that her grandfather might not know what was going on. Maybe Shray was at the heart of the organization. But no. He was an assistant always. And it was her grandfather who ran things. At the heart of this was the famous—and soon to be infamous—Dr. Murray Marks, because this was going to be the end of things for him. And that end was going to happen at GJ's hands. He was going to spend the rest of his life in prison, she knew.

The problem was, no one was out here but herself and Walter. For the briefest of moments, she imagined letting him walk away. She thought about all the times they'd spent together. She remembered going on digs and finding a human skeleton of her own. Looking back, she'd been all of eight. She understood now that her grandfather and Shray had pointed her in the right direction and surely had already known the skeleton was there. But they let her claim the find, and she'd spent all day carefully brushing away the dirt and sifting for finger bones exactly as she'd been taught.

With clearer insight, she understood what a very odd thing that was for an eight-year-old to know—but it didn't matter. It was what she had known. She still couldn't say for certain if her parents had foisted her off on her grandfather and he'd willingly taken her, or if they'd simply let their constantly begging daughter finally get on a plane and go see the man that she'd probably loved best all her life, and now he was here in the woods.

She knew who he was even without being able to hear his voice. Without being able to see his face. She could understand by the outline of him, the shape of him, the way he gestured. There was no doubt in her mind that it couldn't be anybody else. If she stood up and let him see her, he would have no doubt to who she was either. It was something she considered. The way the two men were talking, gesticulating off in the distance, illuminated slightly by the moon, GJ understood Shray was telling her grandfather that he'd found her inside the compound.

She could see her grandfather shaking his head. The hat he always wore, apparently even now into the deep of woods at night, made it very clear what his motion was. She could almost hear Shray saying, "Not only was GJ here, but she is now a member of the FBI. A card-carrying agent, and she was here for them."

Walter tugged on her again, and GJ realized she'd risen up ever-so-slightly to get a better glimpse of the two men. *Shit*, she thought. She needed to keep her training foremost in her mind before Walter took it upon herself to remind GJ of the same. Training said you trusted your partner. Training said you let the partner with the most experience in the situation lead the way. Training said you recused yourself if you were too involved in the case.

Well, she was at least going to recuse herself from making some of the tactical decisions. She turned to Walter and whispered, "Your call."

47

W alter took a deep breath. There was absolutely no way this wasn't going to suck monkey balls. They were about to arrest her partner's treasured family member and if they didn't arrest him, then it would suck worse.

However, she had to make a plan. She had to stop and think that this wasn't GJ's grandfather, this was just a man in the woods talking to another man in the woods.

The second man had already been identified as a leader of a group coming to kill a family at their own home compound. The new man was identified as higher up than the one they'd already interrogated.

Stopping for a moment, she decided to be dead certain before she moved forward. And she asked herself: did she have any doubts as to what was going on? Unfortunately, even when Walter thought about it in every possible light, she didn't. She wished GJ could have put a microphone on Shray; she heard little now but could see was the two men gesturing wildly. She wanted to wait, so for now, that was the plan.

For any subject, she should make sure that she had ample evidence before she moved in for the arrest. If she arrested him and he could state that he hadn't yet done anything illegal, then she couldn't yet get him into jail by way of a court of law.

She still had her doubts about how courts of law would be useful in her dealings via the NightShade division. Or what would happen if anybody had to say anything in court about the fact that the de Gottardi-Little family was known for shape-shifting into were-wolves. That trial would devolve very quickly, but she was still interested in getting this man out of here, getting him in jail, and breaking up his band of merry men with silver-bulleted hunters.

She was waiting for him to make a move.

She and GJ sat like that, crouched, silent, beyond the line of sight of the two men there in the woods. Sadly, they were slightly too far away see anything useful.

Walter made a motion to GJ and they scooted slightly forward. It took a while. The two men talked animatedly as the women moved in. In Walter's imagination—by the time they were close enough to hear—the two men would likely say, "Great plan," and walk off and she and GJ would have gotten nothing, but she had to try. So slowly, step by step, GJ and Walter crept forward through the woods, headed for the two men.

Walter's goal initially was to get close enough to hear. By the time they arrived, it appeared the men were done with the preliminaries. Walter assumed they had already had the discussion about GJ. The way that Murray Marks reacted at first, it appeared that he hadn't liked what Shray had to say. Walter did hear at least a few final snippets.

"Do they have any of our people?"

"Not that I'm aware of," Shray said. "Though we do have a couple who haven't yet checked in."

Walter wanted to pump her fist in the air. *Good*, because they'd sure gotten a couple of good shots on some of the family members. They'd fired live rounds at her. And silver bullets or not, Burt de Gottardi was correct: it would kill you as well as any other bullet would. She'd taken out one of their people and probably one of the howls in the distance had been another one or two going down. She listened.

"Can we gather who we have?" GJ's grandfather asked. "We need to decide on our next move."

That turned her plans immediately upside down. She didn't know why she hadn't thought of it except maybe just that this was a shit situation. If the hunters gathered the troops, if they reorganized and came back again, there was going to be another live-round gunfight and that wasn't something either side could afford. Even though she didn't like these people, even though they were the perpetrators and she had gladly returned fire when fired upon, she was not going to let another showdown happen if she could avoid it.

That was her job, first and foremost. It was an interesting shift from being a Marine, from being sent out with zero control into an area where bullets already flew to being a lone wolf of her own, able to make decisions, and sometimes stop the bullets before they happened. There was something satisfying about it when she'd completed her task in Hogan's Alley. But here in the real world, where shit was already way more fucked up than any exercise they'd run, Walter wasn't so sure.

Turning to GJ, it was even more important now that she keep her voice low because if they were close enough to hear, then they were close enough to be heard. Walter said to her partner, "We have to get them now. I want to use you as bait."

48

GJ gulped. She rarely actually gulped, but this was probably the most nerve wracking thing she'd ever have to do. Sure, she'd successfully defended two theses to a room packed full of strangers while professors tore apart her ideas and made her stand up and defend all the research she'd done. But now, walking forward in the woods was far, far more difficult.

First, as per the plan, she and Walter separated so that by the time the men saw her—when they looked back to where she'd come from —it would not appear there was another person with her. She also, as she pointed out to Walter, needed to appear that she'd walked a straight line from the compound. Anything else would look suspicious. So her path needed to appear as if Shray had escaped and she'd simply followed the man. Why no one had shot at her, she would say she didn't know. Maybe because she was Murray Marks' granddaughter.

Slowly and carefully, and for the first time here on her own, she separated herself from Walter and headed the opposite direction. There would have been something comforting if she could have heard Walter moving through the trees and the brush. It would have allowed her an auditory method of pinpointing her partner, but she had nothing. Though she had a tracker on Shray Menon, she had nothing on Walter, and Walter was silent as a ghost. GJ could only hope that she was half as good.

Periodically, the two women stopped and looked for each other, but by the third or fourth check, GJ had lost sight of Walter, either it was that dark or there were too many trees in the way—or maybe Walter was just that good. She saw no signal now and she was on her own. She was going to have to make the call of when to stand up and start walking toward the two men. Still, she made a few more stops and starts, getting herself to a point she was pretty certain was directly between them and the main house of the compound. Then, with several slow, deep breaths, she stood up behind a tree and slowly began casually walking toward them. She made it only five steps before her grandfather, looking over Shray's shoulder, saw her.

"GJ!" he cried out with excitement as though he was happy to see her. But there was only a split second when she had her grandfather back, then she watched the expression fall off his face as he realized that his excitement in seeing his granddaughter was now forever altered.

"Grandpa," she said—the name she'd always called him when she was happy. This time though, his response was much more subdued; a simple nod as he waited for her to approach. She considered putting her hand on the butt of her gun and she wondered if she'd ever really known this man. All the travels she'd had with him, the months she'd stayed with him, every summer, the breaks from school, all the phone calls during college where he kept her from giving up and giving in to demanding professors, told her how he dug in the African desert looking for human bones that were sometimes four, ten, twenty thousand years old. So when she had a bad day or a long day or a day that had simply worn her to her own bones, he'd been there. And now?

"Grandfather," she said. This time, it was the more formal, more serious name. She was close enough to reach out if she wanted; lean forward and touch the sleeve of his coat. He wore a gray sport jacket tonight and gray pants—dark colors to blend in with the night. So even though he looked like he could have walked directly off a college campus, he also fit here. And that was something she hadn't known before today.

She reminded herself that he hadn't been lecturing at the Sorbonne and he had lied directly to her. He had also, somehow, been in and out of the lab without Eleri or Donovan finding him, and that was something she hoped to be able to investigate later. But how many times had he lied? She held on to that thought tightly. How many times had she helped him perhaps excavate a human skeleton that he had then stolen and kept for his own collection?

"Grandpa," she said it again. And this time when he looked at her, his expression had completely devolved to sadness.

"GJ. Is what Shray's telling me true?"

She shrugged, knowing better than to answer questions like that. If she hadn't been smart enough on her own, interrogation classes had trained that out of her. "What is it he's saying, Grandpa?"

She wanted to throw Shray under the bus. Not that she *truly* wanted to, but of all her choices here, that one was the easiest.

He asked with incredulity, "You've joined the FBI?"

GJ nodded. It was true, and she wasn't going to call Shray a liar when it would make her the liar instead. This time.

"When did this happen?"

"Almost six months ago, Grandpa. They called me."

"But why *you*?" he asked. The disbelieving tone of his words stung, cutting her deep. She held on to it. She was going to need that pain to drive her in the harsh moments to come.

"They called me because I have an exemplary scientific background. They like agents from all walks of life. They called me, Grandpa, because I *stole bones* from an FBI investigation for my own thesis. Sound familiar?" She was angry and she should have controlled it better, but she flung that one out. *I am truly my grandfather's granddaughter*, she thought. The only difference was they'd caught her early and converted her. It was something she didn't think she'd be able to do for him.

He nodded a little. "Six months. You've been doing this for six months and you didn't tell me?"

A shrug was all she could offer again.

"You didn't tell your mother or father?"

She shook her head again. "What would you have said, Grandpa? You would've told me not to go."

He shrugged a little at that, the same as she had in response to his question. She didn't rehash it with him. They both understood. Being a police officer, an FBI agent, anything other than an academic scientist, was something no one in the family understood. She'd simply taken an exemplary childhood career and turned herself into an instantaneous black sheep. No wonder she hadn't told anyone.

Truth time, she thought. "Grandpa, I have to take you in. I have to arrest both of you. I know what you're doing out here."

"You don't know anything," he snarled the words accusingly.

"I know all kinds of things, Grandpa. I know that you're part of this organization. I know that you've been casting silver bullets. I know that you're trying to get into the de Gottardi-Little house and I know what you're after in there."

That made his head snap back. Shray's, too. For a moment, she watched a play between them as her grandfather glared at his assistant and Shray shook his head. No, he was not the one who'd given GJ that information, but she was not going to let him off the hook. If she could turn them against each other, this might go down a little more smoothly. So she tried to drive the wedge.

"We got Shray. He talked to us, Grandpa. He told us all kinds of things."

"I didn't talk to them," the smaller man insisted. "I told you I talked to *you*."

"But I told you I wasn't there. I haven't been any closer than this tonight."

"I saw you there!"

In their gestures, GJ saw what they'd been saying the first time around. They were merely repeating it now and she was grateful for the insight it gave her. Another wedge to drive between them, because Shray believed that he had—according to Christina Pines and everything he'd said to her—surely seen Dr. Murray Marks stride into the room. GJ understood what happened, but again she was not going to defend him.

"He told us so much, Grandpa. He told us that you were running this organization. He told us how many people you had out there. He told us what you were after." Okay, the last part was a bit of a lie, but GJ didn't regret it.

Her grandfather looked more and more concerned, turning on Shray Menon as he did. His assistant began to hold his hands up and back slightly away, a position of self-defense. A position that he *couldn't* defend, even though he was right. "I didn't tell them," the man reiterated, the heat growing in the undertones of his voice.

"How else could she have learned? That's exactly the things that you know."

GJ stood there for a moment. Then she repeated in the silence that ensued, "Grandfather, Shray, you're both under arrest. I have to take you in. Please come quietly. I don't want this to get ugly."

Her grandfather almost turned and laughed. "You can't arrest me."

And GJ looked to Shray, letting his expression say it all. She'd already taken him down once.

"Grandfather, we know everything." She tried another tactic here. "How do you think we came out here and found you? We had Shray, we interrogated him, and then we let him escape. When they came for him, our people didn't try to keep him. They fired random shots." She looked to Shray then. "Why do you think it was so easy to escape? Do you really think you just walked out of a compound that was that heavily fortified?"

And for the first time she saw it dawn on Shray just what he might have done.

"You led me here," she repeated, but didn't let the idea linger. She was going to blame him for as much as she could. Every idea she could wedge between them was another point in her favor. Walter was out there somewhere and GJ was wondering just how this was going to go down. But she had to keep talking.

"Shray, put your hand in your pocket. We put a tracking and radio device on you. We heard everything you two said. You can't get out of this."

As she watched, the man did as he was told, finding first one empty pocket and then, in the second, the small device she'd placed on him. Only if he was very much up to date on his spycraft would he recognize that there was no recording implement on it at all. It was merely a GPS locator, but she had her fingers crossed that he couldn't tell the difference, not on sight, not in the woods at night in the dark. He held his hand out flat while looking at the tech, inadvertently showing it off to her grandfather. He looked horrified and GJ pushed the wedge a little further.

"He led us here, Grandfather. He led me directly to you. I walked out of the house and followed him. It's why I'm here. And I didn't bring my other agents because I'm desperately trying to have this go down as politely as possible."

"You think arresting me and throwing me in jail is going to be polite?" Her grandfather growled. GJ understood. He was going to fight. And if he fought, she had to fight.

That was when Shray Menon threw the tracking device into the trees and turned and bolted.

GJ surprised even herself with the speed at which she drew her weapon, turned, and shot at the man. She hadn't necessarily made the decision. It had simply happened. *Training in action*, she thought as she watched the red bloom on Shray's back as he fell. She turned back to her grandfather before she could let it sink in what she'd just done.

The man she'd likely just killed had babysat her. He'd taught her so many things. He'd watched out for her, protecting her from the older grad students on site who wanted to tease or harass a little girl, and then a blooming teenager. Now she'd shot him in the back.

Still there was no Walter. Now it was just her and her grandfather, the smell of the fired bullet between them. Hers was not silver.

"Grandfather," she said, shocked by the steadiness of her own voice. It must have been bolstered by her anger; anger at what they'd done, anger that her grandfather and Shray had both lied to her for years, anger that Shray had made a bolt for it and had forced her into the position of firing on him. It wasn't her fault that she was a really good shot these days.

"Grandfather, turn around and put your hands behind your back." Though he lifted his hands at about the same rate as her gun game up to aim at his chest, he did not put them behind his back. He did not agree to her demands.

"GJ, you don't want to do this."

"You're right," she told him. Anything less would have been so blatantly, obviously a lie that it never would have passed. "I *don't* want to do this, so don't make it difficult."

"Then stop. Come with me. You don't know what they are."

This again, she thought. " I know exactly what they are, Grandfather. I've been in your lab studying them. Did you let me down there to try and indoctrinate me?"

He didn't answer, but the blank look on his face said it all. Then, with no warning, he started to step backward.

"No," she ground it out, the harsh sound pushing its way out of her lungs on its own.

He took more steps away from her. When he turned, GJ lifted her gun and moved her finger to the trigger. She watched as the red bloomed in his shoulder and he fell.

49

"Grandpa!" GJ screamed as his older body crumpled in a way that Shray's younger version hadn't quite done.

He fell into the leaves and the debris on the forest floor, face forward. She waited for the sting of recoil from her gun but didn't feel it. As she turned and looked around, she saw Walter coming from the other direction, her own gun clasped in her hand and lowering.

Had Walter shot her grandfather? Had *she* done it? GJ wouldn't know until she counted her bullets. But at this moment, it didn't matter. She'd intended to arrest him and now he was dead. Her racing brain reminded her she did not want to explain this to her parents. Though why that was her primary thought right now, she didn't know. What she did understand was that the brain coped in any way it could and this must be her way.

If her grandfather had been able to tell her mother face-to-face what he'd done, then GJ might have been let off the hook a little bit for this. Bad enough that she'd joined the FBI, worse that she'd told nobody. Worse still that for her first assignment, she'd arrested her own grandfather. But if she killed him, she would be the one left explaining to her mother. She stood there in the dark woods knowing that that would make everything she'd done up until this moment so much worse.

She fell to her knees on the ground beside him, feeling for a pulse, lifting his arm and looking for the wound. That was when he turned over and looked at her, startling the crap out of her.

"Get the fuck off of me," he said.

Holy shit, he was alive and kicking. Walter was standing over the both of them. "I aimed to wing him. I think I did it."

Oh my God, GJ thought. She'd never been more grateful to Walter than she was at this exact moment. Walter admitted to shooting him and she admitted to a nonfatal shot. It was not how they'd been trained. If you pulled the trigger, you did it with the intent to kill. If you pulled the trigger, your aim was *always* center mass. Always the place you were most likely to get the kill-shot. Walter had just violated all that training and had probably saved her grandfather's life.

Now, GJ's anger returned as the old man spit and cussed at her, obviously in pain and blaming her for every second of what happened, even though he'd done what he'd done.

"Grandpa, I'm fucking handcuffing you." She pulled out her zip ties and yanked his hands behind his back even as he let up a howl far noisier than anything the wolves had done earlier in the evening. Walter stood guard over the two of them as GJ finished up the ugly work.

In the distance, she heard an answering cry from one of the de Gottardi or Little people howling in the distance. Another wolf voice joined in until finally there was a chorus responding to her grandfather's cries of pain. It was almost fitting.

Hauling him to his feet, she continued looking for where the blood was coming from. While it was staining his shirt, it did not appear life threatening. In fact, it didn't gush. It barely oozed. Whatever Walter had hit, she'd done it right, and GJ was grateful.

"We've got to check Menon," Walter said. GJ had a stunning moment where she suddenly remembered there'd been another man here. Watching her grandfather fall had erased everything from her mind and she had a very strong understanding of why she should have recused herself from this case. However, Westerfield hadn't let her and she was still questioning that decision.

With her grandfather on his feet, Walter in front of them, she watched as her partner leaned over and checked the other man. He lay prone, a good number of yards away, face down in the debris and leaves of the forest floor.

"He's dead," Walter declared. They didn't have the means to carry him and they were bringing her grandfather in. For a moment, the two of them looked at each other and—under the cover of the old man's growling, snarling tirade at his own capture—they made a plan.

GJ held her grandfather in front of her. Taller than she, he shielded her well; her own face barely peeked over his shoulders. Cranking her arm around and up, she held the barrel of her gun to his cheek. Not a very good spot, probably not lethal if it came down to it, but it made for a good show. Walter stayed behind them, her back to GJ's, sweeping the open space for anyone who might come up from the other direction.

With GJ in the middle and her grandfather in the front it was hopeful they could make it back to the house alive. As they looked around and saw no one in the nearby vicinity, though they knew their shots would likely bring people and fast, Walter pulled GJ's phone out of her pocket and GJ listened as Walter contacted the house, quietly texting in a message. Unable to read it, GJ's educated guess was that Walter mentioned they'd captured her grandfather, killed Shray, and were on their way back.

They went a good fifteen yards before they heard the first rustlings of other people in the woods. The problem was, they couldn't shoot first and ask questions later. They had no idea if what they heard were de Gottardi and Little family members who were still out, still coming in, and still not doing what they had been told to do—or if they were members of her grandfather and Shray's unit still here to kill as many wolves as they could and likely to get at the documents that the unassuming little farmhouse concealed.

"Stay back," Walter commanded the shapes in the night.

GJ reiterated the claim. Only she added, "I have Dr. Murray Marks. I have my gun to his head. If you fire on us, he'll be the first to go."

She could only hope that he was as valuable to them as he had been to her. As they slowly made their way back, though no shots were fired, they heard wolves in the distance again. Hopefully, more members of the de Gottardi and Little clan were safely arriving at the borders and making it into the farmhouse.

But halfway back, bullets zinged by. Instinctively GJ tried to drop—not easy with her grandfather in her command. Walter returned fire, but GJ couldn't afford to. She couldn't remove her gun from her grandfather's face because that was their bargaining chip. She couldn't allow him to possibly make a move.

With her free hand, she steered him and occasionally attempted to check the blood seeping from his wound. She called back to Walter, "Are you okay? I don't think any of them got close."

Knowing Walter, she'd probably aimed high since she didn't know what she was aiming at. Walter wasn't one for crazy shots. Unless people were hiding up in the trees, they were likely in no danger from Walter—but the warning had been clear.

As they got closer and closer to the farmhouse, the rustlings in the woods around them became more obvious. GJ even noticed as she looked off to her left or her right, she could see the shadow people coming nearer, getting bolder. She'd seen at one point the ever-so-slight glint of moonlight off a rifle bore aimed directly at them.

She'd taken the opportunity to swing her grandfather wildly, using him to put a human barrier in between herself and Walter and the rifle.

"I have him! Shoot us and you shoot him." She issued the warning in her best FBI agent voice. "Shoot me, and immediately—even as I die—my hand will squeeze this trigger and he will die too. If you want him to stay safe, you will let us move."

Slowly, still unable to see clearly, she swung her grandfather's tense form back, directing him toward the farmhouse again, and pushed him another couple of steps. She fully expected at any moment to feel a bullet slicing through her side. Then again, she *was* also starting to get a little cocky. She'd expected to get shot since she walked out of the house this evening and so far, it hadn't happened. Though she'd felt all kinds of other things, all kinds of other knives in her back, and other shots straight on, she had not felt that one.

They finally hit the most dangerous part of their little walk: the last thirty yards where the trees cleared and there was open yard up to the farmhouse. Luckily, as they arrived, they saw Wade and Art and Will standing in the doorway. And that was when GJ's ears rang with the first retort of open fire.

50

F*uck, shit, damn, crap.* Walter uttered one word for each time she pulled the trigger, firing back on someone who was closing in on her. But, in the dark, an outline of the shape, a bit of movement here or there was all she got.

Her instinct was to duck, to make herself a smaller target, and to run back into the woods where there was natural cover. None of this was an option with GJ at her back.

"Get down, GJ," she snarled. Luckily, her partner was her partner. Together they dropped low, GJ yanking her grandfather to his own knees even as he protested. Walter didn't care. He could protest until the cows fucking came home. She got off a few more shots, aiming at the people around her, knowing her shots likely glanced off of helmets and tactical vests. There wasn't enough light to get good aim on an open piece of skin.

She managed to hear three satisfying thuds followed by wails, cries of pain, or just the tiny sound a person made when they'd been shot down and fell to the ground. It was disturbingly satisfying.

Old war wounds, Walter thought, that she actually enjoyed that sound right now.

"We have to keep moving forward," GJ whispered.

Walter understood. To her, that meant backward, but toward the farmhouse. She crab-walked a little, firing as she went, and she felt the difference in the slide of her gun even as she counted it off. Last bullet. She squeezed the trigger. The slide came back, sticking. *Shit. Three, two,...*she was ready to go.

Yanking the slide, she swung wide for the person who rushed her as she was reloading, trying to take advantage of the less than three seconds where she wasn't actually releasing bullets. But as he came closer, she had the opportunity to aim.

His shots were going wild and she'd learned to stay calm, to keep her heartbeat low while others drew a bead on her. She cited statistics to herself, that even police on the job long term had less than a forty percent accuracy rate in live fire. All she needed to be was not the forty percent that got hit.

This time, her luck succeeded, and her steady hand earned her a shot that left her quarry flailing his arms up into the air as he tumbled backwards, presumably dead. From the way he didn't move, she chalked it up on her kill sheet for the night.

GJ somehow managed to have hands everywhere. In short motions, Walter felt her partner grabbing for her back and pulling her along until they established a pace that somehow worked. That was when Walter heard it behind her—GJ offered up a sound that could only be the noise a smile would make.

The light that flooded the yard told Walter that exactly what she thought had happened had actually happened. The family had opened the front door. She heard the footsteps, some of them sounds she recognized from when she stayed with Donovan. Paws, maybe. Pads of dog feet coming in sets of fours on the wood, down the steps, and then at last she saw them around her. Several dashed by in streaks; one of white, one of brown, one more silver, as they darted into the woods. Sometimes their legs stretched so far as to look like they leapt and flew into the night as they passed into the shadow of trees, nearly disappearing. But Walter heard their short, dark barks, and the growls as they encountered their quarry, then several screams as people went down. She wondered if a single wolf took on a single human or if, like the wild animals they appeared to be, they were more likely to hunt in packs.

She and GJ, suddenly no longer the only targets in the yard, scrambled inside, pushing Dr. Murray Marks in front of them. Walter, though she still held her gun and swept it, was no longer shooting into the woods. Some of her own people were beyond her now. And like in a game of hockey or basketball, there was always a certain point that you weren't allowed to get in front of. Walter was behind the line.

They tumbled through the doorway as a group. Dr. Murray Marks, though in his seventies, was doing his level best to make the job as hard as possible for them. He too was swearing a blue streak, though Walter imagined he didn't know as many colorful words as she did. She was tempted to challenge him. Instead, she had other more important things to do.

They shoved him to the ground and she listened as GJ hollered for someone to bring gauze and look at his wound. Hunkering down low, GJ whirled away from her grandfather, either trusting that the people in the house had it covered, or having decided that she'd simply had enough and she had to hand him off, because she couldn't deal with any more on her own. Walter understood both options as valid decisions. Wade was nowhere to be seen and Walter imagined that he was one of the dogs she'd seen racing through the yard beside her. She thought she'd seen him specifically, but in the low light, with bullets flying around her, she hadn't been sure.

Art de Gottardi came forward to work on GJ's grandfather with his medical kit in hand and gloves already on. He applied pressure, making the old man squirm and scream. No one cared. Art, in all his medical wisdom, ground out, "Shut up."

Walter thought for a moment about keeping her weapon out, finding a position at a window and taking up her charge. But the fact of the matter was she didn't know the area anywhere near as well as these people did and they were now outnumbering those who came in. It didn't appear any more troops had joined GJ's grandfather's militia and Walter was counting that one in their favor. She wasn't sure she'd be useful. Besides, she needed to catch her breath.

They'd been out for well over an hour, tracking, following, talking, and dragging the old man back. She reported to the others, to everyone and no one in general, to Art De Gottardi, and to Burt, who watched over the area, his gun out the window. Walter let her voice carry to Christina Pines, who clearly wasn't paying attention as she sat on the hardwood with her hands pressed flat against the flooring and occasionally tensed her fingers, squeezing as though she could dig in. Again, Walter had no idea what she was doing, but she still made her announcement.

"Shray Menon is dead. GJ shot him." She wasn't sure quite why she added that last piece. Maybe to let them know that GJ was on their side, that she wasn't going to let the hunters get away simply because she was one man's granddaughter and the other man's god daughter.

It didn't appear that the family had any doubts about her partner, but Walter wasn't sure how she would've dealt with it, or how she would deal with it, if they did turn on GJ. So she worked to quell any antagonism now, before it happened. Though the words had basically fallen out of her mouth, she was glad they had.

GJ sat on the floor near the center of the farmhouse. Staying low, she worked to keep her full body beneath the line of fire. Occasionally, though not often, bullets came through the windows, zinging through the air, and anyone who wasn't down was definitely in harm's way. She could see Walter's decision play out on her face—join the fight at the windows, or to stay low, and watch their quarry? That's what he was now, her grandfather, and she, too, had the same thoughts. Like Walter, she'd decided to stay low.

Her grandfather was moaning and complaining, and why not? He'd been captured by his own granddaughter, and now one of those probably-werewolf-people was pushing on his side, directly on the bullet wound that Walter had inflicted on him. He yelled, as if anyone outside might be able to hear him, above the din of bullets and screaming.

"I'm in here. It's me, Dr. Marks. Come get me."

GJ almost laughed. If she hadn't been about to cry, she would have. "Shut up, Grandfather."

He turned and glared at her, indicating he actually did have all of his faculties in place, and GJ decided it was time to let him in on it. "You're only alive because Walter pulled her shot, and Walter only pulled her shot because you're my grandfather. So you can shut the fuck up."

It was shocking, even to her, swearing at her grandfather like this, but it was far more shocking that he was here trying to *kill* people, that he'd been researching this all along and never told her, that he'd lied to her about being at the Sorbonne. She shook it off. She had to get rid of these thoughts. She was an FBI agent now, and this was her job.

It took only a few moments to take care of her grandfather's wound. That may have been because Art didn't feel he had any more moments to spare on this man, but GJ understood. He quickly had her grandfather bandaged and was leaving him to attend to another patient. She could hear doors opening and closing in the back. She watched as someone else was dragged in through the front door, wounded—only this was one of their own people, or one of their own *dogs*.

Art rightfully turned his attention to the newcomer. A gash was open down the furry leg and a second bullet wound marked his upper torso. To GJ, it looked serious, but if he could get adequate medical treatment soon, probably survivable. She only hoped there was adequate medical treatment here, but the more she watched, the more she was beginning to believe that these people could do just about anything. A feat learned out of necessity, unfortunately.

Wade came in next. In full wolf form, he nosed his way up through the cellar, just as he had done earlier. The cellar door creaking made every head turn in that direction. People dove to help lift it, to help the newcomer come in, but it was just Wade.

He stalked over on four soft feet toward her grandfather, and for a moment, GJ thought her grandfather recognized him. Wade certainly recognized Dr. Murray Marks. His growl was low and deep, and full of such animosity that GJ thought she wouldn't have been surprised if he lunged for her grandfather's neck.

As he growled, GJ took notes. Wade's brown coloring disguised most of it, but around his mouth, there was a tinge of red. There were streaks of it in different places on his coat, too. She wondered if it was his own blood, though she was pretty certain it wasn't. She could see the barely-leashed rage in her friend.

Her grandfather, whether he'd pulled the trigger or not, had caused the murder of the man that Wade loved. Though he was still her grandfather and she still wanted to protect him, GJ didn't know if she could or should protect him from this. The man who had taught her to handle her prizes with care and that her actions had consequences, was going to have to learn that for himself it seemed.

After a few moments of staring at each other, Wade stalked off, definitely the bigger man. Only then did GJ turn and survey the scene with clearer eyes. Then, with things better under control, she and Walter nodded once at each other and, in unison, turned back toward the windows. She wanted to ask, "How can we help?" but she was supposed to be in charge.

Looking for an open space, she racked the slide on her gun and took aim. There was nothing to shoot at, though. While she could see the shapes in the woods and a few out in the yard, it was difficult to distinguish who were her people and who were theirs. Not all of the de Gottardi or Little family members were able to shift into dogs, so it wasn't as simple as looking at the outline to know who to aim at. Unfortunately, the clear targets came with helmets and Kevlar vests, making it even more difficult to determine until the person was close, but she squeezed off three shots and found one of her grandfather's people tumbling backward. For a moment, she thought, *This was the second person she'd killed tonight.*

She emptied her clip one shot at a time into the shadows, and even as she did it, she noticed that the shadows in the woods were slightly lessened. The sun was coming up now, and somehow, this had gone on for far, far too long.

Behind her then, she heard a struggle and turned. As she looked, she watched her grandfather manage to scoot across the floor and wrestle a spare handgun from where it was holstered on one of the family members' legs. With bound hands, he stuck the muzzle under his chin.

51

There weren't words for GJ's feelings. Shock. Fear. Anger. All riled through her as she made a sudden dive.

"You will not!" she yelled.

Though it would make things easier, she understood—even in that split second—that she was not going to allow it to happen. He could not shoot himself and remove all his valuable information from this equation. She'd worked too hard to bring him here, and so she dove onto him not quite thinking about the consequences to herself if he managed to get the shot off.

He was lying sideways on the floor. His feet and hands were bound, though his fingers had managed to work their way around the butt of the gun and shoved it upward under his chin.

As she covered him, she jammed the heel of her hand smack down to the floor in the small space between the barrel of the gun and his neck. She used the leverage to push the gun away and the shot went wide. It flew low across the floor and for a moment she had the briefest fear that she'd managed to kill someone else while saving him.

Heart pounding in her chest, she looked up, trying to assess if anyone else had been hit. She knew that when it happened, the recipient of the bullet often didn't feel it for even the first handful of minutes. They would look around, shocked, having heard the sound of gunfire and wondering who was hit, not yet realizing it was them.

So, she looked for what she'd been trained for. Blooms of red forming on clothing. An awkward limp. An arm that didn't hang quite right. But she didn't see any of it.

Her breathing heavy, she almost wasn't able to get the words out. "Is anyone hurt?"

Even then she watched as her grandfather managed to gather the gun back into his own grip. She slammed his hands to the floor, once, twice, before he finally groaned and let go of the weapon. GJ grabbed it, taking control and standing over him. She shouldn't be this high in the air. She was a target. She was supposed to stay low, but for the briefest of moments she wrapped her own hand around the butt of the weapon. Her own finger slid inside the trigger guard and she aimed it him.

"You will not." She ground the words out through her teeth. Never had a family member made her so angry. Never had *any* person made her this angry before. Even the people who worked with him, those who had been outside taking shots at her and Walter, didn't do this to her. But this? This was the worst.

"Get down" Walter hissed. It was a good save and GJ knew it, but she wouldn't get to do anything more here if she took a bullet to the brain.

Instantly, she dropped to her hands and knees as she heard two more shots come through the house, though she had no idea if they were anywhere near her. They were a sharp reminder of how foolish she'd been to stand. Acting in anger was not what she had been trained to do.

A woman appeared at her side then. She motioned with a fabric bag, and when GJ was unsure what to do with it, but the woman held it out again.

"Put it over his hands and zip-tie it down. Make it really tight so he can't flex his fingers. Then he can't grab anything else."

GJ recognized a good idea when she heard one, and this woman had every reason to make sure that Dr. Murray Marks was not able to get his hands on a weapon again. GJ was grateful they were willing to help her do what she felt she needed to do, even though this man was the one who had run the entire militia out here and had issued the orders to come after the family.

"Thank you," she said and accepted the bag. It took several precious minutes to hold the bag taut while her grandfather struggled. The difficulty was making sure his hands remained in closed fists with the bag pulled tight over them. It took several zip ties to get around his wrist, but she made it happen, watching all the while as Art went from patient to patient. As Walter popped her head carefully into the corner of a window, fired off several shots and ducked back over and over.

Surely, this had to end soon. If nothing else, each side would run out of victims. It almost seemed she was right. As the sun came up, more and more times the doors opened and closed. More and more times, one of the members of the de Gottardi-Little family came back —either walking in as a tired, dirty, or bloody human or the same in the shape of a dog.

The gunfire died down. The people outside retreated and stopped making rushes on the house, as though they were actually trying to come in and rescue Dr. Marks. *It wasn't going to happen,* GJ thought. There was no way Walter would let them get her grandfather, nor would she. One or the other of them would shoot him first. He wasn't going back out, and if it came to that, they would have to cut off the head of this organization.

It seemed the sun controlled the fight. The higher it got in the sky, the fewer and further between the sounds of bullets became. At last, they all looked at each other. Having not heard any gunfire for quite some time nor seen any movement in the woods, most of the outside soldiers had returned to the farmhouse. They crowded inside, stuffing every corner, hiding under every chair and every table. The furniture was overturned and the place looked like exactly what it was—a war zone. Furniture was shattered. Some chairs would never stand upright again, at least not until they had a leg fully replaced or more. Some of the furniture would be going on a scrap pile in the backyard, that was for certain.

They received word from Alicia and her contingent. They'd managed to get to a place that was unknown and to hide everything. As far as GJ could tell, no-one had breached the walls.

She turned to Will Little and asked, "Are your documents safe?"

He nodded. "They didn't even get close."

A small blessing.

The scream coming from the yard changed her mind.

52

Though the urge to pop up and look was strong, GJ fought it. It was likely a trap. Send someone running into the yard, yelling, and get everyone to make themselves targets as they came to look.

Next to her, Art stood to crane his neck out the window. He was barely halfway before Wade grabbed him and tugged him back down. Now fully human looking, he must have changed while GJ wasn't paying attention.

Walter, ever the soldier, had rolled from where she'd sat with her back against the wall. Walter had been done. She'd been relaxing just a little, but the screams pulled her taut like a bowstring again. She pressed her face awkwardly to the wall and GJ thought she must have lost her fucking mind for a minute.

Only as Walter yelled out "Fuck!" at the top of her lungs and popped up, did GJ see that she'd taken advantage of bullet hole in the wall to peek through. It was big enough to see out of and small enough that no one could likely shoot into it. Walter hadn't lost her mind, she was just better at this than everyone else.

But she was standing up, square to the window, gun in both hands, perfect police grip.

She was going to get herself shot. The adrenaline in her system slowed time and GJ thought, *Maybe she knows what she's doing.* And if she did, then it was the right thing to do.

GJ stood up beside her. She mimicked Walter's stance, though it wasn't conscious. Only then did she yell, "Oh shit!" as she saw what Walter had seen.

The man running across the yard was lumpy. Boxy shapes ringed his midsection. As he got closer she saw wires, some of which trailed to something in his hand.

He was wired to blow. Suicide bomber.

Who would think these documents were worth that much except the family? This had been a nice, simple gunfight up until now. Though her face frowned with thought, GJ was already cataloging Walter's shots.

The man zigzagged across the space, thankfully making it take longer for him to reach the house. Walter pulled the trigger over and over but he didn't go down. Fucking Kevlar.

"Get down! Move back!" GJ shouted, twisting as she yelled at all the people.

Her grandfather, bound on the floor, could not get back. That was his own fault though. She and Walter would not make it back if this man made it to the door and blew the place to hell, but that was her choice. She'd enjoyed being an FBI agent, even if it was for just under a week.

Turning back to face the yard with Walter, she registered that Walter's shots had slowed.

Head shot.

They needed a head shot.

Lowering her breathing rate, trying to shoot between heartbeats, GJ pulled the trigger.

53

In the end, GJ couldn't say whether the shot that got him was from her or Walter. They'd been firing pretty simultaneously, and he'd fallen. She didn't want to know. Walter's kill number was likely so high that this one didn't make a difference, and her own was so low that it made all the difference in the world and she didn't want it.

She'd been aiming for his head. But she wasn't sure if she'd made it and the switch had been a "dead man" switch, or if maybe the shot had been off and the explosive had been hit and gone up. She didn't know what Walter was aiming for. It didn't matter.

The blast had rocked all of them back. She and Walter had fallen off their feet. A good thing since the remaining glass in the windows had blown inward with the force. She didn't want to know what the front of the house looked like, though it had stood.

Slowly they slid downward, getting out of the line of sight in case this shit wasn't over yet. It was a full hour later that Walter moved from the window. That to GJ was the best declaration that the fighting was over: when Walter declared it done.

She sat in the middle of the room. Her breathing still heavy, despite the fact that no one had fired a shot since the explosion. Walter had been on high alert for quite some time and it took GJ a moment to realize that what she saw in Walter also reflected in herself. She watched over Walter's shoulder as once again the cellar door lifted and another nose came through.

Only it wasn't the nose of a dog. It was the nose of a rifle and it was aiming into the room.

GJ reacted, certain she was the only one who saw it. She dove, hollering out, "The cellar door!" which probably wasn't very helpful. She tried to avoid the barrel of the gun. Dropping and rolling, she came up on one knee firing into the small space.

54

Walter had sat unknowing as a gun came up behind her. She was in shock. How had she not heard it? How had she not known? Her eyes must have been wide with surprise.

GJ fired into the space of the cellar door and a yelp let them know GJ had hit her mark. Walter turned suddenly, scrambling to her feet with the others, who went and pulled back the cellar door, only to find a fully-armed soldier dead at the bottom of the steps.

One shot, one kill, Walter thought. Turning to GJ, she said, "That was pretty fancy."

"I learned it at camp." Her friend shrugged, and Walter almost laughed. She understood the hysterical reaction that most people eventually had to war. She felt it bubbling up in her now. Three different people rushed down the steps, checking for a pulse to make sure that GJ's shot had not only found its mark, but left the victim completely unable to return.

"What do we do with the body?" they asked. Understandably, they didn't want it in here. They already had a hostage in Dr. Marks. They didn't need anything more. Blood was pooling on the cellar floor, and Walter looked around suddenly realizing that many things were missing. Furniture, windows, curtains. Also, things were added: blood smears and hand prints along the wall and floor as some people had crawled in wounded. There were spots where others had bled out while Art frantically tried to save them. The good news was, most of the time, he'd kept them alive.

Walter wasn't sure, but she believed the number of their own people who had died in this fight was in the five to ten range. She could not count the number of wounded, it was way too high. She could not count the number of dogs she'd seen return with blood dripping from their fangs. And though she'd initially wondered why they would go out when they didn't have hands to hold weapons, she wondered now why she'd questioned that.

Her heartbeat was finally returning to normal. It had spiked again with GJ's amazing roll and shoot. Walter suddenly flashed back to a time—not that long ago—when they'd stood at the range and GJ had picked up her Glock nine-millimeter and Walter had cringed just seeing it in her hands. *What a difference a few months made*, she thought. It applied even to herself.

Christina had begun speaking again. Though she hadn't even moved for a long while, she turned, stood, and finally spoke. "They're gone."

For a reason no one could say—other than they'd been told to trust her, and that she hadn't seemed to have lied to them yet—they all believed her.

Though Walter envied the knowledge, she didn't envy Christina Pines. The woman seemed sad and alone, and unwilling to connect with other people, which Walter found extremely funny since she was the last person who would *want* to connect. Now was not the time for raucous laughter though, and she bit her lip to hold it back. It wasn't even that funny. It was just the adrenaline fading from her system.

With slow hands and heavy hearts, they one by one began the effort of cleanup. Carefully, several members went out to the well and brought in water. Others were sent to scout the outside area, to count dead bodies, and look for specific things.

Walter sent a team out to find Shray Menon's body and bring it back. Though no one wanted it in the house, but it had to be accounted for. Then she asked if there was anyone else out there that they specifically needed. They had Dr. Murray Marks, they needed Shray Menon. If anyone could find the mysterious Harry, that would be great, too, though no one seemed to recognize the name.

It was several hours later that Walter had finally eaten a handful of dry cereal. Her body was giving in to exhaustion. She and GJ had been up for over twenty-four hours straight, and she had to believe most of the people had here too. She was just about to give in when a car drove all the way up to the house and Westerfield emerged.

They offered up brief introductions, and he spoke relatively freely in front of the de Gottardi-Little family. Perhaps he understood that, because of their situation, the family members were in no position to share information with him.

"What happened to the two we arrested?" Walter asked when he finished. Because the last she'd heard, he and Wade had been at the hotel, and then Wade was here and Westerfield was at the hotel with them alone.

"They're in custody," Westerfield said almost as an aside. While Walter wanted to press him for more, it became clear that he wasn't going to offer it. Her Special Agent in Charge didn't hang out and help. He didn't offer information. He simply told them what they needed to do and he took Dr. Murray Marks away.

"Where is he going?" GJ asked.

"Into custody," was all Westerfield would offer. Walter could only turn to her partner and shrug. At least her grandfather wasn't dead.

Walter was looking for a bed when the scouts came back and let her know that they had been unable to find Shray Menon's body. With one simple look between her and GJ, they'd ditched the idea of sleep and gone out into the woods themselves, only to discover the searchers had not made an error.

Walter and GJ knew, they had her phone. They had tracking locations. Though he'd thrown the tracker from where he'd last stood with Dr. Murray Marks, the spot was very clear from the information on the device. Turning, they traced the steps, knowing which way he'd run. Though they couldn't see an exact position where he'd died, they found the spot relatively easily by looking for blood stains on the leaves.

As they checked the scene, they found signs the body had been dragged away. Perhaps there were secrets contained somewhere in his DNA, or on his person. The others might not have wanted Walter and GJ to get their hands on the information.

Though it was tempting to leave the compound, Walter felt they couldn't. Christina said they couldn't. And though Wade told them the others would be fine, and that they had a live-in FBI agent in him for a while, they all agreed to stay and sleep in shifts.

For three days, they waited. No more bullets came, and no more shadows flitted through the woods. A pile of furniture stood in the backyard in pieces, ready for flames. Various people came and flashed FBI badges and took away some of the bodies. Walter even helped with the manual labor of burying the dead.

On Day Four, the last of the others began returning home. While Walter hadn't seen them, she understood now that there were tunnels leading into the cellar that allowed the family to come and go. These were the things that she and GJ hadn't known originally, hadn't needed to. She wondered once again where the documents might be. They'd talked to Will several times, and he assured them that all was safe, but clearly something would have to be done. The family needed a new plan, or this would happen again.

On Day Five, they'd heard no update from Westerfield, other than that the right people were in custody and it was time to go home. Walter called Donovan, but he wasn't home either. And when GJ said, "Would you like to come back to my grandfather's with me?" Walter accepted.

55

GJ and Walter had stayed in her apartment for three days. They hadn't spoken a lot. They'd gone in and out on different schedules, and GJ only had the one large bed. They shared it, though mostly in rotating shifts, sleeping for hours on end.

GJ watched stupid TV, and by the second day, Walter was watching stupid TV, too. They ate what the staff cooked—big, extravagant meals that GJ could only imagine fell into a hollow hole created by almost a week of tension at the DeGottardi-Little farm. Her appetite had returned, along with an ability to bend the truth to the staff. They worried about her grandfather, and she told them that he'd been arrested, though not really what for. How could she? Besides, her NightShade directive forbade it.

She'd called her mother and father, told them the story as best she was allowed, admitted she'd joined the FBI, and found the conversation exhausted her almost as much as the gunfire had. Though nobody said it, she heard an edge of blame in her mother's voice, and she understood.

Her grandfather had been better to GJ than he'd been to her mother, and now, GJ had taken him away. At least that's how it appeared if you only counted how the pieces moved, and it was difficult to explain exactly what he'd been doing. So making her mother believe it was that much harder. Still, the wedge was driven in further, and not between Dr. Marks and Shray this time, but between GJ and her own family.

On the third day, after sleeping a fourteen-hour night, GJ had finally woken up refreshed. She found Walter in the small kitchen of her apartment brewing fresh pots of coffee, as she had done for the last several days, almost one right after the other. Without a word, she'd poured herself a mug, and doctored it up with cream and sugar. It was enough to make the once-black liquid not even resemble coffee anymore while Walter silently frowned at GJ and drank hers straight.

"Walter," she said, "we have to go into the basement lab."

Walter only nodded. They'd both known this. It was part of Westerfield's directive. In fact, though her grandfather was in custody, he had not yet been officially arrested. There were no reports of the firefight at the DeGottardi-Little farm. GJ wondered if any nearby neighbors had even heard anything or called any authorities if they had. She found no official paperwork recording her grandfather's incarceration. There were no charges brought, and she wondered if this was just what happened when you were arrested by Nightshade, when you were arrested for hunting werewolves with silver bullets.

She'd thought they might lock her grandfather up for being crazy and put him in an institution. Her worst-case scenario had been a general population prison—she knew he wouldn't survive it, not for long. But, in the end, it was mostly what she'd expected: a few lies and more normality than not. Instead, her grandfather simply disappeared, along with the others they'd arrested. Westerfield's only answer about any of them had been, "In custody."

Now, she looked to Walter and said, "What were we doing there?"

Walter shook her head.

"I mean, we helped. There was a firefight. We knew the people who were coming. We sorted it out. We managed to bring in the FBI to take away the bodies," But when she summed up the outcome, it wasn't clear anymore. At the time, they'd fired on the people firing on them. A led to B led to C. That had been easy inference. But, this, looking back? Not so easy.

"We didn't even graduate," GJ said. "I mean, technically, we did. He graduated us, but we didn't finish. He pulled us out and he put two completely new officers alone into that situation…"

It had been gnawing at her from the moment they'd been assigned the case. "Did he know?" she asked Walter point blank.

That was the big question, and Walter looked up, suddenly catching on. Had Westerfield known that GJ's grandfather was the head of the organization they were sent out to fight? Had he purposely pitted GJ against the man who'd raised her? Had he used her as bait?

Walter only shrugged back at her, and GJ found she was somewhat comforted at least by the fact that it wasn't obvious to everyone else, though she was still concerned it had actually happened.

They spoke a little while longer, and GJ waited while Walter offered up a phone call to Donovan. The tones of Walter's voice changed when she spoke to the other FBI agent, and GJ found herself smiling. It was good that Walter and Donovan had each other, but, GJ...she really didn't know what to do.

The house stood majestic with a full staff and a trust fund to run it. Westerfield said it was hers now, and just the day before, she'd opened a courier package, giving her the deed to the house, signing over the bank accounts to her. Much of it was in her grandfather's writing, and she wondered if it had been voluntary or forced and if she'd ever see him again to possibly find out.

She listened as Walter signed off, wanting to wait, unwilling to go into the basement lab herself. Westerfield had told her everything in there belonged to her now. Though she wanted to return it to universities and families, he'd told her a clear and concise *No*. By doing so, she would create more problems than she solved. It was her job to go into the lab and salvage any information she could. She wanted Walter at her side, if only to be a warm body.

It struck her that for the first time, as she walked down the long hallway and entered the code into the pad, that her grandfather had now given her the digits to open the door in the paperwork. They'd both known that was unnecessary. It was now her job to change it, though she hadn't gotten around to it yet.

This was the first time she'd openly walked into his basement lab, and it struck her again, harder, that it was now *her* basement laboratory. Wanting to combat the nerves that she felt just walking down the steps, she asked Walter about her call with Donovan.

"Why isn't he home? Is he not on leave?"

"He's out with Eleri. They found another lead on her sister. They're in New Orleans," Walter said.

"Wow." GJ didn't know what had happened with Eleri's sister, though she'd heard hints and pieces. All she knew was that Eleri had become an FBI agent as an adult, after her sister had disappeared from sight in a matter of moments, decades ago.

GJ thought of her own situation and wondered what it might be like to have a sibling like that and to have lost them. She couldn't even handle imagining it right now. So she was grateful that Eleri had Donovan with her and turned back to her own task.

"I'm no forensic scientist," Walter offered on a shrug. "I'm not even a regular biologist, but tell me what to do, and I'll see."

They started by doing a simple inventory of the laboratory, pulling out drawers, and trying to get a grip on every skeleton, every bone without provenance. Walter followed along behind her, asking how she could help.

GJ thought they should also catalog equipment, but five minutes later, Walter said, "GJ, there's a body in the kettle."

ABOUT THE AUTHOR

AJ holds an MS in Human Forensic Identification as well as another in Neuroscience/Human Physiology. AJ's works have garnered Audie nominations, options for tv and film, as well as over twenty Best Suspense/Best Fiction of the Year awards.

A.J.'s world is strange place where patterns jump out and catch the eye, little is missed, and most of it can be recalled with a deep breath. In this world, the smell of Florida takes three weeks to fully leave the senses and the air in Dallas is so thick that the planes "sink" to the runways rather than actually landing.

For A.J., reality is always a little bit off from the norm and something usually lurks right under the surface. As a storyteller, A.J. loves irony, the unexpected, and a puzzle where all the pieces fit and make sense. Originally a scientist and a teacher, the writer says research is always a key player in the stories. AJ's motto is "It could happen. It wouldn't. But it could."

A.J. has lived in Florida and Los Angeles among a handful of other places. Recent whims have brought the dark writer to Tennessee, where home is a deceptively normal-looking neighborhood just outside Nashville.

For more information:
www.ReadAJS.com
AJ@ReadAJS.com

Made in the USA
Las Vegas, NV
01 September 2022